CW00434443

Stories from The Pale

MODERN WOMEN

Ellie Taylor-Brock

ISBN: 9798744163112

DEDICATION

To the Mammy and Daddy for always being there

Family & Friends - the well of inspiration

And

Kieran Fagan for the genuine and kind encouragement

CONTENTS

ACKNOWLEDGMENTS

Edited by

Richard Bradburn

Cover and illustrations by Author, 2021

ALL THE GIRLS

The powerful and emotive sound of Aslan erupts, quite suddenly, streaming out from the corner of the room, spurring us instantly into a frenzy of horrendous caterwauling, prancing and comically mistimed lip sync. It's as if the sound, a musical feast, somehow inflames an overwhelming desire to venture into and become part of the "Crazy World" of the song. Energy and life fill the cramped and cluttered space of the tiny bedroom and the air becomes laden with the promise of a giddy, fun Saturday night – a night of endless possibilities.

To linger in the feeling, I gently shutter my eyes and relish the clarity that floods to all other senses. The feeling is sublime – as if I'm being enveloped comfortingly in the warmth of a well-worn and beloved shawl. Drawing deep methodical breaths, I focus and savour the moment purely for its simplicity and undemanding pleasure. This is where I'm supposed to be! This is where the heart is, and it beats with reassuring gusto.

The band, of course, is just a CD in a very impressive new Philips stereo, bought recently by Kathy and which, to her immense annoyance, has been affectionately commandeered by all members of the McCarthy brigade. A marvel of modern technology, so Mam thinks, and used ceaselessly for its intended purpose which is, of course, to accompany us as we howl along with tuneless abandon to every old classic and modern hit we can lay our hands on. And tonight is no exception. So, with barely a note in key and not a shred of coordination either, we hail the coming of the weekend shenanigans, as Aslan fades and The Stunning remind us of our true agenda for tonight – "Brewing up a Storm".

For one brief moment, as I drift away, lost in thought, the chaos around me seems to fade from my consciousness, only to promptly reappear again in bolder, louder form at the harsh thump of a fallen object. Looking around I see Gemma, my older sister, standing to the left of me, swaying gently to the rhythm of the music. Her long, flowing, blond hair seems almost to move with its own, slow rhythmic wave; a sweet, angelic smile lighting her flawless face. It draws a kind of awe and wonder from me, but only because she stands in such stark contrast to Aubrey, next to her, who gyrates around like a drunken, three-legged donkey. With every clumsy and somewhat comical move, she inches ever closer to the dressing table on which Kathy, her twin, has, for some ill-thought-out reason, decided to perch herself. The fallen object, a bottle of perfume, lies next to the table, where Kathy recklessly tries to balance while simultaneously and unsteadily bowing down to her loyal subjects – that's us of course. For our part, we dance around, somewhat gracelessly, as if we were courtiers at a badly organised and somewhat low-end, medieval ball, waving banners of lacy white underwear above our heads as we bow and courtesy in polite response.

Now for onlookers – if there were any – this might appear as a crude, brash spectacle, or perhaps even a mild curiosity. But for us, the McCarthy clan, it's just the usual, pre-night-on-the-town preparatory shenanigans – the warm-up to those endless possibilities, held in trust by the spirit of the weekend and Saturday night itself.

Suddenly, out of the corner of my eye, I notice Jade's dancing as it swiftly morphs, changing in one seamless motion into a bizarre kind of jogging on the spot, and given that I know for sure this is not some new dance craze, I can only conclude it signals her need to use the bathroom. I also know she's not going to budge right now, for fear of missing out on any of the craic, so perhaps now is the time to move this night on to stage two. With that thought in mind, I immediately decide to throw my lacy banner blindly from my hand, casting it with exaggerated pomp, to the other side of the room. But as soon as it leaves my hand, I'm then forced to gape in absolute terror as it plunges dangerously close to a lighted candle, missing it only by a hair's breadth. Heaving a sigh of enormous relief at the near-miss, I finally turn and reach over to press pause on the stereo. Instantly, the room is plunged into an alarming, almost deafening silence which, truthfully, seems to be more of an assault on the senses than the previous ruckus was.

"Ah Jesus, Rhian, I love that song. Turn it back on!" says Aubrey, a little too loudly and brashly, leading me to suspect that perhaps she's had enough to drink already. Her waning aural perception and inability to adjust her volume levels is a worrying sign indeed.

"In a minute!" I say, with some degree of authority. "Now listen up! we're not leaving this house until we make a toast. So Jade, first off, can you please go do what you need to do! I don't want you distracting me from the order of business!"

Jade takes her cue and runs off out the door, across the landing and into the small bathroom directly opposite – totally disregarding the purpose for which doors were invented. So, in this momentary lull we're all treated to the very disturbing sound of what can only be described as her impersonation of Niagara Falls.

In that moment, a thought occurs to me – you really are blood-bound to love your sisters no matter how gross they can be.

Thankfully though, she at least washes her hands – that's also something we can quite clearly hear – and in no time at all, she's back out and standing to attention. Exactly why is anyone's guess, but at least now I can finally start handing out the glasses of champagne which somehow, miraculously, managed to get poured despite all the prancing around.

The champagne isn't real of course – it's just cheap, fizzy plonk – but it's very nice, cheap fizzy plonk all the same and perfect for the task in hand – toasting Kathy's return. Taking my own glass from the cluttered and rather grotty-looking dressing table top I clear my throat theatrically. Then, with enviable elocution (thanks to our parents' hard-earned cash and the nuns of Loreto Convent) I commence with a most vital and pressing speech, nodding at selected individuals in the process.

"Ladies and 'unladylikes'," – the 'unladylikes' raise their eyebrows a tad disdainfully at this – "as you are all now very well aware, today is an enormously special day in the history of our little coven. Because today is the day that, from this moment forth, shall be forever known, as 'Reunion Day'."

I pause momentarily while the girls give a little clap and bow to each other in haughty affirmation before I continue on.

"It is a memorable day indeed because today is the day when our own, most genteel and dearest Kathleen – or Ms Kathy McCarthy as she shall be henceforth once more known as – became officially separated. Free to return home and be reunited with her mammy. And her daddy. And of course, her truly wonderful sisters!"

I suddenly and deliberately change my approach to a less polished, pre-elocution-lessons-style, reverting to habit for the next part of my speech.

"And Jaysus knows in this country getting out of a marriage is antin' but feckin' easy. Sure, there's folk can get out of prison with a lot less hassle. Do you remember the time Mick Doherty told us about how he snook outa the 'Joy in a laundry truck?"

Pausing for a moment just for effect, I scan along the line of girls gazing intently towards me, looking each one of them directly in the eye.

"Anyway, given the fact that our Kathy is allergic to anything remotely resembling laundry and for that matter, housework of all varieties, then that was never going to be an option for her, now was it? Still, the bird has been released from its cage and is now free to fly, fly, fly ..."

"Get on with it!" shouts Kathy, by way of a heckle, and everybody, including myself, has a little giggle at the theatre of it all.

"As we all know," I say as loudly as I can and with renewed attention to my reinstated, super posh and truly odd accent, "her dear, departed husband ..."

"But he's not dead, YET!" shouts Kathy with a roaring laugh which prompts Mam, downstairs, to bang the ceiling with her sweeping brush handle. Mam has a favourite spot where she likes to whack the brush handle when we get too rowdy, and you can clearly see where that spot is because there's a mark – a brownish, circular stain. Somebody, but I'm not saying who, drew an arrow beside it in pencil and the words "BANG HERE" in clear blocked letters. The poor woman nearly had a coronary initially, but it wasn't long before she finally saw the funny side.

"Ah yes!" I continue, raising my head from its brief (mournful) dip. "But he is a terrible bollocks, and to me, that is a kind of dead."

With my hand pressed tight against my upper chest, a contrived, sorrowful expression painted on my face, I continue on with the performance through the howls of laughter which are now so loud I can hardly hear myself think. It appears that my speech is soon to derail – I'm losing my audience.

"A terrible bollocks, I say ... a terrible bollocks, but a bollocks to our Kathy, no more! Drink up! Get pissed! Live long and ... whatever the feck the rest of that saying is!"

My speech inevitably gets cut short at this point because, quite honestly, I'm getting slightly hoarse and the girls are far too boisterous to be trying to shout over. Besides, Jade has hit the play button on the stereo again and The Stunning are once more urging us in "Brewing up a Storm", though at a slightly lesser volume than before. Mam can be heard (just about) shouting from the bottom of the stairs, something about coming up to redden our arses even though we're probably too big but that won't stop her anyway. We completely ignore her and continue on in the same raucous, cackling blare.

It's seven o'clock on a Saturday evening, in the depths of a very cold and dreary late November, and very soon we'll all be heading into town to continue with the celebrations – well, that is if we ever get ourselves in gear. It's beginning to look suspiciously like this night may very well finish up right here where it started.

In my brief moment of contemplation, I look around the room at all my sisters, wondering once more about the big questions – life, love and our futures, our respective journeys – and sadly there are no great revelations forthcoming. Well, except for one, which is the blaringly obvious image of my younger twin sisters, Aubrey and Kathy, who are now teetering dangerously close to the threshold of that drunken abyss, the one that's all too familiar to them. Believe me when I say this; drunk Aubrey and drunk Kathy never ends well, for anybody. Tonight, it would appear, they're on a mission. Admittedly, the same one they're always on, the "bag-a-man crusade", a phrase coined by their own fair tongues. But tonight, it would seem, they have added to their mantra with a notion of "more alcohol, more likelihood of success", or something to that effect.

I roll my eyes to heaven at the thought, but sadly there is no escaping the reality. Since turning nineteen there has been a noticeable, almost tangible rise in the air of impatience emanating from poor Aubrey with regard to romance. She did, after all, have to witness her twin (and best friend) Kathy marry first, and her actually fifteen whole minutes older. In fact, it would not be an exaggeration to say that Aubrey has, in recent times, conducted herself quite regularly with a large degree of cringe-worthiness when it comes to the opposite sex. The girl, quite frankly, is hell-bent on getting herself hitched, whatever the cost, and now hell-bent with the vivacious and newly single Kathy as her wing woman – so it would appear.

Suddenly, as if reading my mind and having an overwhelming desire to stop me midering, whatever the cost, the girls decide to make tracks. Amazingly, and in a surprisingly dexterous and seemingly choreographed way, like a murmuration, they down their drinks in what can only be described as a cacophony of belching and giggling and move towards the bedroom door. One minute we're in the bedroom, then we're charging down the stairs, full fury, like we had seconds to evacuate lest some impending disaster meet us first. Next minute we're bursting through the kitchen door.

Inside, over by the large Belfast sink, Mam is busy sulking, an all-too-familiar scowl leaving us in no doubt of her displeasure. On this occasion, I'm choosing to believe that the real reason for her pique is because Dad didn't back her up. Instead, he appears to have chosen to continue sitting, reading his newspaper by the blaze of the open fire. But that's because he's a wise man, you see, and he knows only too well that it will end more speedily if he leaves us to our own devices. So out of pure divilment, we all pile over on top of Mam, hugging, kissing and teasing her, good-humouredly. She swats us away with her tea cloth and, with a reluctant smile on her face, informs us for about the millionth time in our lives that we'll be the death of her for sure – it's a guarantee (though funnily enough she's surviving quite well despite all our transgressions). Of course, it doesn't stop there. It never stops there! In addition to that, she also warns us about taking care when we get into town, watching out for each other, minding our bags; the list goes on. Truthfully, I think warning us about perceived dangers is her all-time favourite activity. Of course, we can't deny her the opportunity to off-load either, because it serves no other purpose but to prolong her ramblings if we dare to interject or cut her off in any way.

"Remember girls, look out for each other. I'll be getting a report from each and every one o'ye to see if yiz behaved when ye get home," she says, before turning to me with a pleading look on her face. "Rhian! Make sure everyone stays together. I'm relying on you. You're the one with the sensible head on ye. And whatever the feck yiz do … *do not* … *for one second*, take your eyes off my baby!"

She looks up towards the heavens with an even more desperate and beseeching look on her face, which means that she is laying the responsibility of protection squarely at the foot of the man above – her mentor, leader, weather controller and occasional cake guardian, God above.

Aubrey and Kathy take the opportunity to pull at Jade's cheeks and suck their thumbs in an effort to mock her, but then stop very abruptly when Mam throws a despairing glance in their direction.

I stand looking at my three younger sisters for a moment as they fool around with each other and I know with absolute certainty, gained from years of experience, that it will of course be me taking care of everyone tonight. Gemma may be the eldest but she's not what you'd call leader material. She's way too soft and no one pays any heed to her anyway.

"We will, Ma," says Aubrey with a roll of her eyes.

"And she's not a feckin' baby," adds Kathy. "Sure she's eighteen now, for God's sake. A bleeding aul' wan is what she is!"

Aubrey howls with laughter as Kathy hobbles around the kitchen with her imaginary walking stick, an expression on her face that would make you think she was having some kind of spasm.

"She'll always be my baby no matter what age she is!" says Mam defiantly. "Besides, you know the world out there is full of feckin' nutters. So you guys make sure to keep her safe."

Looking at Kathy and Aubrey right now I can't help but think that, just possibly, all of the nutters in the world are residing in this house, right here, right at this moment in time. Still, I know what Mam is alluding to are the homophobic nutters, in particular.

Since Jade came out, almost three years back, Mam has lived in constant fear for her safety. It may well be the 90s but sometimes it still feels like we're living in the Dark Ages when it comes to matters of sex and sexuality – as if nature didn't design it so. And despite the fact that it is impossible to meet a more honest, honourable and good-hearted person than our Jade, it doesn't stop the "nutters" from hurling abuse and calling out as we walk down the road.

In the last three years we have all been called out on the streets around our estate as "homo lovers", "homos", "lesbos" and various other "O's" that are usually inaudible because they're being called out by some witless coward behind a wall or a tree somewhere – no doubt someone with a lot less moral fibre than my baby sister. Thankfully though, episodes like that are few and far between. Jade may put on a brave face and she has never let on that it bothers her, but appearances can be deceiving and I'd say it hurts her nevertheless. Consequently, it's a worry for Mam even if it is a rare occurrence, so we listen respectfully as she rattles off a few more, trite instructions for us. If the past has taught us anything it has taught us that Mam won't be deterred in her instructions. She needs to say it to gain some comfort and peace of mind, and if we want some brevity then we must maintain a respectful silence and *seeming* attention to her words.

When she finally gets every last syllable off her chest, we then go and line up in front of Dad for inspection. It's been a custom of ours since we were young teenagers that, come Saturday evening, when we were heading out to the local disco or a party in a friend's house, Dad would insist on checking that we were "daycently dressed". His rules were: scant makeup and skirts below the knees. Of course, there were also the customary warnings to accompany these inspections: the risk to our mother's health and how infractions were likely to send her to an early grave; bring shame on the family, blah, blah, blah ... How that woman has avoided the grave thus far is beyond all comprehension. As children, our father was always driving that point – he had us living in constant fear of putting our ma in the grave before her time. So quite simply, skirts up around your neck were a definite no-no. God bless his innocence – he never once thought of checking our bags.

Of course, these days if you're not poured into your jeans or have at least a hint of butt cheek peeking out from under your skirt then you're ferociously overdressed and earmarked for the nunnery, which I think is possibly more of a concern for our parents at this stage in life than any advertisement of availability. After all, they still have five unattached young ladies living at home. That has to be a little scary for them. Anyway, the whole ritual is only done now for the craic. He really doesn't expect us to be lining up for inspection at this stage in our lives. Adding to that, when Kathy moved out, the "line-up" stopped for a period of time because, quite simply, it didn't make sense without her.

Not too long back, Kathy had the bright notion of marrying some random lad she had only just met, when away on a trip to Spain with some friends (not even close friends I might add, just people she knew who invited her along). The whole courting took only six weeks in total – start to finish – before they head off out to Las Vegas, on his money, for a wonderfully deep and memorable ten-minute ceremony which none of the family got to partake in. Surprisingly enough, things didn't work out and ten months later she was moving back in here, to our modest but cosy four-bed semi in Tallaght. We missed her terribly when she left of course, but running off to Vegas with someone you barely know isn't exactly a recipe for eternal love. Still, luckily we didn't have to miss her for too long, and now Mam and Dad have their five little birds back in the nest once again. That' also the way things look set to stay, for the foreseeable future, or at least until Jade and now Kathy finish their respective courses.

Jade is currently studying to re-sit part of her leaving cert and Kathy is doing a bookkeeping course which is being part-funded by the company she currently works for. Then, of course, there's the small matter of Aubrey, who just needs to get off her arse and have a notion of becoming employed or engaged in something on any level. Gemma and I, on the other hand, don't have any excuse for being at home right now because we both work full-time. Gemma's a nurse in Our Lady's Children's Hospital in Crumlin and I teach music out in Ballyfermot. Not rocket science but it pays the bill. Regardless, we're in no hurry to leave our mammy and daddy, just yet.

So, after Dad makes some silly, nonsensical comments about our attire and our need to attend to our morals, just to participate in the ritual, we all hug and kiss our parents, put on our coats, hats, gloves and scarves, and head for the front door.

One by one we step out into the cold night air, Gemma leading the way and me keeping up the rear. I watch them all as they canter eagerly ahead, full of life, enthusiasm and bound to the moment like it were the mast of the Hesperus (before the storm and without the gruesome end of course). Aubrey and Kathy look almost to be skipping along, their arms linked childishly and their heads pressed closely together, rather conspiratorially. Jade, who hovers close to Gemma, is peering intently, almost fearfully up into her face as if some vital piece of wisdom now being imparted might somehow escape her and precious secrets will have been conveyed for less than their true value.

I watch them as they hurry across the green and the notion flits through my brain like a spectre sent to jolt life into understanding; they are the world to me; I love them all with every fibre of my being. We fight, we snipe, we sneer and sometimes we even overlook each other. But when it comes to the crunch each one lays it on the line for the other. Maybe because we're all so close in age there is a greater camaraderie, or maybe it's just luck or faith or even genes – who knows? All I do know is that I could not ask for better friends in all this world. Gemma in particular, with her easy temperament, makes such a natural confidant. Her kindness and her patience are a genuine inspiration and she's so utterly oblivious to all of it: to her beauty and sweetness. In my lifetime so far, I have met many women who, with half her beauty, would wield it like a mighty weapon, to slay and overpower; and with great success, I might add. But not Gemma McCarthy. It's like she doesn't even recognise her own physicality, not even on the basest levels.

As we walk to the edge of the green area that stretches out in front of the line of houses where we live and on through the estate towards the main road where our bus stop is, I can't help but notice how passers-by look at her with unfettered reverence: her flowing blond hair and flawless porcelain complexion, something that just has to be gazed upon; her sweet smile a testament to how oblivious she is to her radiance. It's a curse as much as it is a gift for her because the truth of the matter is that men are intimidated by such beauty, and so they rarely dare to approach her. As a result, she has the most terrible luck in love. I would dearly love to see her meet someone nice – someone who could dare to deserve her – but it is something that seems to elude her with painful persistence.

For a few moments more I ponder to myself about luck and love, until something startles me from my reverie and I look up to see Aubrey and Kathy bolt into action, running the last few yards to the bus. "Bus" I hear someone yell and almost immediately, realising that the bus is pulling up to the stop, I follow suit, Gemma and Jade in tow. Luckily enough we're old hands at this now and even though my body may have been a tad unprepared for the dash, it easily complies and we very fortunately make it, just in the nick of time.

THERE'S A HORSE ON THE BUS

The bus is crowded and noisy, and there's a dreadful screeching, droning sound emanating from the general vicinity of the vehicle's undercarriage. It draws an image in my mind of a giant mechanical beast gasping its last breaths as it struggles to claw a path to its final destination. Coupled with that, and despite the fact that it's still relatively early in terms of Saturday night revelry, the melodious tones of a drunken sing-song can be heard coming from the upper deck. The song, which I can quite easily make out, is "Fisherman's Blues". The main crooner, it would appear, is delighting his audience with a comical and seemingly spontaneous variation on the original lyrics. He has quite adeptly substituted "from bonds" with "your buns" and "I will ride on the train" with "I will ride you on the train", drawing a raucous retort of "whoop whoops", whistling and thunderous laughter from his audience. I can't help but feel mildly impressed by the casual artist's ingenuity and talent as he delivers his rather pleasant-sounding comedy-song-combo.

Aubrey and Kathy hurry to the nearest seats, flopping down and gasping loudly for breath in exaggerated style.

Jade follows, taking a pew directly behind them, while Gemma lingers, waiting on me as I stand motionless beside the driver's hatch.

"You do know that there's a pony on your bus," I say to him, thinking that he's going to lambast me for stating the blatantly obvious as I nod disbelievingly in the direction of the equine anomaly.

"Wha? That's not a fecking pony, ye eejit. It's a Great Dane! You know! Scooby-Doo, like? The largest dog in the world apparently. I have it on good authority that that fella there is a genuine Guinness World Record holder, no less," he says in pure earnest, and with a completely straight face. For a moment I'm not sure how to respond. Instead, I look once more at the lad holding the creature by a piece of rope and back at the driver whom I suddenly realise is surely one of two things and that is either, thick as two short planks, or possible just thick, with no accompanying analogy. And seeing as how these two options are technically no different from one another, I decide to allow him the benefit of the doubt by assuming he's settled for denial over arguing with the moderately intimidating group of teenage lads who are now giving me impatient looks.

The girls all seem oblivious to the creature's presence even though they had to manoeuvre with some skill and dexterity around it to get to their seats. The girls seem not only oblivious to it but, dare I say, relatively comfortable in its not inconspicuous presence as if it were some old and familiar friend or neighbour – Hairy Nelly from No. 5 perhaps. They are completely unperturbed, so much so that, quite regrettably, they are now comfortable enough with loudly declaring the talent on offer tonight as being "of slim pickings". Furthermore, they continue vociferously assessing what is on offer around them and it makes me cringe with embarrassment at every word. For a second or two, I wonder if possibly I'm spending too much time with my head down, focusing inward, working and doing my own thing, and not enough time looking around at the unceasing carnival that I'm an unwitting player in.

I'm not the only one mortified by their crass behaviour either, which becomes apparent by Gemma awkwardly and abruptly grabbing me by the hand to guide me towards a seat at the very back of the bus, on the opposite side from where they're seated, and out of view.

We settle in and promptly turn to gaze out of the dirty window into the darkness beyond, hoping that it will somehow allow us to disassociate ourselves from the awful behaviour of our two younger siblings. Poor Jade, who is perched on the seat behind them, is left with no option but to stare down at her feet, as if in doing so she may be afforded some valid distraction. But for the life of me, I can't think of one thing that feet might do spontaneously and which might help her out in some way; I fear she looks in vain.

"You do see the horse! Don't you? I'm not imagining it or going doolally or anything?" I say to Gemma finally.

"What horse?" she says as unconvincingly as anyone could have ever possibly done. "Yes, I see him! He's been on the bus before and I wouldn't call it a horse, Rhian. It's a pony at best. Your man there has the driver believing that it's a Great Dane *mix*. He says that there might have been a pony in the family somewhere along the line but that that's how Great Danes get to be so big anyway." We both look as incredulous as we possibly can at each other, as if no words uttered at any time in humankind's existence could ever sound more ludicrous.

"Sure, it's doing no harm Ree, leave them at it," says Gemma with a hint of a smirk, before taking a small paperback from her bag and turning to a page bookmarked somewhere near the end.

"It stinks of horse!" I offer weakly, before turning to gaze once more out of the window with an exasperated sigh. Blurry, mucky images flash before my eyes and yet I still see little through the well-coated glass. It's rather hypnotic and soothing and threatens to sedate me against my will. So I decide to sit with my eyes closed, facing forward, hoping against hope that Aubrey and Kathy will take this as a sign that I'm having a nap, which in turn might prompt them to refrain from involving me in any of their loud outpourings of non-wisdom with regard to "this wan", "them wans" and "yer wan's" offensive, garish and just downright "wrong" behaviour. The hypocrisy of their spewings is monumental. But they soon tire of their own ramblings and before long a welcome lull washes over the lower deck of the bus.

Thankfully we're not too long into the journey when the bus pulls up to a stop just outside another housing estate and Scooby-Doo, along with his entourage, disembark. But before they've cleared the entrance, two young girls, who I estimate to be about sixteen or seventeen years of age, barge their way past and onto the bus, cursing the exiting passengers as they go. After paying their fare, they strut up the aisle, oozing attitude while chomping open-mouthed on huge balls of pink chewing gum; before coming to a dead stop directly in front of Aubrey and Kathy. Neither of my sisters pays any heed to them despite their obvious presence and attempts to draw attention to themselves.

"Would ya look at the state of your wan – the lesbo?" says the taller of the two girls in an exaggerated drawl, before shooting a glance towards her companion who in turn gives a little flick of her hair in acknowledgement and support.

For a brief moment, the words hang in the air as if suspended, desperately trying to claw their way into understanding. I look at Jade who fidgets a little in her seat, clearly intimidated by the two young women, and just as I'm about to get up and go over to sit beside her, Aubrey bolts up from her seat, fire visible in her eyes, in her countenance, in her every atom. I am quite startled by the spectacle myself and shrink back in the seat, content to watch and observe.

"What the fuck did you just say, ya scaldy weapon?" she hisses, spittle landing squarely on the girl's face.

I look at Gemma who seems nonplussed by the theatre that is unfolding before us and cautiously ask her, "Do you think we should intervene?"

"No! Let's just see what happens. Mam warned her. Remember? After she punched Sally Keogh's young one. She said if Aubrey puts her hands on anyone ever again, no matter what they say to Jade, or any of us for that matter, then she's going to be in so much trouble. And she wasn't joking either."

Kathy pulls at Aubrey's sleeve and I can hear her instructing her sister to let it go. But there's no question about it, Aubrey is having a hard time holding herself in check.

"Say that again! Go on! I fecking dare ye!" she hisses while Kathy continues to tug at her sleeve half-heartedly, fiddling around with her bag at the same time.

"Wouldn't waste me breath!" says the rather startled-looking and now red-faced young girl with mock bravado. Her friend, who's obviously realised that Jade is not alone, pulls her anxiously towards the stairs, trying hard, but losing the battle, not to look terrified. As she backs away, she makes a gesture with her fingers and her tongue and it's like a red rag to a bull. Aubrey makes a valid but thankfully futile attempt to go for her, but oddly enough can't seem to move. In the few moments it took for this argument to escalate Kathy had, with great foresight, managed to clip the strap of her bag through the strap of Aubrey's, which she has slung across her chest and then latched round the handrail. The two girls take their opportunity and bolt up the stairs, while Aubrey struggles briefly to release herself. For a moment she can't quite work out what's going on and her confusion inevitably burns her fury out. When certain that she's finally calm Jade reaches over and unclips the bag strap. Only then does Aubrey realise what was preventing her from moving.

"Ye bitch!" she says with some amount of residual surprise. "That wan deserves a good kick in the hole."

"Yeah, and if you give it to her, you'll get a kick in the hole yourself," says Kathy with a slight smirk on her face. "I just saved your ass, so sit down and relax your cacks."

"Go on ye hooer, feck off!" she shouts towards the vacant stairwell, before turning to ask Jade if she's all right. Jade giggles nervously, nodding at Aubrey before turning to look over her shoulder at myself and Gemma, her lips pursed in an attempt to suppress a laugh.

Almost immediately, calm is restored and the hum of casual chatter begins to rise up around us again.

It's not too long before the bus reaches its destination and when it does, I take a peek over at Aubrey and Kathy. It's hard to ignore the looks of relief on the faces of those passengers sitting nearby, as they too prepare to exit the bus. However, I let myself believe that it was the comments made by the other girl that really offended, and that thought settles the feeling of discord that had gripped me for most of the journey.

The bus stops at the Central Bank and when we finally get off, I head straight towards the pedestrian crossing giving the girls no option but to follow me and therefore no chance to make a hazardous crossing where they just alighted – through the chaos of the city-centre traffic.

Aubrey and Kathy have already declared that they will be going no further than they can throw a stick tonight and that they will sup at every bar within a twenty-yard radius of where they stand at this very moment in time. Aubrey proceeds to draw an imaginary line in the air, just to more clearly delineate that boundary. I'm afraid to count how many bars that may encompass but you can be guaranteed that in Dublin City it's going to be *quite* a few and no question of it.

After we cross the road safely, both Aubrey and Kathy take off running again and leave Jade trailing behind, which is not an uncommon occurrence. However, she seems unsure of whether to follow or just wait on Gemma and me as we linger, too obviously, before ambling at a ridiculously slow pace in pursuit of them. They disappear into the alleyway at the Mercantile and Gemma and I pause to look at each other, grinning sarcastically.

"Remind me again how I keep getting suckered into these things?" I ask with good humour.

"Come on guys!" urges Jade as she waits briefly for us to muster the enthusiasm. We clearly take too long because she succumbs and disappears into the alleyway after them.

By the time Gemma and I stroll through, linger a little more and then push open the heavy teak and glass doors into the bar, which is only literally minutes later, the girls have already hooked up with a group of people at the bar and are flirting unashamedly with the male members of the group. Jade is standing slightly apart from them, looking awkward, which again is not entirely unusual for her, but on this occasion, she seems to want to be a more comfortable part of the social group. For this reason, Gemma and I beckon for her to join us as soon as we have settled ourselves at a table with our drinks in hand. She hesitates momentarily before coming to join us. In that moment I can see, and not for the first time, the difficulties Jade faces on too many occasions. She wants to be part of the younger, more energetic social group, but she has little in common with either Aubrey or Kathy who, for their part, are oblivious to her presence as well as our absence.

We sip our drinks and observe our surroundings quite contentedly for some time before any conversation is necessary. It's a very pleasant thing to be able to do and something that is rarely permitted for any long period of time in the McCarthy household – a comforting silence –

and I feel a warm sense of satisfaction in this moment, as well as a measure of relief at managing to acquire probably the last remaining seat in the place.

"Yer man over there is giving you the eye, Gem!" says Jade, finally breaking the silence.

"He is too!" I interject and then nod to a small group of four people, who at one stage were with the group Aubrey and Kathy are talking to now, but almost immediately after we entered the bar detached themselves when a nearby seat became available. The "man" we are talking about is a rather pleasant and attractive-looking red-haired guy with the warmest smile and kind, soulful eyes. He's very well dressed and immaculately groomed and is perched almost reluctantly on the edge of his seat, like he can't decide whether he wants to stay or not. His hair is a floppy kind of style, but smart, and is genuinely the nicest shade of almost-auburn red that I've ever seen before – not that I'm biased in favour of redheads or anything, but it is quite a fetching shade. I immediately decide that I like him tremendously. His three companions, however, a dark-haired man and two very genteel-looking ladies, can only be described as the most miserable-looking companions a man could ever be cursed to have in tow. The guy in particular, who is a little less polished than the others and who may very well have been hauled here, kicking and screaming from a studio where he was auditioning for a role in "Desert Island – The Sequel", judging by his attire and countenance, looks positively sorrowful.

"Oh stop, guys," giggles Gemma. "He's probably just looking over here because he's facing this way. What do you want him to do, look at the ceiling?"

We all look towards the ceiling at the mention of it and shrug in unison.

"I bet you anything that Ma could wear a hole in that ceiling up there too, with her scuab, if she had half a mind to," says Jade with a little giggle.

When we look back down a bolt of horror runs the length of my body as I see Kathy swaying drunkenly in our direction, bumping into people as she goes. When she reaches our table, she nearly bowls over it and it's clear that she's way beyond redemption at this point.

Apparently, herself and Aubrey had been drinking on the bus from a naggin that was in Kathy's handbag, which might go some way towards explaining the carry-on of them on the bus and the state they're in right now. This of course I know, not because I witnessed it first-hand, but because it's being relayed to me at this very moment.

"Come on over and join us girls," she says with more than a hint of a drunken slur. "You're such a boring shower of shites just sitting there looking around yiz."

I turn to look at Jade and then Gemma before clearing my throat and uttering, with Oscar-winning delivery, "Sorry! Do we know you?"

Gemma and Jade giggle at this a little because Kathy is now so drunk that she is genuinely and momentarily confused by my words, but before she can gather her wits about her Jade decides to proffer her tuppence-worth as well.

"Listen, if ye don't piss off *young wan*, we'll get the bouncer to throw ye out!" she says loudly enough for people around us to hear and I can't help but giggle myself when I see some of them prick up their ears.

"Shh!" says Gem. "Stop messing about or you'll have us all thrown out."

At this stage, it is safe to assume that Kathy is either too drunk to comprehend the theatre of it all or the alcohol has sapped her of all interest in putting any more effort into enticing us, so she turns and walks back towards her increasingly raucous group, giving the detached foursome, close by, a nose in the air as she goes.

"Oh, I wonder what that was all about," says Jade. "Did you see that look she gave them?"

"Yes! I most certainly did," I say, a little conspiratorially.

"What do you think Rhian? You're always great at working stuff like that out. Give us your take on it?" says Gemma, a little excited by the prospect of some profound insight or maybe just hoping for a bit of juicy gossip that I'll have to make up as I have no notion of what transpired in those few moments before we entered the pub.

"Well, I've been watching them since we came in and they were all part of the same group at first – that crowd that Aubrey and Kathy are with right now!" I nod towards the bar before continuing. "However, I reckon that they're a bit pissed off with the antics of a certain pair of unladylikes – except for your fella of course, Gem," I say, giving her a little wink just to let her know I'm only kidding. "They probably fancy that they're too good for our lasses. Look a little stuck up to me if I'm being totally honest. See your man there with the black hair? We'll call him Grumpy just so we can identify him. Well, he's been rolling his eyes this last ten minutes without a hint of a let-up. I reckon he's probably one of the most miserable looking so-and-sos I've ever seen in me whole, entire life, if the truth be told. Now! I'm not averse to the possibility or suggestion that I may be a little off the mark on that score – which of course I'm not. But you asked for it and I have given it to you – my profound, ill-informed and entirely correct synopsis of the current social dynamic within the aforementioned groupage," I say with a snort, a laugh and a certain degree of smugness before settling back in my chair, a self-satisfied grin lighting my face, waiting to see what response I get. And as God is my witness, I could have predicted what that exact response was going to be.

"Oh, I don't know. They look lovely to me, Rhian. You can be quite judgemental by times you know," says Gem in her usual, super-irritating, *non-judgemental* kind of way.

I don't know why I get asked for my tremendously accurate opinion just to be told I'm wrong.

"I think you read way too much, sis," says Jade quite honestly. "I genuinely didn't understand half of what you just said. Got the gist all right but hell, you talk in riddles sometimes and I think sometimes you make words up. 'Groupage'? What the hell ails ya, girl?"

We all laugh at the contorted grimace on Jade's face, even Jade herself, before returning to our silent reverie once more.

Looking slyly over at the foursome once again, just to reassure myself that I'm on the mark, I resign myself to the fact that Gemma is indeed the one who has got things wrong, particularly about the lovely bit. And definitely with regard to the two women and Grumpy, though I haven't entirely written off ginger at this point – us redheads need to stick together! That, at least, is one thing I will not be challenged on.

"Right, I'm off to the loo and when I get back, we're taking Jade somewhere else," I say, getting up from my seat with a flourish and a smile. "It's your night out too, hon, so we might as well bring you somewhere that you can eye up the talent if you've a mind to." With that, I head off around the bar in the direction of the toilets, Jade trotting enthusiastically behind me with a few suggestions about where exactly we could go.

Her enthusiasm isn't the slightest bit dampened by the foul smell that hits us when we open the toilet door and even though I hurry to get out as quickly as possible she is intent on holding me up by lingering to apply some makeup. I gaze at myself in the mirror for a moment and a flame-haired woman I barely recognise looks back at me. I know it can't be, but I'm almost positive that the woman in the mirror is possibly not the same one that left the McCarthy house earlier. Her hair looks like an explosion in a wool and mandarin-orange factory, which prompts me to silently curse the scourge of misty rain. When we left the house this evening, it did, unfortunately, spit rain relentlessly from the time we left the house until we got on the bus, and rain and my hair do not go very well together. When we left, I had a lovely head of almost straight hair, blow-dried to perfection for a change, and with so much more effort put in than I normally care to give to my appearance. But the rain has turned it into a heap of curly, wavy chaos and now it's beyond taming. I wonder why I even bothered.

When we were kids Mam used to always encourage us to eat the crusts of our bread saying that it would make our hair go curly. And in all our innocence we ate them because she made curly hair sound like a good thing. Truthfully, I wish that I'd had the sense to chuck at least a few of those crusts into the bin when I had the chance. Still, it's only an old wives' tale. Genuinely, I don't think I ever realistically had a chance of dodging the curls if the truth be known.

"Jade! I'll see you outside when you're finished. I can't stand the smell in here anymore," I say, wrinkling my nose and pulling my sleeve over my hand to cup my nostrils.

Jade grunts in response as she is unable to speak, and I allow myself a little snicker at the sight of her methodically applying lip liner to her upper lip with all the skill and precision of a transfixed toddler, before I turn and leave.

In the ten minutes that I have been in the toilet, the pub has filled up considerably more and I have to push my way through the now tightly compacted crowd which is blocking my route back to the table. In my efforts I accidentally bump into the dark-haired guy – Grumpy. He moves aside and gives me a very haughty nod before moving on through the throng himself.

When I get back to the table, I see that Gemma has been joined by her smiling admirer and his two female companions. He seems very happy to finally be where he had designs on being and I notice that he sits more decidedly on his seat now.

"Rhian! Can I introduce you to Simon?" she asks when I

draw close enough to hear. "And this is Kelly and Moira! Kelly is Simon's sister and Moira is her best friend. You just missed Matt. I think he's gone to the bar. Sorry!" she says, looking to the group who are now appraising me like I was some prize market bull. "This is my sister Rhian!"

"Hi, Rhian! Lovely to meet you," says Simon, getting up from his seat to shake my hand, quite enthusiastically.

"Nice to meet you, Simon," I say before turning to nod and smile at the two ladies who have evidently chosen silence over polite greetings. I make a mental note to dislike them a little bit more definitely now.

"Simon and Matt are over from England on a business trip. They're partners … *business* partners," she clarifies. "They have their own company. Property! Isn't that right, Simon?" says Gem with a look of childish admiration on her face.

Simon nods his head with equal adoration at Gem's eloquent introductions and so she continues on, encouraged by the approving gesture. The noise level in the pub has reached that certain level when conversation becomes more of an effort than an enjoyment among a group, causing me to drift in and out of the conversation. I struggle to hear and consequently only pick up bits of what she says.

Apparently Simon and Matt build, buy, sell, restore and do practically everything with properties. They have a particular interest in restorations but the bread and butter of their business is building. Blah, blah, blah! Now they're branching out and having a look at the Irish market and while they're visiting, Matt has decided that he just has to buy a little retreat in the west of Ireland. Blah, blah, blah. Because he thinks it's one of the most beautiful places he has ever seen in his life. Blah, blah, blah. And it would also appear that he has heaps of money but no personality – that last bit I made up myself and only because in the meantime, Matt returned from the bar or wherever he was and seated himself in the chair by the window where he now sits in what can only be described as miserable contemplation. I wonder for a moment if it would be at all possible to buy yourself a personality, before my brain sparks amazement at how much Gemma and Simon managed to cram into ten or fifteen minutes. Maybe I was in the loo for longer than I thought?

"So you like the west of Ireland?" I say, directing my statement/question squarely at Matt, inviting him to join the conversation.

"Yes!" he says, nodding but not elaborating, before looking away. The silence sucks up the energy around us, immediately igniting my mischievousness in near tandem.

"Excellent … and who would doubt that for a moment," I say quite theatrically while turning to engage everyone visually. "It's only too clear by your voluminous endorsement of it," I continue, with just a hint of a smirk on my face.

Simon and Gemma let a reluctant giggle slip from their mouths and I feel a warm sense of superiority wash over me before my logical self starts conjuring up a telling-off for the more spontaneous side of me.

I don't know these people at all and I couldn't care much about their opinions of me, but it's evident that Gemma is getting on very well with Simon. As soon as the words are out of my mouth and the snickering has ceased, I make a mental note not to be a smart arse for her sake. To do that though, I'm going to have to leave.

Grumpy gives me a look of unbridled disdain – I haven't impressed him – so I make my move to go before Jade, who has been hovering over me, spontaneously combusts.

"If you'll all excuse us please, we have an errand to run," I say, taking Jade by the hand. "You know where Kathy and Aubrey are if you need them Gemma but I won't be too long anyway. I'm entrusting you with the safety and well-being of my sister while I'm gone Simon," I say, turning to look accusingly at him. He nods and smiles sweetly at me and then at Gemma, clearly delighted at having been given such a desirous task.

Gemma looks briefly down at her feet with a shy smile before returning to her conversation with him and he in turn continues to gaze at her like a love-sick puppy. His two female companions are engrossed in conversation with one another and Matt is … well, he's just sitting there, looking awkward and lost.

Kathy and Aubrey can be heard from somewhere off to the left of the bar so I just wink at Gemma as I head out through the door with Jade by my side. I dare not look in Matt's direction but I can feel his eyes on me nevertheless.

Out the door and up to George's Street we go.

THE HEART OF DUBLIN

At almost twenty-two years of age, I'm not exactly what you'd call a beaming specimen of worldly wisdom, and my formal social life is but a mere half a decade in swing. Nevertheless, in all that time, in all the places I've ever been to, I have never once come across a single individual who doesn't have a favourite bar or bars, or style of establishment where they like to do their socialising, and which matches with their values, maybe even aspirations, or plain and simple needs. I know that's a very broad statement if ever there was one but still, we like what we like and that's the crux of it. So when it comes down to choice of establishment, my tastes vary quite dramatically when compared to Jade's. However, we do both agree that this bar in particular, the one she likes to call "her local" despite the fact that geographically it doesn't come close, is somewhere we're both happy to while away a couple of hours, or even an afternoon in. It also confers a great sense of relief to be able to escort my younger sister, and more importantly, leave her somewhere that I feel this level of comfort with.

But despite that we nevertheless have, as a group, strict

rules with regard to safety and support when we're on a night out, particularly when we venture into the city centre. Either myself or Gemma will accompany Jade to one or her favourite bars, and it makes no odds to us once she's happy. When she has hooked up with friends and is okay with being left alone, we more often than not head away to do our own thing. Only on the very odd occasion will we stay with her for the entire night. That depends on our reason for going to town in the first place. Then, at an appointed time and predetermined spot, we all meet up again, all five of us, to make sure that everyone gets on the Nitelink and home safely. As things normally go, Kathy and Aubrey tend to socialise as a single unit, most of the time, as do Gemma and I, so it makes sense that we more often meet at the pub where Jade has been drinking. Unless she has someone reliable to see her to the bus stop, which tonight, I'm quite satisfied will be the case, because no sooner are we through the door of the pub than a very tall glamourous-looking guy runs over to hug her excitedly and whip her away from me. My eyes follow them as I wonder at his beauty and salience, and more importantly the obvious attention he has paid to his appearance. His medium-length, dark brown hair, enviably styled, is of a lustre and depth of colour that reminds me of pictures from glossy magazines perched conspicuously on the shelves of trendy bookshops, and his attire is awe-inspiring. He has a fitted, berry-coloured sequinned frock, just below the knees, hugging an inch-perfect figure, and the entire outfit is accessorised to a standard that I personally, could only dare to dream of pulling off. He sports a pair of patent berry stilettos that raise him a head-height over the tallest person in the room, elevating him as if by design – to be gazed up at in reverence or perhaps simply just to catch the eye of everyone he passes. Unsurprisingly, people turn and stare, transfixed, like the starving might look upon a banquet.

I'm momentarily bowled over and a flood of insecurities

rush to the forefront of my mind, waiting to find reassurance. I hesitate, pondering on my inconspicuousness in comparison, and the crowd at the bar shrinks me further. I'm uncertain about whether or not to tackle the chaotic and crammed throng in front of me.

In the end, I decide the only option is to dash and squeeze into a small gap that's only child-sized and which places me precariously under the armpits of two very tall, muscular men, who incidentally smell like a breath of linen-fresh air. They look down at me and smile with a slight hint of amusement before moving to allow access through. I smile and thank them, warmed by this simple act of human kindness.

While waiting on the glass of cider I've just ordered for Jade, I contemplate a strategy for my risky, drink-carrying foray back into the crowd in search of her again. It's close to 9pm on a Saturday night so understandably the pub is pretty much at full capacity right now. The atmosphere is light and cheery and for some reason doesn't seem quite as claustrophobic as the other place was.

When the barman hands me the drink and my change I head off in search of my sister and despite the dense crowd I have no difficulty finding her. She's standing on the other side of the bar with a large group of men and one woman. The guy in the sequin dress is loudly and excitedly explaining to her that he has plans to do a comedy dating act in a pub up near Stephen's Green which he can't quite remember the name of at the moment because he's "Oh God, all over the place" and I suspect that's because his brain is scrambling to catch up with the stream of information pouring from his mouth. Apparently this new venture of his is going to be the next big thing.

It's clear that I don't have to worry about her now and so I simply decide to hand her the drink, give her a quick hug and remind her of what time the Nitelink is. Then I turn to navigate the thronging masses once more and exit via the door I just came through moments ago.

Once outside I stand for a moment looking around, savouring the hustle and bustle of Dublin City social life. I watch the giddy lovers clinging to each other as they stroll up towards the Arcade, the fashionably dressed young men and women hurrying excitedly to some evening's delights, even the contemplative strollers gazing around them, or with heads bent down staring into their internal worlds. They all add life, sparkle and zest that seems to dance and flow around me. It's such a hearty feast for the senses, seeming to draw light and energy into some immaterial, spiritual compartment within me.

Memories of travels, of faraway cities, people and customs, flood my mind, and I feel overwhelmed with a sense of connection to this city. I know in an instant and with unalterable certainty that not one of those cities or locations I have ever visited, although modest in number, would have a hope of tearing my heart from this place, my home, Dublin City. There's something uncomplicated about this city's essence, this modest metropolis; there's honesty and warmth like nothing I have ever felt anywhere else before. I love it with every fibre of my being. I hate it sometimes too but only in the way that someone does when they overindulge their passions and need to pull back for a time. In the end it always wins me round again. And truthfully, I'd stand here all night observing it if I could, but unfortunately, I've noticed that a nearby drunk, paper bag in hand, is swaying in my direction with a toothless smile that has my name written all over it. I recognise him from other occasions when we've been in town and although he's harmless enough I don't want to get stuck talking to him. He's horrendously incoherent and a little mad to be honest. So, in a pre-emptive move I leave my very enjoyable platform and head to the next destination.

The girls had all seemed pretty content with how their nights were going when I left. Aubrey and Kathy were whipping up a storm and wooing the lads with drunken abandon, while Gemma was finally getting somewhere with a real flesh and blood male. Jade also seemed like the proverbial "pig" and so I feel that, perhaps, on just this one occasion, I can indulge myself by going for a coffee rather than hurrying back to the chaos of the bar. Joining Kathy and Aubrey is not too appealing to me and I don't want to get in Gemma's way right now. I want to wait a while. So, with that in mind, I head off in the direction of Grafton Street in search of somewhere to have a coffee. Where I don't mind, as long as I can sit contemplating by a large unobstructed window and gaze out at the world going by, while also reading a little from the exciting new paperback stashed in my oversized shoulder bag. So, with full intentions of only sitting for a while; just long enough to give Gemma time to make some headway, I stroll off up the street.

On the odd occasion when we all come into town shopping together, an exercise that I despise most fervently, I have the habit of planting myself in Bewley's on Westmoreland Street with my book in hand to wait out the retail frenzy in peace and solitude. More often than not Gemma accompanies me for at least part of the time. I like to think of it as my city-centre haven and it would be my first choice of locations if not for the late hour. But as luck would have it, I come across a perfectly satisfactory fast-food restaurant that has exactly what I need, a big window for observation and contemplation. And so I purchase my coffee and sit happily sipping and reading, sometimes looking up to watch the world go by as I languish indulgently in the hard plastic chair that surprisingly enough is not that uncomfortable.

Two large coffees later and more time than I had intended to linger, I look up momentarily and to my horror, see Matt strolling by on the other side of the street. Looking over, he changes his direction towards the restaurant.

Something on his face, however, tells me that coffee was what caused him to change his direction because as soon as he draws nearer, he spies me sitting by the window and I see a look of horror flash over his face, probably the same one I had two moments ago. It was the kind of look you might see on the face of someone caught wholly off guard and cornered into something very unpalatable. He heads straight past me to the service counter, trying hard to alter the expression winning over on his face, giving me a reluctant nod as he goes.

Promptly I place my book back in my bag, take my coffee in hand and head out the door and back towards the pub where Aubrey, Kathy and Gemma will no doubt be still waiting on me. Dallying a little, I take time to savour the memories that flood back as I tread the familiar route, indulgently surveying my surroundings.

The drizzling rain from earlier has cleared away nicely and the night is quite pleasant, with a gentle, barely discernible breeze licking around me. With December looming, the shops are already adorned for the Christmas season and the streets are lit up in an elaborate and uplifting style with lights twinkling, flashing and glowing all around. The window of Brown Thomas's is a wonder to behold and, peering in, I'm transported back in time to my childhood, to a scene where Mam and Dad have brought all five of us into town to see Santy in Switzer's. We queued up that day, alongside the window that fronts onto Grafton Street, staring in at the moving figures and waiting our turn to be enraptured by the big bearded man in the eye-catching red suit. Standing now, probably in the same spot I stood in many times as a child, I try to breathe those memories, to flood that sense of wonder back into my soul. Leaning close to the building that still bears the sign of Switzers discreetly round to the right, up Wicklow Street, I linger in the comfort of old memories.

"Ahem!"

A voice from behind startles me a little, sending my visions off into oblivion like the thousand minute shards of a shattered light bulb. I turn to see Matt standing, now mute, looking at me as if I'm meant to respond to a throat clearing in some obvious and coherent way. For a moment I contemplate responding with a similar throat clearing followed by a "to you too", but decide to behave instead.

"Matt, isn't it?" I offer, just because I'm feeling the tiniest bit charitable.

"It is! And you are?" he asks, raising his eyebrows and adding, "I'm sorry, I didn't catch your name earlier!"

"I'm Rhian but you can call me Ree!" I say desperately scrambling for a way out of further conversation and away from him altogether. "Gemma – you know, the cute blond talking to your friend Simon – she's my sister: the eldest. And Jade, the lass I left the bar with earlier, she's our baby – the youngest, I mean."

He furrows his brows in a quizzical and mildly derisive manner, and for some bizarre reason, despite feeling a little discouraged, I still decide to continue on with my ramblings.

"Aubrey and Kathy, whom I suspect you met earlier in the night, are also sisters of mine – younger sisters, twins actually!" I continue on, realising that I have failed epically at my attempts to cease conversing with him.

Partly because he intimidates me a little and partly because I dislike his apparent snobbishness and also partly for unknown reasons, I continue to ramble on. It's very disconcerting but I seem to be somehow not in control of it at all.

"Anyway, I'm heading back there now. What about you?" I finally conclude and he doesn't immediately answer, so I turn to leave.

"I'll walk with you!" he states in quite a startled manner, as if by turning I had just prompted him as to what comes next. "I'm heading back myself," he continues as he moves to follow behind me. "We don't come to the city centre too often so I thought it would be nice to explore a little," he adds as if to explain his presence, his reason for being here at this moment.

Now it's his turn to ramble on and for a guy that couldn't find words one minute, he certainly conjures a few in the end. I scramble around in my brain but maddeningly can find no appropriate substitute for "go away, please" and so I'm left with no option but to walk with large strides as briskly as possible to limit the amount of time I'll have to spend with him.

Rounding the corner onto Wicklow Street I take a sneaky peek up at the Switzers sign and smile to myself before pounding on up the road leaving him to try and keep pace. It proves to be entirely within his capabilities as he has a substantially longer stride than I do and it's not long before I have to slow down and pace myself a little just to draw enough breath. The silence now is a little uncomfortable for me and the end of Wicklow Street seems quite a distance off still. Up ahead I notice a man sitting half in, half out of the doorway of a closed, unlit shop front, a cup laid out in front of him, his head bent, a sign in his hand. As I draw nearer, I can see that the sign is asking for money for a hostel for tonight. Without breaking my stride much, I quickly rummage in my pocket and retrieve two fifty pence coins, depositing them into the cup as I pass. Instantly I have this sense, an almost palpable feeling, that Matt wants to make a comment, right before he actually does.

"You shouldn't do that, you know," he says, with a measure of reserve that has no place in such bold or direct statement. It makes me dearly wish that I could shed my irritatingly frequent need to not offend and tell him to feck off. But instead, I choose the less direct approach.

"Oh really? And why is that Matt?" I say, stopping to face him directly. But he doesn't respond, he just stares at me rather intently in an uncomfortably appraising kind of way and so I turn once more and continue on my way, feeling a little bad about my abrupt tone. So I decide to smooth things over a little.

"How are you enjoying your trip so far?" I ask, eventually.

"I must admit, it's growing on me a little ... Dublin, I mean! The last time we were here, well, I wasn't too impressed. It's just different to what I'm used to," he says hesitantly and I get the strong sense that he's trying to choose his words so as not to offend. Of course, any words that might slight my dear beloved Dublin or Ireland in any way would be guaranteed to do that and I have no doubt that he knows that. I smile inwardly at his obvious discomfort and attempts to awkwardly navigate the English language before throwing him a lifeline.

"I suppose it's the same for anybody; what's not familiar can be a little strange. You'll get used to us before long. You might even come to like us." I say, offering him a little smile before turning away from him again.

The pub is now happily in my sights again. As we approach the door, he speeds up a bit, moving ahead to open it up for me and so I nod a thank you, smiling gratefully as I walk past and into the warm, welcoming hum and heat of the interior.

Inside, the pub seems noisier and more chaotic than before. Gemma is still sitting chatting with Simon, the same drink in front of her by the looks of its dead, uncarbonated appearance. His two female companions are now at the bar with their coats on as if they expect to be leaving at any moment and Aubrey is passed out on the seat where the foursome had been sitting earlier. Kathy is sharing a small table a little distance away from everybody else with some guy I don't remember from earlier, and she is being uncharacteristically civil for a change. Maybe it's not my sister at all; maybe this is some doppelganger or alien take-over that I'm witnessing.

Matt, who had been standing patiently behind me for the last few seconds, half in and half out of the doorway, finally moves around me and positions himself in front.

"May I get you a drink?" he offers awkwardly and for a moment I contemplate having just one small tipple.

"No thank you!" I say quite sweetly. "That's very nice of you but I need to get my sister moving or we'll miss the Nitelink. Unfortunately, we didn't leave the house till … well, much later than we normally do, and as everybody is on a budget saving for Christmas, we won't be having a late one tonight," I say politely. Mark excuses himself to go to the bar, gesturing to Simon who declines a drink before turning to check and see if Gemma would like a fresh one.

I'm a little distracted now as the big wooden framed clock on the wall is telling me that we probably only have about ten minutes before we need to leave. I nod to Gemma before hurrying to the Ladies and back out again in record time. When I return Matt is moving to sit down, right beside Aubrey's slumped carcass. She groans loudly and turns to rest her head on his shoulder. The look of horror on his face is almost comical. Not for the first time tonight I delight in his discomfort while mentally scolding myself in tandem. It's not that I like seeing him uncomfortable, but it's a comical sight nonetheless.

After about four or five very long minutes I finally manage to rally all of the girls and we promptly exit the pub after Simon eventually releases Gemma from the longest hug goodbye ever witnessed by humankind ever. Before you know it, we're all running down the road desperately trying to catch a bus that is three minutes away and which is leaving in about two minutes. It will be a true miracle if we make this one tonight.

But luck is on our side and not only do we make it in time but Jade has saved our skins by purchasing our tickets and sparing us further delay. I immediately slump into my window seat and watch the world go by as the bus promptly speeds off towards its destination.

Aubrey is now slumped snoring away on my shoulder while Kathy, who is sitting on the seat across from us, gazes quietly out through the muddy window. Gemma and Jade, who occupy the seat behind myself and Aubrey, are talking excitedly about their night's exploits. From what I can glean, Simon has invited us all to a party at his place next weekend. Jade is wondering if she can bring this girl she met a couple of weeks ago but only managed to hook up with tonight, as Gemma repeatedly assures her that Simon insisted on it. Kathy apparently will be able to see Bill (the guy she was sitting with apparently) at the party, which Gemma assures Jade is wonderful news. Bill is a colleague of Simon and Matt's and he came into the pub after I left so unfortunately I never got to formally meet him, but he's a gent by all accounts.

I drift off to the sound of their low banter and when I finally come to again, we're thankfully nearing our stop. Kathy and Jade have to practically carry Aubrey off the bus, but when the cold night air hits her she becomes re-energised, re-invigorated and back to her loud, garish self.

Walking up the road and across the green area that lies in front of our house, I finally get a chance to ask Gemma about Simon.

"He's so lovely Rhian! Amazingly sweet and kind-hearted," she says dreamily.

"Gem, you think everyone is sweet and kind-hearted," I reply.

"He is though, Rhian. And we had so much to talk about. It was amazingly easy to talk to him," she says by way of further expounding his graces. "He wants us all to join him next weekend. Himself and Matt have leased a property in Ballsbridge near the RDS for the next few months and they're having a bit of a get-together with friends and neighbours. It's to help with networking and integration and stuff like that. He said that we can bring partners if we like. Jade is going to bring Amy with her. Oh, I'm so thrilled for her. She's been talking about this Amy for so long and now they're finally going out. It's just wonderful," she says with obvious delight. "And Kathy will get to see Bill again. Those two have so much in common. Bill is a building contractor and Kathy used to help out with Brian's building company. I know it was admin and bookkeeping but you learn things, don't you? Anyway, they seemed to have plenty to talk about."

It's lovely to see Gemma so excited and so alive as she continues to tell me about what occurred after I left with Jade. Kathy was a little drunk early in the night as I remember quite well. Then she switched to soft drinks, probably realising she'd had enough. She seemed quite sedate and down at one point and Gemma reassures me that, assuming it was probably because of everything that had gone on in recent times, she decided to go over to her. However, before she got a chance to, that guy Bill came up to her and before long, she had abandoned Aubrey and was sitting down talking like a civilised human being. No table-top dancing or wild antics. No loud exclamations or garish judgements. Maybe our Kathy is finally growing up.

As Gemma brings me up to speed, my eyes drift towards Kathy just as we're nearing the front gate of our house. She looks a little contemplative, maybe even a tad despondent. Separation can be hard on people. I'm pretty sure that nobody goes into a marriage planning for the day they break up, the assumption being that with such powerful emotions there is no question that success and longevity will be the outcome. In fairness, when it feels that real it should come with the guarantee that you will be able to weather the ups and downs, but unfortunately that's not the way life works. It's a challenge – all of it, and you have to keep battling if you feel it's worth saving. As it so happens, none of us knows what went on between Kathy and her ex, Brian, so it's hard to know what to say to her or how to deal with it. I think all that you can do in these circumstances is to avoid making assumptions and be there, for when you're needed.

When we reach the front door, everyone starts calling dibs on their place in the queue for the bathroom. Aubrey somehow manages to place herself first in that queue and to be honest nobody argues – I think we all want to see her in bed and asleep as soon as possible. The rest of us set about removing make-up, getting undressed and putting away our coats, bags and other bits and pieces, eager to get to bed.

Gemma and I share a bedroom, being the two eldest, while Aubrey and Kathy share mostly everything because they're inseparable anyway. Gem chose to forgo the box bedroom when it was offered to her, in favour of bunking with me, and so that meant that Jade could have the smallest room all to herself. I think the reason why she wanted a room on her own was primarily because the antics of women bother her so much and also because she proclaims to have very little patience for all the giggling, chattering and relentless discussions about men. Her room is a shrine to neatness and order but with very little of the female touch to it. Aubrey and Kathy's room on the other hand is pure chaos which they blame on the fact that Kathy left and then returned, turning it upside down on both occasions. The truth of the matter is that I've never seen it in any other state in my entire life. You have to search for space to put your foot down on the floor to even enter the room. The floor is littered with piles of clean and dirty clothes, hair products, shoes, unidentifiable gadgets and general debris. Whereas, mine and Gemma's room … well, it would bring to mind the tale of Goldilocks and the three bears, not too neat, not too messy – just right.

When I finally get my turn at the faucet and have my bed in sight, the house has turned from girls' locker room to baby's nursery and the silence alone is enough to put you to sleep on the spot. Gemma is already away in the land of nod and so I thread quietly along the side of my bed for fear of waking her.

As I sink into the soft, sheathing warmth of my leaba, pulling the crisp, newly washed covers up around my shoulders, I ponder the night that was and can't help but think about Matt and Simon and what very different worlds we come from. Their world is one of wealth and advantage, while ours … well, we certainly want for nothing but we are also not the type of people who drive Mercedes or rent houses in Ballsbridge – which is fine of course. What we do have is a roof over our heads, food in our bellies and love in our home and our hearts, and there are many who don't even have that much. But as romantic and as philosophical as "being thankful" is, the reality remains. This is a dog-eat-dog world we live in and money is power. It's no secret that people will do almost anything to claw their way towards the icon of power, aiming to position themselves more advantageously. I think also at times that people get confused, too. They seek power thinking mistakenly that it is a good companion. For me, it boils down to this one thing: knowing what matters to people that I share my life with. Being comfortable and assured that we have the same core values. Not the have-or-have-not aspect, but more the what-drives-you aspect of people.

I guess that what has been bothering me all evening about Matt and Simon is that they are clearly men with power, and I wonder at whether they will have had to struggle or fight to claim position in life. Besides that of course, Matt's aloofness, his standoffishness, poses too many questions for me. Is it a sense of superiority or is it just plain old social ineptitude? Do family and love or even friends and charity mean more to them than material things? I need to understand these things about people to be content with engaging with them.

With thoughts of power and personal struggles swirling

round in my head I feel the sleep take hold of me and I let go with great willingness. These subjects, which I've mulled over many times in my life, are not about to keep me from my much-needed rest tonight.

COMMUNITY

The next morning I'm awakened by the sound of the telephone ringing and that inevitably penetrating yet low murmur of conversation, followed soon after by Mother Hen making her usual Sunday morning declaration, something about going to pray for sinners. Her hope, of course, is that someone/anyone will miraculously see the light and join her, thus offering her a glimmer of hope in what might be a vague resemblance of pious reawakening. All she gets in response are some enthusiastic "goodbyes" and a loud "see ya". I pull the covers up over my head and relish that delightful feeling of drifting back towards warm, cotton-soft oblivion. But just as I'm beginning to surrender to it's comforting embrace Gemma whips the bedclothes away from me with cruel disregard for the lack of *actual* warmth there is in the air in late November.

"Come on girl! We're starting the collection today," she says with an undisguised measure of delight at being up before me. And I can't help but notice a certain unfamiliar energy radiating from her, which I'm almost sure will have me worn out by the end of the day.

"Oh look at you, with your big smilie head on ya. And

44

let me see now … what could be the reason for that, I ponder? Hmm. Or should I be asking 'who' is the reason for that? Would it perhaps be somebody by the name of Simon? Was that him on the phone?"

I move to place my finger so it hovers just above my lips, setting the scene for a brief but calculated spectacle of theatre. Then I offer her a quizzical, cross-eyed and somewhat comical look to enhance and boost my performance.

"You know … you two could have some *mighty* craic altogether, playing that game 'Simon says'."

I reposition my index finger against my cheek now and feign contemplation before continuing.

"Simon says, get your kit off! Simon says, giz a shag young wan! Simon says, where's me feckin' breakfast, woman?"

Laughing heartily at my own humour for a moment or two, I contemplate the viability of recovering the duvet in some artful and hopefully imperceptible move, as the desire to cocoon myself lingers tantalisingly. But such foolish notions are swiftly quashed when I glance up at Gemma who stands, steadfastly, looming with an expressionless yet defiant look on her face.

"Yes! All very humorous Rhian. The girls have already christened him Simple Simon. But yiz can say what yiz like. It doesn't bother me. Just get your backside out of that bed because I am *not* going around this estate alone," she says with a very weak tone of authority, but a tone that leaves me in no doubt of her determination, nonetheless.

"Jade is gone out to meet Amy for coffee and Aubrey has been cute-arsed enough to lock the bedroom door so I can't pull her out of her nest. Kathy went AWOL, something to do with the flat and some loose ends, blah, blah, blah … She wouldn't let anyone go with her, which doesn't matter anyway because I rang Martin Callaghan, one of the neighbours, and asked him if he wouldn't mind keeping an eye out, maybe pop in to see that everything is okay. Just in case Brian's about and tries to gives her any jip. He assured me that he would. Rhian! You're my last hope, lass."

She's right, and I know it. There's nothing left for me other than to roll my eyes in hopeless despair, before hopping out of bed with the energy of an overexcited toddler on Christmas morning and bounding into the bathroom to multi-task with the skill and dexterity of an Olympian. In no time at all myself and Gemma are heading for the front door with our mother's wheelie bag in tow, gathering hats, gloves and scarves to wrap ourselves like swaddled babes, eager to commence this year's collection.

The Christmas hamper collection, which is a well-established tradition in our family, goes way back as far as my memory serves. It was the brainchild of our Aunt Bev and Aunt June, along with some of their friends, neighbours and of course, Mother Hen herself. In the beginning it was a simple concept which centred around the collection of tins, non-perishables and various other suitable bits and bobs to make up food hampers for the old folks in the community. I believe it was Bev who first formulated the notion and then she put it to Aunt June who was more than happy to jump on board and help set a plan in motion. Bev is my mother's older sister and first girl in a group of eight siblings. Her cohort, Aunt June, is their sister-in-law and wife of their eldest brother, Uncle Dickie. The whole idea, which took flight many moons ago, has now fondly come to be known as the "food run" or "hamper run" – it alternates. One day soon my aunts hope that our generation will take over the running and organising of the "food run" and keep the tradition alive. I personally have serious doubts about this, given that some of my sisters' sense of charity and selflessness are a tad wanting, to say the least. After all, it has become a bit of a mammoth task in these latter years and even the hardiest would find it a daunting project to commandeer.

In the beginning, when it was just for the old folks around the immediate area, it was a manageable enough task, but now it's a bit of a logistical nightmare and something akin to disaster relief.

The hampers themselves typically include all the food essentials for a Christmas dinner, plus a little extra. The whole exercise is a spur for human kindness with people from all over the community as well as local shops and businesses rallying to help, as well as donate. Two weeks before Christmas Day we all get together to do the final package and wrap, ready for imminent delivery. Copious amounts of liquor is used to lubricate the mechanisms of this finely tuned and productive "hamper-making enterprise" which is why I always expect the days to end in riotous shenanigans, an expectation that is, more often than not, met fully.

For me, and for most of the others I would imagine, the holiday season starts when the hamper collection itself starts and that day tends to be around the end of November, beginning of December – and always on a weekend. Everyone makes a concerted effort to try and schedule things so that there is at least a week to solicit help and donations and a week to construct the hampers, and then all going to plan we should be able to deliver our masterpieces in plenty of time for the big day. Today, the 27th of November, is the perfect opportunity for us to set the wheels in motion and it's also the reason why I put up no resistance when Gemma came to haul me from my warm, inviting nest.

The day itself is a bitterly cold and uninviting winter day, so we wrap ourselves up like mummies before heading off towards the farthest reaches of the estate to start on our planned route. If history is any indicator, it will be a long day and the key to efficiency and expedience is how well we have planned our course before this moment.

The gentleman who lives at number one, Mr Byrne, who is eighty-five years of age and a bachelor his entire life, will be our first stop of the day. He will also, without any shadow of a doubt, be our greatest challenge. Though tremendously likeable, he is what's affectionately known as a rogue; or at least he was in the old days when he had his wits about him. Today he is the neighbour tasked with setting the tone for this bitter cold morning.

As Gemma and I near the end of the road and turn into the small gate at the edge of Mr Byrne's very large and unkempt front garden, we look at each other with a knowing grimace, bracing ourselves for what's about to come. For a second or two I hesitate, poised, with my hand on the knocker, before striking it with some gusto against the brass plate. Resigned to our fate, we stand, guarded. After only a few moments, the sound of the door first being unlocked, then unlatched and then unchained, can be heard before Mr Byrne finally slides his head out from behind the smoky, brown-glass-panelled front door. First, it's a slow and cautious reveal, then, quite abruptly he flings back the door and positions himself, hands on hips, as if to exhibit himself. His shirt is open, his fly down and his face is almost swamped by the largest, gummiest smile I have ever seen in my life. To make matters worse, his trousers are barely covering the goods and I have an awful fear that they're not going to stay where they are for very much longer. Speed is of the essence here and God knows Mr Byrne is not one to let callers go easily.

"Ah, Rheeny, Gemmy! How are my two favourite ladies this morning?" he croons excitedly.

"We're grand, thank you for asking Mr Byrne, and how are you this fine Sunday morning?" I say with a certain amount of Dickensian style while shouting at the top of my lungs for him to hear me. Mr Byrne is as deaf as a post – when it suits him of course.

"All the better for seeing your lovely faces at my door,"

he says, smiling very mischievously. "Come on in! I have your stuff right here in the sitting room," he says excitedly.

Though Mr Byrne will himself be in receipt of one of the hampers, like most others in his position he also likes to contribute a little as well. However, we suspect that this is more likely part of a ploy to gain an ear for his many, lengthy and often-told tales.

"We won't if you don't mind, Mr Byrne. We have so many houses to call to today and if we were to stop at every one of them, sure nobody would get a hamper this year," I say this knowing full well that if he gets us through that door we'll never get away and bless him but his house is in such disarray it's difficult to be comfortable in the place.

"We'll call back for a visit during the week though if that's okay," I continue in a half shouty kind of way, before covering my mouth and whispering to Gemma briefly. "We'll send Ma. She might even do a little tidy up for him. Looks like he might need a little helping hand."

"Ah girls, you're breaking an old man's heart. Wait here one moment and I'll get that stuff for yiz," he concedes, turning to head back into the sitting room. Gemma and I look at each other and smile.

We wait in silence for a few moments more, listening to the distant rustling and clanking of bags and tins somewhere in the house. Before too long Mr Byrne appears at the door again, holding up a heavy-looking bag in front of him, gazing at it with a puzzled expression.

"Yes Mr Byrne, that's for us! Remember!" says Gemma in a slow and clear drawl.

"Ah! That it is!" he exclaims with an air of delight before handing over the bag.

We thank him, advise him to close the door as quickly as possible to keep the heat in and then turn to go. As we're heading back down the path, he calls out to tell us to call back again tomorrow, or the next day, or whenever we can. We reassure him that of course we will, before cantering off out through the gate and on to our next location, a knowing glance passing between us both.

As we work our way through the next couple of listed collection points, my memories are gently nudged by the warmest sense of contentment, as fond images rush to remind me of why I love this community so much, and its clan of colourful characters. With no great fortune or rank to lay claim to, they make do with a wealth of personality and life which oozes from every atom and fibre. With just the simplest of human attributes to offer, they are all that is needed to endear and delight those curious enough to give them their time. Characters like Mr and Mrs Walsh who live at No. 5. Mrs Walsh is a retired librarian and always on hand to tell a tale or two whenever an occasion calls. Both herself and Mr Walsh are faithful contributors to all community events, most notably as our resident Santy and Mary Claus. Mrs Walsh, who is well into her 70s, is a sight to behold as she heads to the shops in the afternoons, dressed in clothes that you'll only ever see on teenage girls. Brightly coloured fishnets, leather minis, tutu, ripped jeans; she has them all. To accompany whatever ensemble destined to be the pick of the day, she sports the deepest shade of hot red lipstick, which is undoubtedly put on in the dark because it never hits the mark. It's as if she applies it without the use of a mirror, while driving, one-handedly, down a winding, bumpy country lane. It is the strangest sight to see. But these things – they're just superficial. The truth is, they both have a warmth and depth of character, like eternal children or innocents, and they never fail to bring a smile to the faces of all those they meet. They are the colour and the light in our local masterpiece of human life.

Much the same as our next call; Mr and Mrs Finlay, who live at No. 13. We like to think of the Finlays as our own home-grown celebrities, known not just within the community but far and beyond as well. They have a garden which is very often described as a suburban wonderland and has attracted the attention of various local and national newspapers. After rounding the corner and passing the Walshe's house, who are unfortunately not in today, Gemma and I turn in through a set of brightly painted ornate gates covered by an arched trellis, the entrance way to a tiny piece of heaven.

Mindful not to disturb anything, we tread with painstaking care; moving from one strategically placed stepping stone to the next. As we work our way steadily along weaving through a myriad of decorative garden ornaments, our eyes are drawn to all the wonderful treasures. All around we see brightly birdhouses, dotted among the various signposts pointing to coveted destinations, enormous colourful cartwheels, old water pumps, various unidentifiable but intriguing mechanical parts, elaborately adorned milk urns and more gnomes than anyone can count, all collated into something awe-inspiring, something spectacular.

Myself and Gem are so careful in how we advance that we barely make a sound, and Mr Finlay doesn't notice us until we're right up behind him. He's hunkered down by a group of three disparately posed gnomes with red hats and white beards, which are located adjacent to the front door. He talks to them in a low conspiratorial voice that's almost a whisper, making it difficult to hear exactly what's being said with any certainty. On seeing us, finally, he pats each of his stone confidants on the head, rises and turns to greet us.

"Good day to you young Gemma," he says in a jolly, assured manner, nodding to her quite haughtily. "Good day to you young Rhian," he says in exactly the same way, turning and nodding to me in duplication.

"Good day to you too, Mr Finlay!" I say in rather the same style as his own. "Can I just say, your garden looks fantastic today, like every other day of course. You certainly do keep yourself busy with it. It's a credit to you," I continue, while surveying the treasures around me.

"Oh, thank you very much Rhian, kind of you to say," he replies, while beaming and gazing around himself. "You're here for the hamper items! I'll just grab them for you. I have them ready and waiting inside the door!" he states before moving to retrieve a bag from the front hall.

Moving to take the bag from his outstretched hand, we see Mrs Finlay who waves and smiles at us from the entrance to the kitchen, just behind her husband. She has a small Pomeranian cradled lovingly in her arms which she stokes gently while whispering in its ear. Three other balls of canine fluff yap and leap at her ankles, clawing for attention. Her freshly blue-rinsed hair is coiled around giant pink rollers, loosely but elegantly covered by a brightly patterned scarf. To complement the leafy design of her headscarf she wears a vibrant green tracksuit and enormous fluffy white animal shippers on her feet. They look suspiciously like they might trip her up should she try to move in them. We wave back to her, smiling affectionately, call out a sincere thank you and head on our way again.

Before long we're back, working along our route again and a little closer to our house with every step. Gemma takes a list from her pocket every now and again, crossing off names and ticking the next. Technically it should be Mr Baker that follows the Finlays but Mam has scribbled a note beside his name stating that he's 'NOT IN', along with a drawing of a face. It's a simple enough symbol; a small circle with two dots for eyes, a hook for a nose, a curved line denoting the mouth and a U shape lolling from the corner of the curved line. The drawing is upside down, which is the symbol Mam always uses, in relation to Mr Baker when she wants to indicate that he is not available, emotionally. Gemma and I look at each other knowingly and decide to move on. However, before we do and as if to confirm Mam's home diagnosis, the face of Mr Baker appears, partially obscured and somewhat dishevelled at the corner of the top bedroom window. From where we stand, just at the end of the small pathway that leads to his front door we can hear the thunderous sound of footfall as he pounds down the stairs moments later. Half expecting him to open the door we wait momentarily – unsure. After a little time has passed, we notice the flap of the letter box inch up slowly and the low, barely distinguishable sound of Mr Baker telling us to feck off.

"Go on," he repeats, a little more audibly. "Feck off, with yiz! Or I'll set the dogs on ye," he states quite unthreateningly. Of course, Mr Baker doesn't have any dogs, but he probably feels that such a threat might send us on our way more speedily, which we do, lest we cause him any further aggravation.

People say that he used to be a civil servant but no one truly knows. He has a penchant for telling very high tales and if any of these tales were to be believed then it could be reasonably construed that he was in fact a secret agent, spy or some such covert, undercover individual in his professional past. He's not a terribly old gentleman, but clearly he's seen some hardship in his life and this is etched painfully onto his tortured face. He once got very drunk and ran up and down our road stark naked, not even a pair of socks on, shouting, "Fuck it, fuck this shit, fuck the whole lot of it", over and over again before he hid behind a bush yelling at us all to hide, "they are coming". The poor sod had to be hauled off by the Gardaí in the end and we didn't see him for weeks after that. When he finally did come back, he was a changed man. Since then, he has remained uncharacteristically quiet for the most part, so it's generally assumed that he's now on some very strong medication. To be completely honest he looks like a man who's asleep on his own two legs most of the time, which kind of says a lot.

At lunchtime we pop home for a quick bowl of soup, the house buzzing with activity and chock-a-block with bags, parcels and loose donation items. I'm curious to know how well we've done overall this year and so myself and Gemma speculate a little on just that very notion, comparing years gone by.

As the day wears on and we move from house to house, returning to our own occasionally, to unload and grab a cuppa, we finally begin to see the light at the end of the tunnel. The last few houses lie tantalisingly ahead of us. At this stage I can feel the weariness begin to take hold and Gemma teases me good-humouredly about my old age and looming twenty-second birthday. As usual the girls will be donating to the collection for the turkey vouchers instead of buying me a present but I have no doubt that a celebration will be on the cards as well.

Our last call of the day and the one we deliberately left till the end, is to our dear friend and close neighbour Patricia Mooney. Patricia lives just five doors away from our house and every year she gets one of the hampers, with all the extras that can be crammed into it. Her story is quite a tragic one and you'd have to have a heart of stone not to shed a tear on hearing it.

Patricia used to live in the west of Ireland, on a very large beef farm that had been in her husband's family for generations. Those in the west who know her well say she lived a hard but idyllic life in one of the most picturesque parts of the country. Sadly, on one otherwise ordinary day many years ago, her devoted, hard-working husband collapsed and died of a heart attack while out in the fields tending to the cattle. Patricia, at the time, pregnant with her ninth baby and not far off giving birth, lost the love of her life that very day – her childhood sweetheart – and the pain was almost too much for her to bear. The poor woman was left with eight babies, barely a year between any of them, and one on the way. Her heart torn in two, she had no option but to move to Dublin to be nearer her family. There was just no way for her to rear nine children and run a farm by herself. Patricia is a waif and no mincing words, a beautiful, heartbroken waif that'd tear the heart out of you talking so longingly about the west of Ireland from Valentia to Inch Beach and on up to Ballybunion. Admittedly, she has settled well back in Dublin for now but her heart is still roaming aimlessly round the ring of Kerry searching for the soul of her departed love. The farm, which is in Dingle, was taken over by her brother-in-law, and never has a moment gone by when she hasn't talked about the day she'll return. When the kids are all grown up, that's what she says. And although life is tough right now and she struggles to make ends meet I firmly believe that she will indeed return to that farm in Dingle one day. She's a determined woman, a woman with many mouths to feed and little to do it with, hence the reason why she receives one of the hampers every year. However, Patricia is also on our call list for hamper donations because regardless of her circumstances she still likes to make a contribution of her own, which is usually something she's made or that the kids themselves have made, and Gemma in particular loves to call on her and spend time with the children. Her eldest daughter Colleen, who will be sixteen soon, aspires to be a nurse, just like Gemma.

Finally, we reach Patricia's house. Walking through the gateless entrance we trudge up the small gravelled path leading to the front door and almost immediately the door swings open and we're greeted eagerly by Colleen herself.

"Hi," she sings, with more inflection than letters allow, and then immediately grabs Gemma by the hand, leading her into the house eagerly. I trot obediently behind.

Patricia is in the kitchen, standing amidst the steam of the many cooking pots on the hob.

"Hi girls," she says, turning her head momentarily from her kitchen sauna. "That basket there on the table is for the hamper and Colleen has something to give to you, Gemma," she says, nodding to Colleen who hovers impatiently nearby, fidgeting excitedly. She ducks momentarily into the sitting room, returning almost immediately, dragging a black plastic bin bag behind her with exaggerated effort.

The bag is brimming over with soft toys, all handmade from the offcuts of housecoat material kindly donated by the ailing Glen Abbey lingerie factory nearby. Patricia reliably informs us that a friend of hers who still works there okayed it with her boss to take some of the scraps which were earmarked for the bins and donate them for repurposing. Colleen, along with some of her brothers and sisters, cut out a simple pattern for small teddy bears and, between the sewing machine (used for the main body) and their skills with a needle and thread, the children made a total of seventy-five, soft toys of various colours for the children in Our Lady's Hospital. Gemma and I are gobsmacked, to say the least. The teddies themselves are delightful, truly flawless little treasures, and will be a wonderful uplifting gift for so many of the children over the holiday period. Gemma is speechless. She can't utter a word. This spurs Colleen to jump up and down clapping her hands with delight.

Thankfully Gemma eventually sparks into life, moving forward to hug Colleen tightly, thanking her over and over. The ruckus and activity bring more of the children pouring into the kitchen.

"Thank you so much … from the bottom of my heart," says Gemma with tears welling up in her eyes. "I can tell you this – when the children get these beautiful teddies, it's going to make their Christmas. You guys are so good!"

The children are delighted with this and shoot question after question as well as endless nuggets of information at her. She patiently attends to each and every one.

I turn to talk with their mother.

"How are you doing Patricia?" I ask

"Not bad at all and yourself, Rhian?"

"Oh, sure I can't complain," I tell her honestly. "Where's Fionn these days? I haven't seen him around for a while. Is he still playing the bodhran?"

"He is to be sure!" she says with evident pride. "He's off down in Dingle again. His uncle Richard says he has the whole farming thing down to a fine art now and any time he feels like coming back and taking over is fine with him. Poor man should be well retired by now."

Fionn is Patricia's eldest and, at seventeen years of age and soon to sit his leaving cert, it's hoped that he will return to Dingle to take over the running of the farm at the first opportunity. He travels back and forth from Dublin during holiday periods and on the odd weekend, and his uncle, who is married to the sister and only sibling of Patricia's deceased husband, has been coaching him for the last couple of years. Truthfully, the family are eager to have them all back in Kerry as soon as possible and I have no doubt Patricia will be back there just as soon as Fionn is finished his leaving cert.

"Colleen, Mary, Sean, Derry, round up the troops and get the table set! Dinner's ready," says Patricia as soon as she hears a lull in the chatter of the many children jumping up and down around Gemma.

"Come on guys!" she repeats. "Get the table set and let Gemma alone," she says, momentarily turning to look at the rabble, winking at me and nodding in Gemma's direction with a sympathetic frown.

"Before I forget, Rhian, will you tell your mam thanks for the mince pies? They hardly touched the table before they were gone, but I'm sure they were delicious nonetheless! Not that I'd know," she declares before laughing a knowing laugh. "There's enough dinner here too, if you ladies want to stop and eat with us," she offers, without stopping for a breath.

"Oh, no thank you!" I reply. "Mam will have our dinner warming for us so we'd better get a move on."

The children let out a chorus of divergent moans and groans of discontent as myself and Gemma begin moving towards the door. Gemma repeatedly hugs each one of the children, thanking them all over and over as she goes and before long, we're off down the garden path once again and heading towards home at last.

On the short hop back up the road Gemma gushes over how wonderful the children are and how amazing Patricia is to be doing such a sterling job on her own, and I have to agree, wholeheartedly. If it's one thing you can say about Patricia Mooney, it's that she puts her heart and soul into everything that she does and top of that list, are her kids. As a result, they are a delight to be around and such wonderfully skilled and artistic individuals. Patricia herself holds demonstrations in the local schools and community centres, showing kids how to weave, knit, sew, crochet and even make butter. She also teaches classes for the summer project so I can testify to her skill and artistry. Dwelling on their circumstances makes my heart ache a little. So, I try to focus on the happier aspects of all the lives of those around us, and thankfully there is plenty of that to mull over too.

It's a genuine relief when finally we get to walk through our front door at last and as expected, the bounty is immense. Mam, along with her crew who have already left, spent most of the day sorting all the stuff. The front room looks like a warehouse in the making. There are tins of peas, beans, tomatoes, pineapple chunks, condensed milk, spaghetti and soup stacked neatly on one side of the room and biscuits, puddings, cakes, crackers, jars of mince, pasta, rice and condiments stacked neatly in groups on the other side. In the middle, like an island in the sea of food, are the miscellaneous items such as fizzy drinks, dilutes, Christmas crackers and the like, as well as empty boxes donated by the shop up the road, and rolls of wrapping paper and cling film kindly supplied by the local wholesalers.

Over the next week or thereabouts, we'll go out in the

evenings for an hour or two only, endeavouring to tap all remaining sources, aiming to finish accumulating what is required so we can reach our target.

Gemma, as usual, is on different shifts in work so it's not always possible for her to accompany me on these trips. Nevertheless, we'll all band together and I have no doubt that somehow it will all get done. Gemma's work shifts can be long and exhausting and as she volunteers at the hospital too, I try not to bother her with hamper stuff, but instead ask some of the others to help out in her place. But I don't hold out much hope of that happening, as history has taught me that you'll get one good day out of most of them and rarely anything more. Besides, at this time of year the girls have more social engagements than they can attend; helping out is low on their list of priorities.

True to form, I'm left to forage on my own for the next two evenings even though I have to try and fit in some rehearsing, for an upcoming session in Temple Bar as well as the community classes, which are on Wednesday evening this week and next week. This year, thankfully, I only have the two: fiddle for beginners which is at five o'clock and the intermediate level which is at six o'clock. The classes, which take place every winter over eight weeks, won't finish up until Friday the 16th December, a week later than they normally do. They are, however, a little more straightforward than, for example, the classes organised as part of the summer project, mainly because they're all indoor-based and typically centre around arts, crafts and music, making them a little less time-consuming overall. Still, there's a lot that goes into organising them. The classes, which take place on Monday, Wednesday and Friday evenings as well as Saturday and Sunday mornings, are all run by local volunteers. They are an excellent way of giving kids a focus during the lead up to Christmas when, let's face it, most kids get a little stir crazy. They also offer those who wouldn't ordinarily be able to afford lessons an opportunity to obtain some basic skills with which they can springboard off.

Nevertheless, it's an exhausting and hectic couple of days and as a result, I totally forget about my birthday. By the time Wednesday arrives, I'm so focused on preparing for the class and getting music sheets done up, that I'm taken by surprise when Wednesday morning finally arrives.

Mam and Dad are the first to wake as usual and they waste no time ousting me from my slumber with what can only be described as bellowing jubilations, followed by awkward hugs, a birthday card and a new pair of pyjamas. As is customary in our house, the birthday girl, or daddy, as the case may be, gets first spot in the bathroom queue and celebratory pancakes for breakfast, after which I head out to work into the driving sleet and snow. It's a frosty but surprisingly pleasant day, in all its transient white fluffy splendour. Thankfully the snow doesn't stick and the day seems to fly by in a hue of fun and pleasant, small gestures from all I meet. After work I head straight to the Community Centre where all the kids are waiting to start class and when I walk in, they launch into a hodgepodge of sounds that I know are meant to be, and are desperately aiming to form, a cohesive melody that almost sounds like Happy Birthday. It's rather sweet actually.

Later on, at home, we have homemade chocolate cake with a single, solitary candle perched in the centre, and all the girls rib each other about how old we're all getting. They're all adamant that the real celebrations will be this weekend at the party, and for the first time in a long time I'm looking forward to what has now been termed "our posh party".

Apparently Simon rang Gemma first thing Monday and again on Tuesday to make sure she was still coming and, even though they made several attempts to meet up, they only managed to slot in a quick cuppa in the hospital canteen on Wednesday morning. Between her having to cover extra shifts in work and him getting called away for one thing or another, it was just very difficult for them. So, I suspect Gemma will be looking forward to Saturday too.

As the week progresses further, the front room becomes more like a genuine warehouse with Mam and my aunts sitting among the boxes each evening, sorting and packaging all the necessary components to make up the hampers. All the monetary donations were used to purchase vouchers for turkeys and hams, bottles of wine, mulled punch and cheap fizzy plonk which are placed into the hampers that are now finally beginning to take shape. Mam made a rake of mince pies in advance as usual and everyone sits around eating and drinking tea, coffee and hot chocolate with their delicious pies in hand while the suspicious aroma of whiskey laps through the air around us. It's lovely to come home in the evening after work to a house that is buzzing with life and purpose and, of course, the odd homemade mince pie or three doesn't hurt either. The sight of all the sweet little old ladies with their frothy coffees in hand, big goofy smiles on their faces trying to pretend like the coffee is as innocent as their expressions, warms the heart.

By the time the weekend approaches there is a definite air of anticipation among the girls and it's clear that we are all well and truly ready for a good old knees-up. The need to let off some steam and shake off the exhaustion of the week is evident in every word and deed. So, when Saturday finally arrives, the "getting ready" process is a monumental affair. Firstly, it starts a little earlier than it would normally, with Aubrey pounding into the bathroom with drive and purpose, declaring that she is going to find herself a rich auld fella with a dickie ticker so she can finally live the life she was meant for. Nobody pays too much attention to her banal ramblings. I say a silent prayer that she'll find sense before she does find a man or it'll be another McCarthy disaster in the making.

The sad truth of the matter is that we don't get invited to very many parties around our immediate area anymore, not since the last little disaster, the one that will be forever known as "the unholy reveal". It has now become part of McCarthy legend, and not in a good way either. The party that was the scene of this unfortunate event was in a friend's house just up the road at the back of the local shops. Crissy Maxwell, who went to the same school as us and who was once a very good friend of ours, always had the best parties around. It was guaranteed that we would always get an invite to every one of her get-togethers, that was, until the day Aubrey got drunk and decided to flash her boobs, which ordinarily goes down quite well or, best-case scenario, nobody is sober enough to notice or care. Sadly, on this very unfortunate occasion, Chrissie's parents came home a little earlier than expected and almost at the same moment as Aubrey whipped up her top, the dad walked through the door, eyes ready to pop from his head. The old fella must have just abandoned all reason for a split second because he made the weirdest sound like he had just dipped on a rollercoaster just before lunging towards Aubrey. Most likely the poor old guy wanted to bring the spectacle to an end but unfortunately what happened was that just at the same moment Aubrey fell backwards off the coffee table and onto the couch, Chrissie's dad landing on top of her. The party ended quite abruptly at that point and the old guy got into a terrible fluster trying to explain that he was trying to cover her up, which sadly his wife didn't appear to believe. She also gave Aubrey a fair old tongue lashing too. As a result, we've been black-listed and Aubrey's reputation for rowdy and tasteless behaviour has become the staple for gossips all over this estate.

So, as tonight is a rare and wonderful thing, I'm going to make the most of it myself, put a decent amount of effort into getting myself presentable and enjoy every moment of it. However, the sound of Aubrey and Kathy fussing in their bedroom about who's wearing what and who owns the top in the first place penetrates my enjoyable reverie and I think about going to referee. The pair of them swap clothes so often that they're beginning to lose track of who owns what and it's now becoming the norm that they will argue about clothes on a Saturday night.

"What are you wearing tonight, Rhian?" asks Gemma as she stands before the vanity mirror contemplating the option of a tailored navy dress which she holds up in one hand, versus her little black number which she holds in the other hand.

"I think I'll wear my black skirt and that white chiffon blouse of yours if you don't mind?" I say while deftly applying my make-up using only a small handheld mirror.

"Of course, go ahead," she urges. "That blouse looks much better on you than it does on me anyway," she offers sweetly. "Which of these do you think I should wear?" she asks, frazzled with having to make the decision herself.

"Gemma! You would look beautiful in a black sack so don't stress about it too much. Though if it were me, I'd bring out the big guns tonight," I say pointing to the little black dress.

The sound of elevated voices coming from Aubrey and Kathy's room has reached fever pitch at this point and so I finally get up from the bed where I've been sitting happily for the last while and go and investigate.

When I enter the room, Aubrey turns to me with flaming cheeks and spittle on her chin.

"Rhian, will you tell that cow to give me back my top," she shouts, pointing to the cream blouse that Kathy is wearing.

"Firstly, Aubrey, that top, or blouse as it is, belongs to Gemma. She loaned it to you about three months ago and has asked you for it back about a dozen times. So, can you two pipe down and grow up?"

"Oh, that's the blouse! I didn't know what she was

talking about, but now that you say it. Okay, then tell Kathy that Gemma gave it to *me* and that she has to give it back to *me*," says Aubrey with renewed venom.

"Can you guys not go one Saturday night without fighting?" I ask in exasperation.

"Yeah, we can! If she fecks off back to her husband and out of my bedroom," says Aubrey with a hint of shame on her face at the obvious realisation that she has just now crossed a line.

"Aubrey! I hope you never find yourself in the same boat and then expect support from your family," I say, glancing at Kathy who's hurt by the comment and is removing the blouse very dejectedly.

Before anyone has time to say another word, there's a firm knock at the front door and Mam shouts out for someone to answer it. Gemma is in the bathroom and calls out for someone else besides her to answer it and Kathy and Aubrey fold their arms in defiance. Jade as usual is avoiding the melee by hiding out in her bedroom and so I reluctantly leave the scene to go open the door.

Heading downstairs I listen intently, hoping that the girls will not resume the argument. Thankfully all remains quiet for now. When I open the front door there's a gentleman standing there looking very dapper in a black suit and cap, posing rather regally with an expressionless look of purpose on his face. Looking past him, I see a limousine parked at the kerb, which immediately explains the attire.

"Erm … I think you may have the wrong house here," I say, even though I suspect he doesn't.

"Is this not where Ms Gemma McCarthy and her guests reside?" he asks. And without waiting on an answer adds, "I *was* given this address."

"Oh right, then yes! You are at the right house. This is indeed where Ms Gemma McCarthy and her guests reside. Though we're partial to being called her sisters," I say, giving him a gentle, air-nudge with my elbows and the broadest smile I can muster. He doesn't crack a smile but stands poised, as before.

"Can you give us ten minutes, we're not quite ready, just yet," I ask with a more serious countenance.

"Yes of course, madam! I'll wait in the car for you," he says walking back to the limousine.

I close the door and race back upstairs.

"Hurry up girls! There's a limo downstairs waiting on us."

Aubrey and Kathy who have already put their differences aside and are hugging, disengage and run into Mam and Dad's room to look out of the window. Gemma gives me a knowing glance and Jade comes out of her room with her coat and bag in hand all ready to go. I fly back into the bedroom to put my clothes on and grab my stuff, and by the time we all get down the stairs to say our goodbyes Mam is already outside offering tea and mince pies to the driver.

THE PARTY

What a sight to behold! The sleek, dark blue and pristine silver body glistening majestically under the dim light of the half-crumpled street lamp, stretching out in elegant style, from the end of our neighbour's drive up beyond that of our entrance. Occupying a spot where two average vehicles would normally quite comfortably fit. In all its stately and imposing splendour, it is without a shadow of a doubt, unlike anything any McCarthy has ever seen before. And what a confusing myriad of emotions it conjures at first sight. Even now, as we wind our way through the streets and side roads of Dublin, it's hard to put into words – to express – just how unsettling it is to be coupled with such overt extravagance. On one level, initially, there's a sense of overwhelming fascination, followed quickly by that of disconnection, as if somehow you are not entitled to be part of, or occupy something so decadent. As if to do so would cement you as an interloper of shameless proportions for all eternity. But then there's also this strange, gnawing dimension of unfathomable awkwardness, of having no benchmark, no prior experience by which you can proportion correct behaviour. And it is that, the awkwardness, something I'm quite accustomed to, which holds firmly on this journey. It is that dimension, which I had to suffer through, while half the neighbourhood came out to have a gawk at us before we left. Of course, this was not made any easier by our mother who insisted on running upstairs to get the camera so that she could take a few hundred million pictures, just for posterity, and Dad of course, who for his part, had more than plenty to say on the matter.

"A waste of fecking money," he declared. "When you could just as easily hop on a bus down the road, for nothing more than a few shillings." Such utterings, expressed with whole-hearted conviction and monumental gusto, and yet retracted with equal resolution, as he begrudgingly admitted that, "sure if some gobshite wants to waste daycent earnings", on his daughters, then who was he to argue? After all, it was certainly none of his business! But I think honestly, it may have been the sight of the mini bar, or maybe it was the enormity of the seating area – room for five grown women and not one of them touching the other, that finally swayed him. I smiled as I glimpsed a vague, if not slightly reluctant look of approval on his face when we moved cautiously away from the kerb.

His confusion and exasperation are not unique, however. Truth is, we're all very much out of our comfort zones with this one. And what's even more telling is the silence that has lingered on the journey so far, a silence that quite simply is not a McCarthy trait, especially when there is no shortage of that well-known and much-loved jaw lubricant, alcohol, on board. Not cheap plonk either. Our host quite generously supplied us with several bottles of Dom Perignon, no less. Not the kind of thing you carry home in a brown paper bag from your local supermarket, that's for sure.

The sight of the empty bottle sitting in front of me elicits a grin, in turn nudging me back, out of my daydream, to the here and now. With one hand tightly grasping the slick, cold metal of the rear passenger side door and the other hand lazily caressing the cool, soft leather of the upholstery, my attention slowly returns to my sisters, who had momentarily faded from my cognisance. Jade, who doesn't seem to be all that consumed by the luxury surrounding her, appears uncharacteristically quiet nevertheless, and that's saying something because she's the quietest one of us all. Even Kathy is surprisingly devoid of criticisms and quips, while Aubrey just gapes unceasingly, seemingly incapable of closing her mouth at this point. Her gaze darts from floor to bar, then from corner to corner and back again. On the other hand, Gemma, I suspect, is silent for a totally different reason. My guess would be that perhaps she knew all along that we were going to be picked up but said nothing because she thought it might elicit less of a reaction, with less time to conjure that reaction.

"So Gem! Did you know we were being picked up?" I finally ask.

"Yes I did!" she says rather decidedly. "And I said nothing because I knew you, for one, would insist on getting the bus and I didn't want anyone getting all hyped up over it." She darts her eyes in Aubrey's direction who thankfully misses the gesture.

"Well, seeing as how you've hoodwinked us all so mercilessly, I think we deserve another glass of that fancy-looking champagne there. We may as well make the most of it," I state, with equal measure of assurance.

"Oh, do you think we ought to? One bottle is enough," she says with an edge of uncertainty.

"Of course!" interjects Aubrey as she finally comes too, snapping back to reality herself. "He wouldn't have put it there just to be looked at. It's not a feckin' work of art, that we're supposed to *gaze upon admiringly*. It's liquid! You drink it! With your God-given gob. Come on Gem, hand it over," she says, with her hand thrust defiantly towards the bar.

"I guess not!" says Gemma retrieving the second bottle, uncorking it and pouring five small glasses of the effervescent nectar. Of course, we did have to have a glass to toast when we first set off but it was an awkward celebration and nobody was too confident in going any further. But the air of tension that lingered for a while seems to have dissipated somewhat, making room for normality to return; and normality generally doesn't make room for abstinence in our world.

"I'm okay! I won't have anymore," says Kathy to a stunned audience. "I'm cutting back. Think I might give it up altogether and take up jogging, get myself all fit, like," she adds, and the renewed, but momentary silence in the limo is beyond comparison, it's stark and disbelieving – alien even.

"I'll have hers!" says Aubrey, promptly breaking the silence once more and then abruptly swiping the extra glass with her free hand. "It's that fella she met the other night, you know. He's all into his keep-fit and that kind of shite," she says with the barest hint of a sneer in her tone. She then raises the same glass to her lips and downs the entire contents almost in one go. Entirely ignorant of her lack of tact, she then belches so loudly that I'm sure I hear her glass faintly ring out under the stress and resonance. If Kathy was contemplating some response to that comment it is soon forgotten, as the whole group erupts into thunderous laughter and banter.

The silence, now well and truly dispelled, is but a distant memory as the rising chatter of the girls fills the interior of the limousine. I watch as they sip and snack a touch awkwardly while the driver navigates the home stretch, towards Ballsbridge.

Marvelling not for the first time at how quickly time flies when you're having fun, and indeed how quickly you get to where you're going when you travel in such style and comfort, we finally make it to the edge of Ballsbridge. Soon the limousine is pulling up in front of a very grand house on Shewsbury Road. At least I think there's a house there somewhere. The stone walls are exceptionally high and for the most part the structure is obscured by vegetation. Our driver deftly positions the vehicle, up alongside the kerb, directly opposite a set of very large, black wrought iron gates which would appear to have been left open in anticipation of our arrival. One by one we clamber out and head through onto the gravelled front drive that lies beyond the impressive gateway. Just inside there's a girl, standing, smiling broadly, waving gingerly at us. She has very short, almost shaven dark hair and a raw beauty that to me seems almost delicate, angelic in its form. Her petite, round face, atop a slender, tall frame is continental in look and there's something boyish in her comportment. For a moment I'm struck by a familiarity in her, like I've seen her before, and no sooner has my brain posed the question and recovered the necessary information than Jade runs from the direction of the limo into her arms – this is the famous Amy.

With an over-exuberance, Jade introduces us all as we walk towards the front door of the house, the splendour of which is truly regal and intimidating, comparable to nothing I have ever experienced first-hand before. What is of mild comfort though is the sense that the others seem equally as awestruck as I am. We dally a little to take it all in as the limousine driver strides ahead of us to ring the doorbell. By the time we reach the door Simon has already appeared, eager to greet us. He says hello to each one of us individually before Jade introduces Amy to him and him to Amy. In his now trademark conviviality, he welcomes her warmly and faultlessly but without hardly taking his eyes off Gemma for more than a second or two. His smile is unfaltering through the whole process.

After the introductions, he leads us through the front door into the hall which, without exaggeration, is probably as big as the entire footprint of our now dwarfed abode and

I'm tempted for a moment to shout out just to see if there's an echo. But I refrain, and instead follow on after him as he continues towards a large set of ornate oak doors, past a truly enormous dual staircase and into the lounge. This also, is an exceptionally large space, sparsely occupied by very smartly dressed people sitting and standing in various locations, mostly in pairs, or the odd small group. Some are sipping from cut glass crystal tumblers, some from gilded wine goblets, and the sober and sombre setting makes me mentally pat myself on the back for correct choice of attire. We all seem to have guessed the code for this one right this evening. All the guests who are sitting down are doing so on an array of enormous, darkly shaded and tastefully worn brown leather couches. They chat and sip their drinks to the sound of barely audible classical music and I can't help but imagine Aubrey hopping up on top of one of the beautiful rosewood tables, pissed out of her head doing her "Patricia the stripper" routine. It makes me smile a little to think of it.

Moving slowly around the room, Simon methodically introduces us to all his guests and I find myself nodding absentmindedly while half aware, trying to take in my surroundings at the same time. I push to the back of my mind a gnawing feeling that I'm being rude, which isn't the case because truthfully Simon is only interested in showing Gemma off to his guests – it's not *our* undivided attention that he needs.

"Gemma is a nurse," I hear him saying, this time to a group of suited gentlemen, one of whom is a tall, very handsome older looking gentleman I recognise as the same person Kathy was sitting glued to last Saturday night in the bar – Bill Sheridan.

"She works in the Children's Hospital in Crumlin and, I might add, she works very hard indeed," he continues, a look of doe-eyed admiration on his face. "I've tried relentlessly to drag her away from her duties to come have dinner with me this week, but unfortunately to no avail. Instead I've been forced to make do with stolen moments and fleeting rendezvous."

Despite his complaints, Simon's face is alight with admiration and adoration and it's very evident he could gush about Gemma all night long if he was let. But Bill, I suspect, may well have been introduced to Gemma already, as he appears to have decided that introductions have been more than sufficiently covered. Breaking away from the group he moves to engage with Kathy who had remained discreetly at the back of the group up until now. Jade and Amy take their cue also and move off towards the bar, which is situated in the far-left corner of the long, rectangular-shaped room. The bar itself runs half the width of the back wall from the corner, over to the enormous glass-panelled patio doors and is manned, no less, by two actual living bartenders, in uniform, the very idea of which seems superbly immoderate to me. The two girls stand leaning on the bar completely engrossed in each other while waiting on their drinks and I can't help but notice that my sister, although she isn't a big girl by any stretch of the imagination – voluptuous and womanly – but not big, makes Amy look decidedly slight and even more waif-like in close proximity. I ponder at the possibility of how disappointed men must feel when they finally realise that the stunning creatures standing before them are so totally and utterly inaccessible to them. I feel momentarily sad for the disappointments of others as my brain conjures scenario after scenario of possible human heartbreak. The girls move off from the bar after being handed their drinks, and settle themselves onto one of the oversized couches on the other side of the room, at the same time as I myself reach the bar.

The volume on the record player catches my attention at this point, as it inches slightly higher and higher still, and when I look around, to my horror I spy Aubrey, examining the controls. Casting a critical eye in her direction she responds by promptly giggling and walking off, looking at the ceiling, feigning innocence in a very obvious way. The more upbeat and seemingly rather suitable sound of the Eagles has now replaced the previous, sombre, sedate tune and admittedly it adds a little dash of life and light to the atmosphere. Given that the volume is at a reasonable level also and nobody seems to mind (I notice a bit of toe-tapping beginning to erupt around the room), I allow myself to relax, finally. Turning to the barman I order a glass of red wine and wait contentedly as he retrieves a glass and begins vigorously buffing it with a crisp white linen cloth.

By the time I have my drink in hand the room has livened up a little bit more and there is a distinctly more relaxed atmosphere beginning to emerge. The girls appear to be settling in well too and Simon, it would seem, has finally managed to expound Gemma's graces to the entire room; some have even been given the revised, extended version of the tale of Saint Gemma.

I look around and notice Kathy again – she appears very comfortable as she lounges on a fine old chaise longue by the large front window, Bill perched by her side. His attention is unwaveringly focused on my sister who notably has no drink in hand. The same however, cannot be said of Aubrey, who has a drink in both hands and is circling the room, appraising everything in it like she's about to put a serious offer in, on, not only for the property but its contents as well. It makes me a little nervous for some reason.

Simon and Gemma come and join me at the bar just as I take my first sip of the wonderfully smooth Merlot, and they both order champagne even though there is a waiter circling the room with glasses already poured. The extravagance of it all is hard to ignore.

"Rhian, Gemma tells me you're a keen reader and a master fiddle player too," he says with the cheeriest of delivery.

"I do like a good book for sure, Simon, but the master fiddler bit might be a slight exaggeration," I state confidently as he points to a closed door just across from us, on the opposite side of the room. The door is wonderfully ornate with the promise of great treasures beyond and instantly I'm giddy with curiosity.

"That's the library in there," he says. "It's very well stocked and if you want to borrow any of the books, you're more than welcome. Sadly, I have no fiddle. Or I'd insist on you entertaining us all," he declares, feigning a look of sadness.

At that moment a couple walk into the room and right on cue Simon hops up, taking Gemma by the hand and hurries to greet them. The champagne flutes remain on the bar and Gemma gives me a backwards glance that's half apologetic and half-amused.

"Sorry, Rhian! Talk to you later," she says before I'm *just about* out of earshot and so I take my drink and move to where Jade and Amy are sitting.

In the short time we've been here the pair have managed to expand their little group by pairing up with the two ladies from last week, Kelly and Moira, and they all look like they're getting on extremely well, smiling and laughing quite comfortably.

"Rhian! Do you want to have a look around the house?" asks Jade quite excitedly. "Kelly said she can give us the grand tour."

"I'd love to! Yes, please!" I state eagerly, delighted at the prospect of getting to see the treasures that lie behind the intricately carved and enticing library door.

Immediately everybody springs up from where they're seated and without hesitation, Kelly happily leads the way back out into the hall, by way of the doors we came through earlier. I note that these too are of similar design to the library door, with beautifully detailed carving and what looks like an oil rub rather than varnish, making it appear almost worn and antique-like.

The house intriguingly has a great deal of history attached to it, though it didn't strike me as a particularly old-looking building from the brief glimpse we got of the exterior. Kelly narrates this quite concisely and with an air of uncertainty, as if she heard it, can't remember it and is on some level reinventing and perhaps embellishing a little. In truth it doesn't matter because the enjoyment is in the visual aspects of the house, though the history is welcome nonetheless. Our guide leads us up the stairs and briskly through almost every room, before directing us back downstairs again and finally towards the intriguing library door – one of two entry points to the room, so we're informed. This particular entrance sits slightly back, out of view, and just under the hangover of the sweeping landing, and Kelly eagerly leads us through the door into the room, while mumbling something about Simon and his love of books. She circles the room slowly, heading towards the door on the other side and after informing us that she'll be right back, disappears into the lounge. The rest of us continue ambling around the room freely and I for one gape mesmerised at the towering bookshelves that cover every wall right up to the underside of the mezzanine that spans the length of the back wall. A simple wooden staircase leads up to the mezzanine where even more bookcases cover the upper portion of the walls.

The room itself is of course, nowhere near as big as the lounge but holy God it is a big room for books nevertheless, with every volume in the place perfectly alphabetised and in pristine condition. Some of them are old and possibly valuable as well. There is every imaginable genre from crime to horror, to romance, reference books, encyclopaedias … everything you could wish for.

Circling the room several times, I finally stop at a large mahogany bookcase, take a copy of *Lady Chatterley's Lover* from a lower shelf and flick through it. Jade, Amy and Moira stroll around the room gazing up and down at the volumes and soon Kelly returns with a waiter in tow. The sound of music floods the library through the now open door and it seems alien, out of place in this space of quiet study and meditation. I look down at the book I hold in my hand. It's one I've read before, but this particular volume intrigues me as it looks old and on carefully opening the front cover I see it is indeed a very early edition – something amazing to hold in your hands. It brings to mind a memory of an old oak tree in my grandmother's garden, her urging me to stand still and pretend I was that tree: to imagine, to visualise history sweeping around and past me – time in fast motion. I would stand, eyes shut, pretending the gentle breeze that lapped around me was time itself rushing by. What has such a tree lived through? What has such a book been part of? What life and history has been made during its existence? I imagine shadows of things past, dipping and rising, swooping all around in fast motion, and I'm entertained and elated by the fantasy.

Placing the book carefully back in its spot. I join the girls who have all amassed at one section giggling and flicking through the pages of the *Kama Sutra*. When I approach Kelly she indicates to the champagne sitting on the tray, left by the waiter. I decline, before moving off around the room again, circling back to the section marked "reference books". A familiar name jumps out at me and so I carefully slide the volume from its place to closer examine the front cover. It reads *Pure at Heart*, by Stuff Smith. I'm not familiar with the guy myself but some of my students, who fancy they know just about everything there is to know about the world of fiddle playing, have raved about this guy. Personally, my taste in musical composition doesn't extend much beyond the boundaries of the Emerald Isle and is well-grounded in our traditional forms, but out of pure curiosity I leaf through the relatively new-looking book just to get an idea of the man behind the classroom chat.

"There you all are!"

I turn abruptly to see Gemma standing in the doorway to the lounge. "There's food being served if anyone wants to come and get some," she says, without moving from her position in the doorway.

The girls are still intrigued with the pictures in the book, loudly expounding the merits of one position over another while laughing hysterically at times. They look in her direction but don't respond.

"Very important research being done at the moment, Gemma. I don't think food is high on their list of priorities right now."

"Ok," says Gemma quite sweetly and with a puzzled look on her face before disappearing back into the lounge.

I hesitate a moment before deciding to go and join her and so I move to return the book to its vacated spot. Just as I'm about to slide it fully into place the door to the hallway, which is just behind me, opens up quite abruptly and Matt walks in. He startles me so much so that I accidently drop the book to the floor and let out a sharp gasp.

"Apologies! I didn't know there was anyone in here," he says, a little awkwardly.

Mr Matthew Devine, as I now know him to be, stands hesitantly before me in his tweed coat and leather gloves, briefcase in hand. His face is frosty-looking, the outdoorsy type not the cold, angry type (though I suspect that's just one masking the other). He promptly lays the brown leather case down on the reading table beside me and moves to pick up the book which I'm ignoring in my shock.

"Thank you," I say in a near whisper as I glimpse him eyeing the cover before sliding it slowly into its spot. I can feel the cold air that clings to him moving to surround me, and a shiver runs through me. The air fills up with the faint aroma of quite pleasant aftershave, but I can't help but feel uncomfortable at how close he is to me. I can't move right now either as to do so would be too obvious and might appear rude, so I hold my ground as if being tested on my ability to endure and remain expressionless. Adjusting my facial expression a little, to remove any trace or hint of how uneasy I feel right now, I slowly rise from my hunkered position and casually move back towards the desk.

A loud burst of laughter from the girls causes Matt to turn, quite startled himself.

"Research," I say with a grin on my face and he looks momentarily puzzled.

"Matt, come here!" orders Kelly. But Matt doesn't move from his spot. I suspect he's not the type of person to ever respond to unceremonious direction.

"Come! Tell me how in God's name is this even possible," she says, holding up the book for him to see the cover.

"The *Kama Sutra*," I say with no expression on my face.

"Yes, I see," he says, sighing heavily. "Kelly, I'm afraid, can be a little unguarded at times and also quite easily led. I must apologise for her."

The notion that he needs to apologise for a young girl doing nothing more than having a little giggle over pictures in a book is frankly quite astounding to me. But more than that, the inference that perhaps others around her, one of whom is my sister, are the reason for behaviour that he finds unpalatable is genuinely quite annoying to me. So I smile politely, turn around and head back into the lounge after giving him a neutral smile and nod of my head. Jade calls out and dashes to follow me; Amy, Moira and Kelly quickly follow.

The room has filled up quite a bit more since we left and it's hard to spot where the rest of the girls are all loitering at this point. Scanning the room with my almost empty glass still in hand I finally lay eyes on Kathy. She's sitting in a different spot now but Bill is still by her side and still steadfastly focused on her. There seems to be what I guess is an orange juice in her hand and even more extraordinarily she's being civilised. It's odd. Maybe, while I was off in the library, aliens came and abducted the real Kathy and replaced her with this courteous and sober being from another galaxy.

Scanning further, I finally lay eyes on Aubrey too, who despite the fact that she is titillating a group of men in the far corner of the room, appears to be surprisingly well-behaved. Something is amiss here, even if she does appear to be drinking alcohol. Chances are her good behaviour won't last too long though. Gemma of course, is still by Simon's side as he continues to make the rounds of the room.

A waiter and waitress move from guest to guest with platters of canapés which look truly exquisite, and suddenly I'm struck by how much easier this is than I had thought it would be. Feeling somewhat more relaxed than I was moments ago I head towards the platter, that to me, appears to carry some particularly delicate-looking morsels.

"Rhian, come and sit over here with us," says Jade, dragging me to join Amy, herself and the two ladies on a large brown leather couch.

"Rhian, I never properly introduced you to Amy," she says rather proudly, before launching into a brief biography. Apparently, she works as a DJ in the same pub I accompanied Jade to last weekend. But her day job is a lot less exciting. She works for the civil service and finds it boring as hell. But it pays the bills.

"The club keeps me sane and you get to meet the most amazing people," Amy interjects, giving Jade a cute little side-glance and giggle before sitting back in her seat to allow Jade to continue where she left off, with some guidance of course.

Jade smiles back at Amy before explaining that her father, who is French, lives in a small town somewhere south of Paris, while her mother who is Irish, lives in

Galway apparently.

"They're not together anymore," state Amy quite matter-of-factly. "But my father, he comes to Dublin to visit, whenever possible. He's quite fond of Dublin, and of course, I go to visit him whenever I can," she concludes, before turning to Moira and Kelly to tell them about some wild party that she DJ'd for recently.

Up close Amy is even more beautiful than she first appeared. Her skin is a flawless caramel colour and I notice that she has a few tattoos and piercings, though very discreet and tasteful. When she speaks her accent alternates between French(ish) and a strange mixture of Dublin meets west of Ireland. It's the oddest thing to listen to. She could be talking away in a kind of French accent then say something like "Jaysus" in the middle of the sentence in perfect Dublin speak. Both herself and Jade take periodic, sneaky, lingering glimpses at each other when they think that nobody is looking. It's quite sweet actually.

As we're chatting away, Simon beckons to Kelly to come join him, which she immediately does, and Moira promptly follows. Jade takes her cue to quickly inform me that the two ladies are a couple but apparently nobody is to know because it would cause problems. The father, it would seem is a firm and fixed homophobe, having said as much on many occasions. As well as that, caution should be exercised around Matt who is quite close to old Mr Hendy, Simon and Kelly's Dad, and who himself has professed a belief that homosexuality in his opinion appears to be a thing of fashion these days. Though not an outright condemnation in Kelly's estimations, it is nonetheless felt to be a smallness of mind regardless. As Matt constantly seems to find fault with Kelly's choices and behaviour, she is not willing to incur any more criticisms or censure. I wonder, at hearing this, whether Matt's perceived slight of my sister earlier was indeed some aversion to her sexuality and I vow internally that if that is to be proved the case then I will dislike him even more for such ignorance. Putting it from my head, I turn my attention back to Jade who informs me that herself and Amy are only going to stay for another half hour or so before slipping off into town. They're staying at Amy's tonight apparently. She lives in an apartment in Temple Bar and Kelly and Moira are going to join them but need to slip away discreetly a little while after Jade and Amy leave. It warms my heart to see Jade with her social cup brimming over. I've never seen her this full of life in all my days and it fuels my good humour and abandon for the rest of the evening, even though Matt's seemingly condescending face appears intent on gawking at me from various locations around the room throughout the evening.

When it's finally time to head for home I'm only too delighted to climb back into that limo again and leave it all behind. Poor Simon though, or Mr Hendy Jnr., to give him his full title, seems very reluctant to let Gemma go and for a brief moment I start to wonder if indeed he will let her go. Eventually, we all climb into the limo and it soon moves to whisk us away, back to where we came from. On the journey home, Kathy seems unusually quiet and when I mention it, Aubrey, hops in, only too delighted to tell us all why.

"She's mad into old Billy-Bob", says Aubrey with a weirdly startled grimace on her face, "and you know, he is a bit older than she is – more mature – more notches on his belt as they say! You know what I mean," says Aubrey, laughing exaggeratedly at her own humour while winking at Kathy who looks on stony-faced. "Anyway, she doesn't want to mess things up by coming across all silly and immature and well … not having her shit together. But more to the point, he works for Simon and Matt, and is, right now, doing some massive job, extending and renovating part of an old historic building – or something like that. He told her that the "project" should have been completed last year but the contractor they originally hired turned out to be a *bleedin' fraudster*. Mind you, they admit that they may have kind of rushed into getting someone to do the job initially because of time constraints. But how could they have known? It looked like a legitimate company on the face of it. But as it turned out, one of the so-called engineers who worked for the company was filing invoices for money he was actually pocketing himself. We're not talking pennies and pounds here either, it was thousands, and not only that, but Simon and Matt weren't the only victims either. This gang of *"charlatans"*, as Posh-Bob calls them, left a trail of devastation behind, when things finally fell asunder on them. Horror of horrors, the owner of the company was Willie Connors! You remember that gobshite, don't you? The baldy fecker from up near the chipper?"

We all nod in acknowledgement and stare, waiting on her to continue.

"So here's the really juicy bit," she adds before pausing, nodding and continuing in a slow, deliberate drawl. "The so-called engineer who was pocketing money was none other than Brian O'Farrell himself, who to my knowledge only ever worked on building sites as a labourer."

Having finally finished her tale, Aubrey sits back in her seat, seemingly quite satisfied with her efforts and a silence descends among us. The clear rhythmic hum of the limo's engine is the only sound to be heard as everyone sits contemplating, processing, looking vacantly to one corner or another or off into space. Now we always knew that Brian was the type of person who at the drop of a hat could lay his hands on whatever was needed and which just always happened to fall off the back of a lorry. But this is grand scale; this is beyond what any of us could possibly have imagined. Not to mention the fact that, well … what are the odds of us crossing paths with some of his victims?

"So, let me get this straight," I say, trying to piece the puzzle together. "Brian, or at least Brian and some other gobshites, set up a bogus company, pretended to have engineering qualifications they didn't have, took this job on – among others, pocketed thousands of pounds and never did any work? And now Matt and Simon are out for his blood?"

"Kind of!" says Kathy rather sombrely. "They did do some work. But none of them are qualified engineers or certified for that matter. They're just a gang of out-of-work brickies and plasterers. *And I'm not defending them by any means* but if I know Brian O'Farrell he would have thought it was well within his powers to pull this crap off, especially with the likes of Willie Connors at the helm. Except it didn't work out. It was all too much for them and soon their so-called buddies started to jump ship: when clients came looking for their money back or their jobs completed. Brian had taken money for jobs and had nobody to help him finish the work – and no way of certifying it. So he disappeared too."

"So how does that reflect on you? Or why would you be worried about what Brian did? He's your ex now. Not your problem," I say, quite perplexed.

"Aww, but she's mad about Billy-boy! Did I not say? She doesn't want him to find out that she's connected to Brian. It's too much of a coincidence, Rhian. Nobody would believe that she just happened to be related. She thinks it would look very suspect! And I have to agree with her. If I were Billy, or Simon or even Matt for that matter, I would think Kathy was up to no good. I mean, look at her. She's well dodgy looking," says Aubrey with a big grin, nudging Kathy in the ribs playfully.

"How would he find that out? Besides, if he has anything between the ears he'll work out the truth of it for himself before long. I mean, what kind of eejit doesn't do their research before handing over wads of cash to someone anyway?" I ask, genuinely confused.

"By all accounts, the company looked legit on paper and they had done some jobs that were all above board, so they gave those as their references," Kathy informs us.

All the way home, out of the limo and into the house, through the usual bedtime rituals, the girls continue to chat and muse over the dilemmas in their lives and I can see that Kathy is weighed down by the whole Brian saga. Before we climb into our beds to go asleep, I knock in to her room to see if she's okay.

Aubrey is snoring her head off in the bed next to her while Kathy sits, propped up against her pillows, gazing off into the distance.

"Can I come in?" I whisper

"Of course! Come on," she whispers back.

"Look, hon. I'm not an expert but you know what they say. If it's meant to be it will be. Don't be fretting about what Bill will think of you. If he's a genuinely nice guy and truly into you then it won't matter. I know you and Brian didn't work out, but we all make mistakes. Take your time with this one. Make sure it's all for the right reasons. If I were you, I'd tell him everything. So if he bolts then you know that there are things that mean more to him than you and honestly you'll have dodged a bullet. If he is genuinely into you then he'll have no issue and you never know, he might even be supportive. Either way it's a win-win for you. Get your man or dodge a bullet."

"You're right, Rhian, I know. Still, I think it's too late. Matt and Bill were talking just before we left; they were looking over at me. When I went to say goodbye, Bill was acting strange, not like he had been earlier in the night. Jaysus, Rhian, I think I'll give up the men as well as the drink. Neither seem to bring me any luck."

We sit in silence for a moment, both of us in contemplation.

"I'd give up the men meself if I had half a chance of catching one to start with," I say and we both stifle a little giggle before I get up, hug her briefly and tiptoe out of the room, turning briefly before pulling the door behind me.

"It'll all work out! Don't worry! I promise!" I whisper before winking at her and heading back to my room.

A DAY OUT

The next morning Gemma, Kathy and I head out on the hamper run again and the hours are spent in a hue of mostly, pleasant, Christmas-fuelled banter. At every turn, on every street, dazzling arrays of string lights and opulent displays brighten and liven our way. Elegantly adorned evergreens wow and mesmerise us, while people in high spirits, dashing about with feverish purpose, radiate the magic and wonder of the season. Christmas fever has taken hold.

Earlier on in the week, it had been decided that we too would coordinate ourselves for a day off mid-week, en masse, to do some Christmas shopping of our own. The only thing that remained was for us to iron out the finer details. Of course, this undoubtedly requires an extraordinary amount of tense discussion and debate, so ultimately our pleasant Christmas-fuelled banter turns to talk of the imminent day out.

As a result, two things are now crystal clear to me. Firstly, and most importantly, said day out, from my perspective, will most certainly *not* include the "shop till we drop proposal", now being put forward by Kathy, even if I do concede that *some* Christmas shopping needs to be done, and done *soon*. After all, things are going to get a little "bargain crazy" out there before long and no sane person wants to wait and get caught up in all that madness. Secondly, the hampers are all but near completion, barring the loose ends, which is very reassuring because now it's reasonably possible to take a day off without responsibilities piling up. Like most people, my last day in work will be the 23rd of December, so that doesn't leave much time if you're expecting to cram between then and the big day.

Considering how busy it all gets at this time of the year and how eager I am to get the shopping trip over and done with, nobody is too surprised that when Thursday arrives the girls are all ousted from their beds at the crack of dawn with as little tact and finesse as any human being can muster. The sight of them all humours me immensely, as I watch them slowly come to life, like images from a zombie movie I once saw where the walking dead dragged themselves around laboriously until the scent of living flesh wafted their way, spurring them into increasing momentum. Thinking on this, while entertaining myself with whimsical fantasies, I work my way through the morning's preparatory rituals along with my siblings, and it's not long before we're happily on our way.

When we do finally find ourselves jostling through the massing throngs on Westmoreland Street, it's not long before the girls are brought to a maddening standstill as they endlessly debate the merits of Henry Street versus Grafton Street. For me, there's only one decision to be made and that's whether or not to linger with them a little longer, out of politeness, or deposit myself immediately inside the doors of Bewley's Café. So, having given the matter little or no consideration, I happily say my goodbyes and exit the melee with resolve and purpose. After all, coffee and a vanilla slice beckons, while life or death decisions about choice of most advantageous viewing point for consumption of the desirous vanilla slice, *must* be made – and soon. Luckily, at this early hour there's even a choice of such spots and, with both coffee and cake in hand, there is nothing to do now but exhale and commence enjoyment of the McCarthy Christmas shopping expedition, 1994.

"I won't be long," says Gemma, who pops her head through the doors momentarily, a clear look of cake envy plastered all over her face. "Literally just the Body Shop and Eason's and I'll be back to join you for one of those. Looks delicious!" she states before disappearing back out the door, leaving me free to cram the cream cake into my mouth the only way I know how, messily, and with total disregard for the poor employee who will have to clean the God-awful mess up after me. The table now looks like an explosion in a pastry factory. Sadly, a long time ago I had to resign myself to the fact that there is no fast and elegant way to eat vanilla slices, especially when you're cursed with the inherent compulsion to consume cake at breakneck speed, as if to delay might put the very existence of your cake at risk. I fear it is the legacy of living in a large and very hungry family who cruelly try to swipe the food from your very mouth at every opportunity. And with that thought in mind, I take my cue to deposit the last morsel of delicious flaky goodness into my mouth with all the finesse of a pig at the trough. Having no mirror to assure myself otherwise, I'm now confident that, most likely, I look like someone who just got caught up in the very same aforementioned pastry factory explosion. Finally, I get to sink into my chair like a woman on the crest of a wave of contentment and start to read my book while sipping on that cloud of cotton-wool-like coffee heaven.

After some time has passed and two more coffees, neither of which I finish, Gemma reappears with a large coffee and a cake of her own, taking a seat eagerly beside me.

"What are you reading now, Rhian?" she asks with

genuine interest.

"It's that book I borrowed from Simon's place," I say, showing her the front cover. "Are you guys going to be meeting up so you can give it back to him for me at any stage?" I ask, looking up briefly from the page to see Gemma finishing her éclair off, leaving no sign that food had ever been before her.

"Well, it's very hard for us to meet up properly, with my shifts and his work. Any time we've tried to do it this week it just hasn't worked out for us. Having said that, he is meeting some friends in town today and we agreed that if we crossed paths then it might be possible to while away some time together. But sure, who knows?" she says with a suspicious glint and the barest hint of a smirk on her face.

That smile! A prelude to future events was exactly what I thought it was because, no sooner had she cast it and as if her words had somehow, magically conjured them, Simon and Matt, along with two other gentlemen, come striding over towards us, coffee cups in hand.

While chatting they had somehow gotten past me and it's a mystery how, though I suspect not so much of a mystery to Gemma.

Simon is grinning from ear to ear, and for the first time I notice how radiant my sister looks today, perched somewhat mischievously beside me, dressed in what can only be described as her Sunday best.

"Oh, did I mention that I told him we would be here – at just this time? I hope you don't mind," she says quickly and without looking directly at me but still managing to draw a napkin across my cheek with pinpoint accuracy while getting to her feet.

"I sincerely hope that wasn't the blob of cream I was saving for later." I joke.

Gemma moves to hug Simon and greet his companions before everyone else is swiftly introduced and just like that, my peace and quiet is shattered into a million tiny shards.

I'm once again forced to endure the company of Mr Matthew Devine, wet weekend extraordinaire and desecrater of Christmassy cake-cramming vibes, and I'm not particularly happy about that. Simon however, in stark contrast, almost makes it bearable, with his cheery, effortless and polished social graces.

"Ladies, what a pleasure it is to meet you," he says with evident sincerity. "Where are the others? Off shopping I suspect."

His enthusiasm is exuberant.

"Yes. They've been gone this good two hours or more now but chances are they won't reappear for another couple more – at least," says Gemma cheerfully. "Rhian despises shopping, so she always opts to hide out here in Bewley's and I hate to leave her alone too long. Though I imagine she'd prefer if I did."

Simon gives us a brief summary of what's going on in the world of property and investments, and while we listen courteously, the sound of a fiddle drifts towards us from a nearby group, off to our left. The four lads and one girl appear to be a party of students sitting several tables away from us. One of them it seems, has been suitably encouraged by the rest of his friends to take out the beautiful instrument and is joining forces with a cohort tin whistler for an impromptu recital. It's a familiar jig to me because I teach it to my students, and I notice that everyone at our table has now shifted their attention towards the performers and the promise of something truly enjoyable.

"Beautiful!" whispers Gemma, as the sound lifts into the air with their growing confidence and the clear approval of all around.

"Are they as good as they sound, to the average person's ear, Rhian?" she asks without truly expecting a response. This I suspect, because she immediately turns to Simon's new pals to explain her reasons for asking me the question in the first place. In doing so she offers them a little too much information about my personal life, if I'm being honest, but I have to bear it because it's probably the only flaw that Gemma has – talking too much when she's uncomfortable. I feel my cheeks begin to redden, but also, I feel the need to keep a brave face for my sister's sake because I know she'll be well aware of how much I despise being exposed in this way and equally unable to stop herself.

"Rhian! Play for us, will you please?" pleads Simon. "I would so dearly love to hear you," he says. And before I get a chance to protest, he hops up and goes over to the group of students to solicit a fiddle from them. I can already feel my cheeks burning a deeper shade of red and the room starts to close in around me as they beckon for me to come over and join them.

Reluctantly, and to some degree resigned to my fate, I move over and take the proffered instrument, trying hard to act as if it's the most natural thing in the world and that I practically live for getting called to perform at every possible opportunity.

After making a quick adjustment to the tuning, noting what a beautiful and expensive instrument it is, more expensive than anything I own, I look up and to my horror realise that one of the young boys who is part of the musical group, and who has the most colourful knitted hat atop of his head, complete with giant bobble, is one of my students. At this time of year, it's not uncommon for them to afford themselves early Christmas holidays, so it shouldn't be such a surprise. Still, it is a college day and I'm sure he's now sizzling with mortification.

"Sorry, about this Séan. I bet when you came out today you didn't think you'd end up in Bewley's with your teacher," I say as a means of dispelling the awkwardness.

"Wha … Oh, Jeeze … I mean jeepers, I didn't recognise ye, Miss. You look kind of normal, like. Not teachery. You've got clothes … not that you don't normally have clothes but nice clothes and hair an' stuff …" he fumbles about, flustered and caught off guard. And then, taking a long, deep breath, he has another go.

"Here Miss, can I get an A if I just shut up and play that jig again."

Evidently he has managed to recover his mental faculties, as he now turns to grin triumphantly at his group.

When everyone seems ready to go, I place the fiddle under my chin and count us in. A cascade of musical notes bursts forth, swirling and flowing around us like unseen spectres, as the uplifting sound of the Swallowtail Jig lights up the room. The energy is palpable all around as the youngsters tap their feet and whoop and cheer, goading onlookers into dance and participation. The tune nears its end and Séan circles his head to indicate that we repeat once more.

A jig, a reel and a bit of improv later, I finally protest enough to be allowed to return the fiddle to its owner and head back to my own group. Half the populace of the café, who moved to get a closer look, relocate themselves back to whence they came, as a chorus of raucous cheers and applause rises through the air. Séan and his team take to their feet in a flourish of exaggerated bows as I slip quietly over to my table. The excitement in the café slowly abates and everything soon returns to normal save for the faintest sound of excitement coming from the students who are already preparing to leave.

Séan, it seems, can't resist the urge to have a word as he passes by the table.

"Terrible example you're setting for us youngsters, Miss! Mitching, of a Thursday no less, and disrupting the peace and tranquillity of a very respectable establishment. Shocking. Might have to report ya to old frosty jaws in the morning if I don't get that A!" he says before erupting into howls of laughter in unison with the whole group. The young girl at his side, pushes him towards the exit with an affectionate smile and they spill out onto the street outside. The life and energy seems to follow them and we all wave and smile as they move off.

"It's probably about time I went looking for the others," I say when the quiet is finally restored.

"That was amazing. You're a very talented individual, Rhian," says Simon in earnest. "Who'd have known that so much talent could exist in one family alone," he gushes.

"Thank you, Simon. You're too kind. But if you ever do that to me again, I will have to kill you. Slowly."

He laughs a little cautiously while I try unsuccessfully to hold a stony expression. He's the type of person you can't be annoyed with. The sincerity and warmth just ooze from him.

After a few more minutes of discussion about the pleasures of music and art, all the while Matt gawping at me half menacingly, I decide that it's time to leave. But before I get a chance to vocalise that thought, Mr Devine decides it's now time to converse.

Turning to look at him briefly, to avoid being impolite, I'm suddenly struck by a revelation. I never gave it much though until now but in close proximity, he does have the most amazing dark and brooding eyes. Right now, with a less irritated countenance, he almost seems quite pleasing on the eye. With a shudder, I promptly push the thought from my mind in renewed determination to find him rigid and intolerant, and reinvigorate my efforts to stay focused on being stony-faced.

"That was indeed incredible – a truly pleasant experience. You must practice a lot. Do you?" he says rather uncertainly.

"Thank you, Matt! I do as it so happens! And I teach, so that requires a fair bit of playing, and I practice whenever possible, mostly at the college, and not so much at this time of year – too much on. Still, you have to be mindful of staying ahead of these guys. They're super-talented young people."

He smiles quite sweetly but doesn't respond and I try and resist the urge to fill the silence which is genuinely hard for me.

"And of course, there's also the summer holidays," I say, failing miserably at my attempt to remain silent. "Three months is a long break so I tend to fill some of those weeks gigging. The midlands and the west of Ireland are great spots during the summer months! Tourists love the traditional music," I say, trying desperately to find a way of stopping. "Do you play an instrument yourself?" I enquire, finally seizing the opportunity to hop off the crazy talking train.

"Unfortunately not! I would have loved to but my father was very clear about that. The arts were for dreamers and time-wasters." He falters, looking a little awkward. "Apologies, I don't mean to be rude but it was just his way. He was a very driven man and business was his focus. We clashed a bit on the subject but he was a man who was used to getting his own way," says Matt with a sudden look of shock on his face as he realises that he has crossed some boundary regarding personal revelation. A look, fleeting but undeniably tangible, is there and gone, a clear mark that he has just shut down.

"Well, that's a pity. Especially if you had a genuine interest. Still, it seems to me like you're good at what you do. So I'm assuming you must on some level enjoy it and get some fulfilment from it?" I say, in a non-probing sort of way, a sudden instinct to allow him the option of avoiding having to respond, prompting my tact. As I suspected, he has derailed the communication tracks, the confirmation of this evident in his silence. So I do what I do best – I babble on for another bit.

"Of course, I personally didn't realise, when I was younger, just what I was getting myself into. It's too handy to have a musician in the family. Never a dull party, even if

I do say so myself. But never a minute's peace either. Every Christmas without fail, the fiddle comes out and I'd complain only it gets me out of having to dance with Uncle Des. Now, the less said about that the better," I say with a nervous laugh. Matt laughs a little too and I'm quite surprised to see his face with such lightness to it. It has a strange draw for me.

"If you'd like to come and see me play again, you're more than welcome," I say without much thought, quite surprising myself. "I'll be playing in Temple Bar this Sunday, early evening. It's a casual, impromptu kind of thing but always good fun. Gemma can let Simon know the details. Sure, why don't you all come along? It's a great venue and I believe the Guinness is very nice there too."

Just as I'm beginning to warm to Mr Devine the peace and comforting hum of the café is promptly torn apart by the harsh and pitchy sound of Kathy and Aubrey entering the café, fighting and swearing like a pair of delinquents. Matt looks appalled, which doesn't surprise me, but when I see Simon grimace I feel instantly wounded.

Hopping to my feet with lightning speed, I turn to Gemma. "Think that's our cue to go, girl!"

"I'll follow on later, Rhian, if you don't mind," she says with a little uncertainty, and I'm over to the door before the girls can comfortably reach our table, ushering them back out onto the street, a brief nod and wave to Gemma as we go.

Catching a glimpse of Simon's expression out of the corner of my eye I'm relieved to see a definite smile. Maybe it was the thought of Gemma leaving and not the girls' brash behaviour that soured his face in that moment. Waving goodbye to all inside the café we move off up the street, as Jade, who had been standing just outside the door, pivots rather theatrically and follows behind.

"You pair are making a holy show of us. Pipe down," I say, turning to look at them directly. They're both ignoring each other now which is ironic. Pity they couldn't have reached that impasse before they got to the café. Neither responds and so we all continue on our way.

"What were they fighting about this time?" I ask Jade as we convoy towards our bus stop.

"Well, it was quite funny," says Jade with a little chortle. "Aubrey was trying on a pair of jeans and they were as tight as a nun's knickers on her which she knew of course because she had to get down on the floor to haul them up and get the zip to close. Anyway, Kathy was helping her up off the ground and the pair of them were cod acting and between the jigs and the reels Aubrey fell and ripped the jeans."

I throw my hands over my face in exasperation while Jade continues to recount the events for me, all the while giggling at my reaction.

"Don't worry!" she says in a comforting tone. "She bought the jeans. But she was pissed off and told Kathy that she was going to have to get them repaired because it was her fault. Now, if you want me to repeat what Kathy said then you're going to have to show me some ID. It's rated 18, adult content – not for the faint-hearted," she laughs with genuine amusement.

"You're alright! I don't need the graphic details. Just tell me this and spare my faint heart. How much of the alphabet did she use?" I say, humouring myself.

"Pretty much every possible letter. Except maybe X, Y and Z. But yea, I'm going with pretty much everything else. Lots of use of the letter 'F'. And I mean lots and lots of 'Fs'. Oh! And one very obvious 'C'. I definitely heard the 'C' word."

For a moment I don't react. I think it's the shock, but this prompts Jade to give me a clue.

"It rhymes with 'punt'," she says, looking at me with humour splashed across her face – her eyebrows raised and fixed, comically.

"Oh dear Lord, she did not!" I whine, pathetically. "Tell me you're joking."

Jade shakes her head slowly.

The girls have now reached the bus stop and I can tell that they are trying to broker some sort of truce so I stay back a little to chat with Jade and attempt to stay out of it.

"So! How are things going with you and Amy?" I ask.

Jade turns to look at me, a big cheesy grin on her face. "Good!" she says rather smugly.

"Just good?" I ask, looking at her with puzzled inquiry.

"Oh okay! Fab! She's amazing. I just don't want to get my hopes up because it's early days yet and well, you know how it is! You dream about it, you want it for so long and when you get it, you're almost afraid to breathe, in case you disturb it and send it scurrying away."

"Great analogy, girl. You make her sound just like a disease-ridden rodent." We both laugh at the idea of that before I look her squarely in the eye. "It'll all work out okay, you know? What will be will be and if she *does* scurry away then it's because she won't have deserved you. You are a good person and she would be mad to let you slip through her fingers. Breathe easy and be yourself. After all, *I* love you just the way you are and I know stuff! I have certified smarts."

I give Jade a hug and we both head over to see how the girls are faring. As it turns out, all is pretty good. They've agreed that they'll split the cost given that they were both to blame and Kathy will get a friend of hers who does invisible mending to restore the jeans to their former glory. Being a friend, this should mean the cost will be minimal and, given that they wear each other's clothes all the time anyway, it makes sense that they split the cost.

As a result of this truce, the bus journey home is very harmonious and the girls happily show off what they bought, passing various gifts and some very risqué lingerie around the bus. When we get as far as the village the bus pulls up to a stop on the main street and a group of lads get on. I estimate them to be early to mid-twenties in age and they're an extremely noisy and boisterous group who appear to be celebrating something. The busman refuses to move on until they settle down and take their seats, stating that the bus is going nowhere till they comply. Consequently, they decide to test the driver's patience by running up and down the aisle pretending to play Gaelic football or something like that. The passengers look on bemused as most of the group jump about, shouting and feigning tackles and passes while throwing their invisible ball. Eventually, disgruntled bus passengers begin to get steadily more irate, airing their annoyance out loud till one of the guys attempts to get his fellow "mime footballers" to settle down – to no avail, however. People on the bus are getting palpably more annoyed with each passing moment, not least of all Aubrey.

The busman makes a curt announcement over the intercom again stating that he's not budging till the lads get off the bus or settle down and he even turns off the engine which seems to ignite the dry embers of some peoples frayed nerves. Shouting and arguing ensues.

Having probably had enough of fighting for today Aubrey leaps up from her seat and marches down the aisle towards the lads.

"QUIET!" she yells at them as loudly as she can.

"You!" she points her finger at one of the lads as we all look on in stunned silence. "Paul Hynes! I know your ma and if ye don't sit the feck down and shut the hell up then I'm going straight round to your place when I *eventually* get home and off this bleeding contraption, and I'm telling her the carry-on of ye." She whips around and points her finger at another lad. "You! Patrick Morris!" The venom in her tone not to be mistaken, as she moves her face to within a hair's breadth of his. Rather than shout she cups his ear and proceeds to whisper something to him that nobody else can hear. Immediately he sits down, his face ashen. They all sit down, and the lad who was trying to calm them thanks her and turns to mumble his annoyance at them for bringing so much grief on the whole group.

After the bus sets off again and everyone is in their seats once more, the guy who thanked Aubrey earlier on, who Jade reliably informs us is Declan Kelly, moves up and hunkers down beside her to reiterate his sentiments of appreciation, several times over. He apologises profusely and asks for some reassurances that she won't say anything to anyone about anything. I'm intrigued, as I'm sure everyone else is, as to what was whispered. The pair of them have a bit of banter for the remaining part of the journey and when we finally arrive at our stop, I can hear him asking for her phone number.

"Ah go on Aubrey. Just one date. If it's as awful as you think it will be then we'll just go our separate ways. You'll get no arguments from me. I promise," he says before licking his finger and crossing his heart.

"Oh, go on then. I'll see you tomorrow at seven. Don't be late 'cos you'll not get a second chance," she shouts back at him as we alight from the bus.

To say that we're all now dying to know the Patrick Morris mystery would be a horrendous understatement of fact and as the bus is pulling off, we all gather beside Aubrey as we walk up the road, waiting with bated breath to find out what she said.

"Well! Dish the dirt on Pat, will ya?" says Kathy when she can't wait any longer.

"What? I have no dirt," she says coyly. "I just told him that Rita Long said he had a tiny willy and that if he didn't shut the feck up, so I could get home, I'd show everyone the picture of it that I nicked from her bedroom. She's always bragging about having it even though I know for a fact there's no such photo. But that fecking eejit clearly doesn't know that. It must be that small, so! Did ye see the colour he turned when I said it to him. Poor fecker. Well, if you're not picky about where ye put your sausage then you've only yourself to blame when it all goes awry."

We all burst into fits of laughter at this as we continue on up the road towards home and across the large green that lies in front of our house.

"Aren't men fierce stupid all the same!" says Jade after we've all finished howling. "Them and their willies. Who cares what size a willie is?" she muses. "They say that size doesn't matter anyway! Right?"

"Not to you it doesn't! Sure, they could have the biggest one in the world and you wouldn't know what to do with it," laughs Kathy.

I look at Jade and roll my eyes. She shrugs her shoulder in confirmation of Kathy's statement and we both hurry on ahead to open the front door and get away from the fascinating discussion of willies.

One by one we march through into the sitting room where Mam and some of the other hamper volunteers are all congregated. It would appear that they've all been having a little tipple or two, while sorting and packaging the remaining handful of hampers. Mrs Dowling from up the road is dancing around the room with ribbon tied across her chest in a makeshift bra style and another piece located weirdly around her crotch and waist, like a cheap G-string. They're all belting out rebel songs while Mam is conducting with two small sticks of firewood. I head into the kitchen/dining area where Dad is sitting, scowling by the fireplace, while the others stay behind to join in the revelry.

"I hope that's not going to go on all night," I say to him when I walk in. "Gemma and I have to get up for work in the morning. What's she been drinking?" I ask him wearily.

"Well, it started off with mulled wine, then they progressed to just wine and then Margaret ran up the road and came back with a jar of poitín. You know your mother can't drink that shite to save her life but she had a glass of it nonetheless, and I've warned her. She'll be sorry in the morning. Sure, leave her at it! She deserves what she gets," he says with a mischievous glint in his eye.

I hate to have to leave the fun and celebrations behind me but unfortunately I need to head back out almost immediately, to rendezvous with some of the other class organisers to go over the schedule for the remaining workshops. When I return at 11:30 the shenanigans are beginning to wind down and by twelve o'clock, as Gemma is finding her way through the front door, Mam and some of the others are helping Margaret out of the house because she can barely stand on her own two feet. Mam herself is looking a bit worse for wear and is already swearing blind never to do it again. Not a drop is ever going to cross her lips for the rest of eternity, apparently.

Then quite abruptly she turns and makes a run for the kitchen sink as we all say a sad farewell to tomorrow's dinner, which unfortunately was defrosting in the very spot where right now, Mam is hurling her guts up. The half-defrosted chicken now looks more like a putrid stew than a gorgeous roast-to-be. I resist the urge to laugh and instead help her up the stairs, as Mrs Dowling and the others finally manage to pull the door behind themselves.

HOME COMFORTS

Despite the late evening shenanigans and the dead-of-night sound of poor Mam vomiting into a mysterious megaphone, I still miraculously manage to get a half-decent night's sleep. By morning, harmony is restored to the McCarthy household once again. By harmony, I mean the usual chaotic rituals whereby we run around shouting dibs, wrestle for the mirror, rummage for clothes and other paraphernalia, and of course everything in this house gets thrown, because no one ever seems to have the time to pass things over with any measure of civility. But even more amazing is the fact that we mercifully get to do all of this without the need to step over a single unconscious reveller, something which has been known to happen on more than the odd occasion in this household. Only recently, after one such impromptu gathering, I woke up the following morning, sometime around 7 am, to get ready for work, and there it was, a body asleep in the bath. It was the rather tortured-looking carcass of our neighbour's teenage son, who, in his defence was a novice drinker. His mother, I was subsequently informed, place a pillow under his head and blanket over him before she left. On that occasion I decided, as clearly others had, not to wrestle with his fairly large bulk, but rather to go to work a little earlier than normal and have a wash in the staff toilets instead. Not exactly my favourite thing to have to do but as the saying goes, 'necessity knows no shame'. Today, luck is on my side and thankfully there's no need for any such drastic measures. Consequently, I arrive to work happily washed and in plenty of time to sit and have a nice mug of tea and slice of toast before classes start.

To add to my good fortune, the day itself is delightfully pleasant and upbeat, fuelled by the ubiquitous spirit of Christmas – an air of festive frivolity engendering a kind of lightness and good humour all about the college. My busking buddy Séan spent half the morning delighting the other students with his exaggerated tales of our antics in Bewley's the previous day, and they, in turn, revel in their embellishment of the tale as it is told and retold throughout the day, growing from a simple performance into an epic tale of adventure and glory. According to the bush telegraph, I was hopping around the place, rocking it to the core, wooing the hordes of mesmerised spectators. I'm pretty sure that, apart from some non-aggressive toe-tapping, I barely moved throughout the entire time. Plus, at the very most, there were possibly a dozen, maybe two dozen rather docile coffee sippers in the place, one or two of whom may have inched a bit closer for a better view. Still Séan, being the flamboyant character that he is, had to have his moment in the spotlight, and just possibly, on some minute level, he may even have managed to elevate my street credibility among the general student body, ever so slightly. So I'm not complaining.

Despite this, however, it's still nice to finally finish up and head home at the end of the working day. What's nicer still is to be greeted by the tantalising aroma of roast chicken, a blazing, crackling fire and a quiet calm that's a rare yet welcome phenomenon within these four walls.

After stuffing myself till I can hardly breathe, I sit lingering over the remains of my dinner, reluctant and possibly even incapable of moving. Soon enough I hear the front door open and close and a few seconds later Kathy appears, coming in from the biting outdoors, via the sitting room and back out into the hall again, without so much as a word. Mam speculates as to why she left so abruptly, while I help myself to one of her roast potatoes, mindful of that fact that they'll be ruined soon, smothered beneath the harsh metal film that will be placed over them to help keep them warm.

If you're not home in time, in this house, to take your plate of food in hand when it's ready, then it gets the dreaded tin foil cover on it and is set upon a pot of boiled, simmering water to keep warm for however many hours it may take for you to answer the call of the gong. After that, it will never taste the same.

Not long after Kathy's appearance, Aubrey too, bulldozes her way through the front door, announcing her arrival quite blaringly, before immediately disappearing upstairs to ready herself, as Mam says, 'for her gentleman caller'. Jade, who hasn't appeared yet and who should have been the first one home, is presumed to have gone straight to meet Amy. Dad of course will be working late tonight. He works late every Friday.

Listening distractedly as my mother narrates the comings and goings of each of the girls before eventually wandering off into the sitting room, I finally begin to feel myself succumbing to the sedative of heat and gluttony. But then her re-entry, quite suddenly, back into the kitchen, startles me back to full consciousness. She comes and takes a seat directly opposite me at the table.

"So, what's this Amy one like?" she says quite directly.

Our mother loves to be kept up-to-date with what's going on in our lives but she has a very good sense of boundaries also. Never too prying, like some parents can be when it comes to their children's lives. But it's a balancing act for her nonetheless: trying to stay informed while also staying on the right side of "the line". When we were younger she used to tell us how, when she was growing up, her mother would always open her mail, even when she was a young adult and out earning her own wage and contributing to the household. Her mother always felt that she had the right to open any letters or parcels that came to the house, regardless of whether they were addressed to her or not, and if the fancy took her, she might have relayed the message or passed the contents of a package to the actual addressee. Mam hated it so much and felt like she had no privacy, and she vowed never to do that to her children.

"You know I don't like to pry," she says a little sheepishly. "Remember what your granny used to do to me? I feckin' hated it. Your father and I nearly didn't end up together because of her."

Mam has told us this story so many times that I'm almost tempted to interrupt her and finish the tale in as few words as possible just to hasten its end but I know she likes to tell it, so I summon the powers of patience.

"We were supposed to meet and go dancing. Your dad had asked me, specially, to a hop in the Kingsway Ballroom in Granby Lane. But he never turned up. He had the flu as it turned out. But I didn't know that because I never got his letter until after the fact which also happened to be after I told him to shag off in very colourful language. I'm surprised he agreed to meet me again after the mouthful I gave him. Anyway, that's neither here nor there. I just don't like prying. But if I'm being honest, I don't know how much is too much nosying, because you younger generation are way more open than our generation ever were. So go on, gimme some idea?" she concludes.

"She's lovely, Mam! Really sweet, and Jade is totally enamoured with her," I say, smiling. "You know how it is when you meet someone you really like and you're afraid of messing it up. Well, she has a bit of that going on at the moment. But I don't think she needs to worry. It's clear that Amy thinks the sun shines out of her arse, just as much as Jade thinks the sun shines out of Amy's arse," I say rather casually.

"You don't have to use the colourful language, Rhian! It's not very becoming!" says Mam with a smirk on her face that makes me doubt her sincerity. After all, she's not averse to using colourful language herself from time to time – whenever necessary.

I pick away at the remains of my dinner again, although I can hardly fit another morsel in me, while emitting soft gluttonous moans which tragically don't deter Mam from lifting a dessert plate off the counter to her left, placing it on the table and pushing it over towards me. Like most Irish Mammies, Cristina McCarthy is what's commonly known as a feeder – always shoving food down someone's throat. Always telling them they haven't had hardly a bite. She says it's a symptom of hard times and having a sense that you needed to eat as much as you could, when you could, for fear it would be the last bit you'd get for a while. 'Waste not, want not' should in truth be our national motto because all the mammies I know use that saying as their personal mantras, seeming to display the exact same trait as our mother, finding multiple reasons why you should eat everything being shoved at you.

"Ahh, I'm glad," says Mam, a little distractedly. "Everyone deserves love in their life," she adds, looking at me rather strangely.

"What's the look for?" I ask curiously.

"Well, it's just that I can't ... I mean I don't know ... like how ... well, what I'm trying to say is – how do they do it? You know ..." She nods and winks in an exaggerated way at me, as I look on bewildered. "You know ... how do they do *'the sex'*?" she says, mouthing the last two words. The look on her face is undisguised relief at having finished her sentence and I valiantly resist the urge to laugh out loud and hug her all at the same time, opting instead for a reassuring smile.

"You're hilarious, Ma. I bet you've been mulling over that for ages. Believe me, mother, when two people want to express their love for each other they'll find a way, and well, after that it's not anyone's business. They're consenting adults, with a right to privacy."

At the mere mention of the word privacy, Mam goes into lockdown. She gives me a look to say that she's satisfied with this being the point at which the discussion should end and promptly gets up to clear away the dinner plates.

"Maybe we should invite her over for dinner this Sunday?" she says, in an effort to move the conversation along. "I could make a nice roast beef. We haven't had beef in ages. It's so expensive and it's too hard to justify buying it when your uncle is so good giving us all those rabbits and pheasants. I still have loads of trout in the freezer from his last fishing trip." Mam stands looking upwards for a few moments, a contemplative look on her face. "Yes, we'll do that," she answers herself. "We'll have Amy over for dinner this Sunday."

Content with her decision she goes about washing the dishes and my offer to help is flatly refused as she insists on me putting my feet up for a bit. I happily comply.

At that very moment, Gemma rushes in, still in her uniform but smelling distinctly of cigarette smoke and aftershave. And given that she doesn't smoke and that the heady aroma isn't quite her variety of aftershave then that can only mean that she was out somewhere with someone after work.

"Ohhhh, get you ya dirty stop out. What were you up to, or should I be asking 'who' instead of 'what'?" I say, smiling my best cheesy smile.

Gemma has a cheesy grin of her own to offer as she

takes the plate Mam offers her.

"I went to meet Simon after work for a bit. He wanted to go out tonight but I can't. I'm only home for my dinner, forty winks and then back in to do another shift. They're short-staffed in work. I'll have my dinner and then try and get a couple of hours sleep if I can."

Mam wastes no time retrieving a dinner plate which she holds in front of Gemma's face. My poor sister shovels forkfuls of dinner into her mouth without even sitting down and Mam takes her cue to grab a dessert bowl also, waiting patiently for Gemma to take it.

"You'll give yourself an ulcer," says Mam. "Chew your food properly!"

"Can't! Spent too much time with Simon. Need to sleep or I won't make it through the next shift." She shoves two more heaped forkfuls of potato, turnip and pheasant into her mouth, nods a thank you while simultaneously refusing the desert and then turns to leave.

"I'm going to stick my earplugs in. Sorry, Mam. The dinner is lovely but I have to sleep," she says before disappearing through the door and thundering up the stairs to bed.

"I'll cover that," says Mam. "She might have the rest of it later before she goes off to work."

I wander off into the sitting room to give the hamper list a quick scan. Tomorrow morning is D-day. Everyone will be coming here at the crack of dawn to start the distribution process. First, we'll sort and allocate deliveries to groups or individuals. Then we'll get confused because someone will change something about and it'll throw everything else off. But that someone will be convinced this change will work better. Then we'll row, voices will inevitably elevate steadily in pitch until someone calls order, and then we'll reset and start all over again. It's always the same routine. Usually we work in pairs but some groups finish before others and then go to assist the rest, so at the end, you could have four or six of us all running around the place together. The rule is that nobody goes till all hampers are delivered so it's in everyone's interest to pitch in and get it all done as quickly as possible. Once the last hamper is delivered, the pressure is well and truly off and the wind-down to Christmas can begin. It fills me with a warm sense of relief and fulfilment as I linger, scanning the room.

Over in the right-hand corner of the room by the window is a pile of hampers earmarked for myself and Gemma. One of the hampers catches my eye because it is larger than all the rest and is sat upon a pile of wrapped boxes, each one roughly the same size as the next. It's all tightly held together with cling film so I can't nosy at what's inside, at least, not with any great ease. But I'm a little curious nevertheless and so I decide I'll just have to climb over the hampers in front of me in an effort to get to the corner and examine a little more closely. At just that moment when I lift my leg, Mam walks in.

"Be careful you don't trip and break your neck, girl," she warns me.

"I'm just having a nosy at that hamper," I say, pointing directly at the one in question, hoping that she will enlighten me so I don't have to go any further. There isn't anywhere to put my feet so I'd be happy not to have to navigate a treacherous route through.

"It's just Patricia's! It's got a few extras in it. It's a large family and she's been very good to me. I've hardly had to buy a stick of butter this whole year 'cos of her, and every time her brother-in-law visits, he brings a rake of chickens and eggs which she always shares. Come to think of it I don't recall buying one chicken this year. The boxes are from us. Nancy and Evan, they need new shoes. They're up and down here enough times that I had a mind to ask them to take their shoes off on a couple of occasions when I had just washed the floors. Then I took a sneaky look at the sizes. I'm pretty sure I got them spot on and sure, I've held onto the receipts just in case; she can exchange them," says Mam rather matter-of-factly. "Won a few bob at the bingo and bought your father a new coat for Christmas. Then I thought, sure that might be a nice way of saying thanks to Pat for all she does. After all, money's for spending and sharing not for saving and worshipping," she concludes with a dismissive, upward nod of her head as if to ward off any discussion or debate on the matter.

I look at my mother with her shabby loafers and her tattered jumper, mended more times than I can count. She could have spent that money on herself and she didn't. She never does. She's hardwired to put everyone before herself. Even when the dinner goes on the table of an evening, she leaves herself till last. Always making sure that others have what they need before she'll put a morsel in her own mouth. God knows she never goes hungry but still she'll never put herself first as long as there's someone else to be thought of first. She is the single most selfless, empathic being I have ever met in my life and it's an emotive thought, just to dwell on how it seems takes its toll on her. I see her ageing more quickly than she should, just out of pure worry and concern for others.

I feel my eyes welling up just thinking of all she's been through in her life and how giving and caring she is in the face of life's constant challenges.

"Mam! Why don't you get an early night! It's going to be madness here tomorrow and you'll need a good night's rest if you're to weather the chaos," I say in a vague attempt to ease her burden.

"Ah sure, I have to make some mince pies for the gang. I'm just waiting a bit till the pastry chills in the fridge. Everything else is ready to go. I just have to make the rounds, fill them with mincemeat and bake and then I can go to bed," she says. "Not long now."

"Sure I can do that. Why don't you get your book and go on up and read and relax for a bit and then you can nod off when you're good and ready. I'm stopping up for a bit so it's as easy for me to do it."

Clearly in need of an early night, Mam doesn't refuse the offer and heads off with a satisfied grin on her face.

I, on the other hand, head back into the kitchen to read the newspaper, scan the few TV stations that our aerial manages to pick up, and consequently time flies by. A little later than I had intended to I start on the mince pies, at which point Dad wanders in, eats his dinner, chats with me briefly about work and life before heading off to bed himself. Gemma too, swoops by like an apparition, on her way back out to work again. Kathy and Aubrey make a very conspiratorial and brief appearance at some stage but disappear upstairs quite rapidly, and for a fleeting moment I think that they're up to something but put it to the back of my mind, deciding to make some buns to add to Mam's mince pie collection instead. It's a lot less work than trying to work out what that pair are up to.

By the time I've finished and cleaned up after myself, it's almost one o'clock, which is certainly a bit later than I had thought. Resisting the urge to linger and sample a bun, instead I head straight upstairs to bed. As I lie waiting on sleep to come, the barely audible sounds of life outside drift in through the air vent above my bed. Firstly, I notice the low hum of occasional cars passing, some near, some farther away. It's quite a hypnotic sound. But then my brain focuses more keenly as a car accelerates, slows and eventually moves from earshot, another one soon taking its place. I fancy that I can determine who the drivers may be, depending on the rate of acceleration, perceived speed and engine sound, and smile to myself at the obvious possibility of being totally wrong. Off in the far distance, the familiar and unnerving sound of tyres screeching can be heard, as somebody goes for a late-night joy ride. My heart beats faster with the fear as endless dark possibilities and reckless outcomes flood my mind, and I try to stir my thoughts away. Soon, another sound comes to distract me, the escalating growls of a nearby argument, followed swiftly by loud indistinct shouting – mostly expletives from somebody who has had his sleep disturbed by the warring parties. The ferocity in the threats seems to instantly subdue those who had been arguing and what follows is a welcome return to stillness and calm. Night time draws me into the void as lingering sounds begin to fade.

The next morning, light moves slowly in to dissipate the gloom of a cold winter day. Eager and full of purpose, I'm out of my bed earlier than normal, knowing that as soon as I'm washed and dressed the house will be buzzing with life and activity and I don't want to miss one moment of it. Mam is already up and offering about the fry up, toast and homemade scones to everyone who comes through the door. The smells around the house are a feast for the senses and the energy is like life itself. Miraculously, all the girls are, for the first time ever, present and eager to play their roles. Jade is the last one to join the posse, clunking heavily down the stairs just behind me. It would appear that she was out till late last night and I'm surmising that just possibly, today will be a struggle for her. But that doesn't matter, she's here and that's what counts. Poor Gemma, who is still in her uniform, looks like death warmed up and could do with having some sleep. But she refuses point-blank. Hamper day is one of those days when everyone rallies together no matter how they're feeling or what else they might have to do.

Volunteers wander in and out for the next while as the doorbell rings constantly. There is a wonderful current of energy running through the house, a current of fun, purpose, even camaraderie. At some point the doorbell rings and much to Mam's delight Amy appears, looking even more radiant than I remember, despite the fact that she too bears the scars of a late night on the town. She gives Jade a knowing smile and they both indulge in a giggle before laying their heads on one another. Everybody is introduced at some length and in some detail, knowing that today is not a day for hurried production – it's a sociable enterprise. Despite that however, it's not too long before the hampers and addresses are being allocated and plans are being laid, scrapped and re-laid. Eventually everyone gets their various roles clear and group by group we all head off.

"Are you going to be meeting Simon this evening Gem?" I ask as we head down the road with the wheelbarrow and six hampers.

"Yes! He wanted to meet up earlier today but I was explaining to him that I'd be doing this and that I'd see him in Temple Bar later. We've had some lengthy phone conversations," says Gemma rather hopefully. "He came into the canteen for a quick cuppa before I started the late shift. It was lovely but there were so many things going on as well that again, we didn't get to talk, just one on one. I'm sure he understands though. He's a very busy man himself. Do you think it would be okay for me to invite him over, at some point over Christmas? He didn't say he was doing anything or going anywhere, but I just didn't want to take it for granted that Mam and Dad and you guys would feel comfortable with him coming to visit," she says, finally stopping to look at me.

"Sure, why wouldn't we want him to visit? He's a gentleman. A delight to be around. Besides, the more the merrier. Mam, Dad and any one of the girls would say the same themselves," I gush, smiling my sweetest smile at her. "You go right ahead and invite him," I state, quite firmly, as we trundle happily off down the road like two kids full of the joy, excitement and expectation of anticipated delights.

THE RIDDLE

I can hardly imagine a more finely tuned enterprise anywhere else on this planet than the McCarthy & Co Christmas hamper run, yet every year, despite our best efforts something goes awry on us. Mostly it's a minor slip-up, like a hamper with no turkey voucher in it, which thankfully seems to always get picked up early on in the process. On one occasion, two turkey vouchers ended up inside a hamper and no ham voucher. Another time there was a hamper left over at the end of the run and no one knew who owned it. A quick run through the entire list and it was confirmed that everyone had gotten their hampers. To this day it remains an unsolved mystery. Then there was this other time when we attempted to deliver a second hamper to an address ten minutes after we'd already delivered one. On that occasion it was more comedy than tragedy and again, nobody lost out. Ultimately, the mix-ups are easily remedied and everything turns out well in the end. Just to be sure though, the following year we put in place measures designed to prevent mistakes from the previous year. This particular aspect of the run, the errors, can be both a challenge and, to some degree, a little entertaining for us also, because, let's face it, nobody *ever* knows how these things happen. It's like some mischievous leprechaun sneaks in when we're having those customary tipples, or perhaps he does it when we're in bed at night. He probably does it just for pure entertainment purposes, moving things around a little so he can delight in the sight of us scratching our heads like a shower of gombeens. As a result, our slip-ups, which are a steadfast feature of the hamper run, have come to be an expected and anticipated segment.

So when this year finishes up without a hump or a hitch everyone is understandably gobsmacked: beyond gobsmacked – doubtful even. To top it off, a box of crackers, the pulling variety, even managed to get lodged under the couch, only being discovered on our return to the house, and yet still every hamper met its requirements. To reward ourselves we decide to pair the pulling crackers with some edible crackers, and a bit of cheese, and of course, cheese and crackers need some of the old blackberry wine to complement them. Understandably, the mood becomes festive and jubilant with that added sense of exhilaration and relief at having successfully completed our task and everyone is on cloud nine. It doesn't take long for our rather civilised and sophisticated cheese and wine gathering to turn into a few more drinks, a little more food and a roaring sing-song.

Unfortunately, I have to drag myself away to get ready and head into town for my sessiún. It's a very casual affair and something I do only from time to time. A group of trad musicians play various well-known and popular Irish pieces at various stages through the afternoon and early evening before the main band come on. The first time I ever played with them I was in the bar in question having a drink with a friend celebrating her birthday. There was no stage and no obvious group of musicians that day and then just very casually people who themselves had been drinking, dotted around the bar, got up from their seats, cleared a small area in the corner of the room and started to play. Initially, I thought it was a spontaneous, impromptu kind of thing but it turned out that they did this every Sunday afternoon, so it was kind of organised but in such a way as to look quite casual. There were several musicians who seemed to switch places with each other and in addition to that, they would encourage staff and patrons to come and sing or join in with songs they knew. On one particular Sunday, after I'd had a glass or two of Dutch courage, I decided that requests for singers to come and join in also included fiddle players, and so I offered my services. The fiddle player, whose name was Louise, loaned me her fiddle and well ... the rest is history. It was a great night and any time Louise needs cover, which isn't too often, she rings me and I happily oblige. Louise needs to be gone by six today and as the group don't normally finish until eight, she asked if I'd like to fill in for her.

When I arrive, the bar is packed to the rafters and, as anticipated, there are no visible signs of an imminent performance save for a single mike stand in the usual corner. Simon, Matt, Kelly and Moira are at the bar and it looks like Moira and Kelly are getting ready to leave. Simon hops up to greet me, a beaming smile on his face as he watches the door behind me.

"Oh, Gemma and Aubrey will be along shortly. Gemma needed to catch up with some sleep; we were out doing the hamper run this morning and she was on a late shift," I say by way of explanation. Simon looks visibly deflated but paints a not too convincing smile on his face nonetheless. Moira and Kelly say their goodbyes and head out of the pub.

"So how does this work? It seems like anyone who wants to play just gets up and plays!" asks Simon genuinely puzzled. "Granted I notice a few faces keep reappearing but is everyone in here a musician?"

"Not really. But it adds to the relaxed casual vibe if

there's a more spontaneous kind of set-up to it. Believe it or not, it kind of encourages people to join in and participate if they like. I got roped into this in much the same way," I explain. I continue to expand on that a little more, outlining how it first came to be that I initially get involved and Simon nods in understanding.

"Can I get you a drink, Rhian?" asks Matt quite abruptly. "Simon, will you have another?"

"No, let me!" says Simon signalling to the barman to repeat his and Matt's order "What will you have, Rhian?" he asks.

"Oh, a 7up will be fine for me, thank you!" I say very decidedly and Simon instructs the barman to add a 7up to the order. After he pays for the drinks, he excuses himself and heads off in the direction of the gents. The silence between Matt and I is a little awkward and I scramble around desperately in my head trying to find something to say.

"So what have you guys been up to since Thursday?" I finally ask.

"Nothing very productive, unfortunately," he says wearily. "We were supposed to be getting started on a project but … well … it's complicated. We have some legal issues to deal with relating to misappropriation of funds by one of our building contractors," he says in exasperation and I squirm just a little, wondering if it's the issue with Brian O'Farrell's crew. "All very boring and terribly time-consuming, to be honest! You seem to have been busy yourselves!" he states.

"We have indeed," I respond and just like that the conversation seems to slip into an easy flow. "I suppose Gemma has probably already been telling Simon about the hamper run?" I ask him, just so as not to repeat the tale and bore him with the details.

"Simon did sort of tell me but to be honest I don't understand exactly what it is. Some kind of hamper business I gather?"

"Well not exactly. It's not a business. It's just a thing that my aunts started years ago when they were young adults. My mam was only a kid at the time so she wasn't involved at first. There were a couple of elderly neighbours of theirs, lovely old family friends whom my aunts and my mum grew up around. They lived all their lives in the same area so they were more like family than actual neighbours. Anyway, it was just about making sure they had what they needed for their Christmas dinner to be honest. Then the 80s came along. They were tough times for a lot of people and so the hamper thingy became something more than just making sure that a few of the older neighbours had their Christmas dinner. It became like a redistribution of supplies. People who had something to spare would give to those who had little or nothing. Of course, that's not just at Christmas time now, that people in our community are apt to be charitable, but the Christmas hamper thingy remained a passion for one of my aunts who continues to rally us all to the cause almost two decades after its inception." Matt listens intently and I take a look around briefly, curious as to where Simon has gone. I see him off over talking to Doc and some of the other musicians. Doc, as we call him, is a jolly, portly guy in his early thirties who looks way older than his years and who organises all the musicians/groups who play in the bar. He's a very good guitarist and can hold a tune fairly well himself.

I smile contentedly to myself, thinking how lovely Simon is and how sociable, and realise that the contentment I feel is at the notion of such a lovely individual going out with my sister.

Even though I've finished talking Matt is still looking very probingly at me and I look back in Simon's direction again just to avoid his stare. Doc points towards the mike stand and nods his head as if to ask me if I want to get started and I gladly hop up and grab my fiddle case from under my stool.

"Excuse me, Matt. I've been summoned!" I say gleefully.

Simon hurries past me on his way back to his seat, a huge grin and palpable excitement oozing from him.

"Break a leg, Rhian!" he says as I pass him.

"Hopefully not, Simon!" I say, smiling broadly at him and it's not long before we're set up and in full swing.

Both Matt and Simon seem to be enjoying themselves immensely, at least from where I'm standing, and over the course of the next hour or so people drift in and out of the bar, some stopping to look for a moment, some lingering to drink and dance. All in all it's a pleasant time and I find myself getting lost in the flow of the music, my head intermittently settling on thoughts that briefly need examining before I return to focusing on the music. Suddenly the small narrow door into the bar flings open and an astonishingly inebriated Aubrey falls through flailing and swearing at two guys, clad in football jerseys who appear to be trying to help her.

"Fuck off!" she roars at them loudly enough to be heard over, not only the music but the loud hum of chatter also.

"I have to see me sister!" she slurs almost incoherently while smacking wildly at the two sports fans.

I turn and look at Doc who nods at me and ushers me to go, knowing that I need to deal with this. So I hurriedly place my fiddle back in its case, grab my backpack and immediately head towards Aubrey and the door.

Simon has already moved from his chair to help her to stand as she's clearly struggling to do so.

"Thank you very much!" I say to the two guys, who laugh awkwardly and immediately turn to leave. Their abrupt departure is a little startling to me.

"Simon, would you mind grabbing me a taxi?" I beg in almost disbelief, and without a word he hurries through the door, returning in no time at all, beckoning for us to come outside.

"Thank you so much Simon and I'm so, so sorry. I know she's 'energetic' at times but genuinely this is not like her at all," I say. There's a little doubt in my tone as I guide my sister, who for all intents and purposes looks like she's just fallen asleep on her legs, outside and into the waiting taxi, waving an embarrassed goodbye to Simon, and to Matt also who has just appeared at the door.

The taxi driver pulls away immediately, having gotten his instructions, and I look at Aubrey slumped in the seat beside me. She lifts her head momentarily and her eyes are almost rolling in her head.

"I only had one drink Ree … it's …!" she slurs almost inaudibly, finding it hard to stay conscious. "That bar across … them lads …"

With that she falls unconscious in my lap and I wonder to myself if she wasn't drinking before she left the house. I've honestly never seen her like this before.

When we get back to the house the driver kindly carries her to the door where my horrified parents greet us. Needless to say, I give him a decent tip before he heads on his way.

"What the feck?" ask Mam and Dad in unison as Dad takes her upstairs to her bedroom.

"Was she drinking before she got on the bus earlier?" I ask my mam. "Was she drinking here?"

"No! She wasn't! She didn't have a drop. Said she was going to have one in town and no more. She left straight after you. Gemma fell asleep and she was trying to wake to get her to get ready but the lass was too exhausted and so Aubrey got a bit annoyed and went off without her. Sure she's not even gone long enough to get into this state. What happened?" Mam asks again.

"She said that she went into the bar across from where I was playing, well, I gather that from the three words she managed to utter and her pointing briefly as we passed. Two lads accompanied her when she came across to me.

Now that I think of it they were trying to bring her back out of the bar. I thought initially that they were trying to help her out, thinking she wanted to go somewhere else."

"Jesus! How many times have I told yiz not to be in town, or anywhere for that matter, on your own and not to turn your back on your drinks. Spiking drinks is an actual thing ye know!" says Mam looking down at Aubrey's lifeless carcass. Dad and I look briefly at each other before looking down ourselves.

"Do you think her drink got spiked?" asks Dad and we all shrug in a synchronised and dejected way.

A noise from behind prompts us all to turn around where a sleepy Gemma stands, eyes half shut, looking in our general direction.

"What's up?" she asks wearily.

"You're on shift!" I say with a weak smile as I usher her towards Aubrey. She looks puzzled.

"We think somebody maybe spiked your sister's drink," says Mam as she walks away and back downstairs with Dad, leaving us play nursemaid.

"Sorry sis! I got her home. You're stuck with her now," I say as I move aside, allowing Gemma to squeeze up past me and over to Aubrey's bedside. "I'm only kidding of course, just want to show my face downstairs, say hello, and then I'll be back up in a jiffy with a nice cuppa tea for us both. You do realize that you were supposed to meet Simon tonight!" I cautiously remind her.

"Oh God, Rhian. I didn't forget. I just fell asleep and that was it – dead to the world. Next thing I know, you guys are banging around in here. I'll call him tomorrow and apologise. He'll understand! Besides I can't imagine he'd be home yet and I really wouldn't feel comfortable ringing the house at too late an hour, disturbing the others."

"I'm sure nobody would mind, Gem. Anyway, I'll be back up in a few minutes." I say before finally heading down the stairs.

Dad's old pal Paddy, who plays a mean guitar, is centre stage in the middle of the sitting room, entertaining all around with a few old favourites, oblivious to the commotion that just occurred upstairs. The heart-swelling sounds of "Dublin in the rare aul times", followed by "When you were sweet sixteen" and then "Dirty aul' town", grace the confines of our cosy little sitting room.

With the evening not entirely at its end, celebrations begin to look, for all intents and purposes, like another enduring session in the making, as even Mam and Dad join in the performances, busting out a few ill-rehearsed moves on the dancefloor-cum-rug. This is the point in the night when usually Aubrey would make a magical appearance in the spotlight, offering to further entertain us with her beautiful vocal ability. But sadly she is conspicuously absent from the gathering and thinking on her I feel rather unsettled. Say what you will about our Aubrey – and plenty has been said over the years, not much of which would be considered glowing commendations – but there isn't a single human being that with all honesty can say that the girl can't sing. Truly she has an amazing vocal ability. Her voice has the kind of power and tone that brings reverent silence to the rowdiest of mobs and rabbles. You can almost imagine that the wind outside stops blowing when she sings, and the birds alight nearby, to hear a sound sweeter than the dawn chorus itself. Tonight however she lies unconscious upstairs, watched over by her loving elder sister, while the rest of her informed family members carry on as normal, plagued no doubt, by the worry of her.

At almost the stroke of ten o'clock, the barely audible whirr of the telephone comes to disturb the ebb and flow as it beckons from the hallway. Gemma, who is probably the only sober person in the house and who's also probably mindful of the fact that we're engrossed, can be heard pounding down the stairs to answer it. After only a moment or two has passed, she pops her head in through the door and beckons for me to come out and join her which I promptly do, setting my fiddle on the window sill so as to keep it from harm's way. The look on her face, when I enter the hall, tells me that it's something unpleasant and just like that, the light and celebratory mood of the day alters irreparably.

"What's the matter, hon?" I ask, with a little trepidation.

"That was Kelly on the phone," she answers, quite sombrely, pausing before continuing. "She's apologised for the late hour but wanted to tell me that they're all heading back to London tomorrow, Simon included of course. First thing in the morning." She pauses momentarily, with a contemplative, puzzled look on her face. "They've decided that it would be best to spend Christmas at home with family and friends, no point in delaying their return. So, Simon says goodbye to us all, though not in person – through his sister, and, well, that's the crux of it. Can you believe that? He didn't even come on the phone himself."

She pauses again and looks at me for guidance but I'm useless. My brain is stuck in gear, not quite comprehending, not quite understanding the significance. He's gone home for Christmas. Nothing odd in that, my brain has decided. He didn't say goodbye in person but there could be any number of reasons why that might be. He didn't say a word to Gemma, my beloved sister who clearly has grown quite fond of him – who was allowing herself to hope and dream and move towards the object of those hopes and dreams. But again, I have no understanding of why. I can see though, by the expression on her face, that unlike me she has a firm and unquestioning grasp on the reality, the finality of it all.

"They're not coming back, Rhian. They're gone for good and he couldn't even be bothered to say goodbye himself – to say anything himself," she says in conclusion, tears welling up in her eyes. I take her by the hand and we lumber up the stairs together to our bedroom, where we sit down on the edge of my bed and sag motionlessly for some time.

"I'm sure there's a reasonable explanation why he didn't speak to you himself," I say doubtfully.

"Like what, Rhian? she asks, the frustration creeping into her tone.

"I don't know. But I'm sure there is one. He's a good guy Gemma, that much I do know, and he likes you, I'm sure of that too.'

"Rhian? Do you think it's because I didn't hop into bed with him straight away? Because I didn't *'put out'* as they say? I know I messed up tonight and I have all the intention in the world of getting myself better organised, especially with work, but at this time of year it's just chaos. I feel like I didn't get much of a chance … to adjust my life and time, to accommodate another person. But I wanted to. And I would have."

The tears that puddle at the edges of her lower lids finally tip over and flow down her cheeks in meandering streams and she quickly wipes them away, composing herself as best she can, a flicker, almost as if she just swept the grief off into some recess – to be stored away forever – passes over her face.

"Gem! I don't think that's the case at all, and if for some *unimaginable* reason it was, then good riddance to him. You deserve better than that."

If myself and Gemma had been running on batteries powered by emotion, right now the light would simply just have gone out. The energy has left us. The dreams of young women are so potent that if they falter or dim from view, like a vacuum they suck the emotion from our souls as they go. We could do nothing but gawp and sit with our shoulders slumped for the longest time.

"Look! Forget about him for tonight and come downstairs. Enjoy the rest of the party. Jade can ring Kelly tomorrow when they're back in London and try to get some more information from her. There's no point in speculating and making yourself miserable. I know in my heart of hearts that there will be a very good reason for him leaving so abruptly, something we're not aware of. So for now we should re-join our guests and celebrate our hard work," I say, with a little more conviction than I'm feeling right now, as my heart begins to wilt and wane a little more.

"If you don't mind, I'll just go to bed. I'm exhausted anyway and this has taken the last of the pep out of me. Aubrey will be okay by the way. She's well sedated but apart from that, it's all good. She just needs to sleep it off."

Without waiting for my response, she gets up and starts to organise herself for bed.

"Rhian! You go on back down to the party; I'll be fine. I need to think. My head is all over the place."

I give her a brief consoling hug and head downstairs to whisper in Mam's ear then put my violin back in its case, and I'm not long in the kitchen cleaning up when I hear the crowd shifting from the sitting room. Mam is very diplomatic when it comes to bringing a party to its end. She's so subtle about doing it that she almost makes people feel like it was their idea.

The departing guests are swift and noisy in their exit, leaving an uncomfortable silence in their wake. Even the girls themselves who arrived home at some point, unbeknownst to me, convoy up the stairs and into their rooms with a lot less noise than they normally would. In the blink of an eye downstairs becomes barren and almost lifeless. Mam, left alone in the empty sitting room, comes and joins me in the kitchen. I explain briefly to her what transpired and the discussion and analysis is both brief and, on some level, consoling. She has an amazing ability to rationalise everything that causes us heartache in our lives and to help build up our strength and resolve. After talking to her for just a short time I immediately get an injection of confidence in Gemma's ability to handle this heartbreak and to find the strength and resolve she needs to move past it. Of course, we'll all be there for her too, to help her and support her in any way we can.

After a few more moments of mulling it all over, myself and Mam head up to bed ourselves and as if someone had drained the house of life and hope, an atmosphere suiting the mood settles throughout the house. It's an uneasy atmosphere and when I get into bed, I have this sense that sleep is not going to come easily tonight. As I watch the hands on the clock move slowly but steadily through the hours, my initial thought is sadly confirmed as my head is set on replaying every word, every expression, every action, over and over, painfully analysing, again and again, depriving me of sleep. What could possibly have driven Simon from the arms of my beautiful sister, when they were so enamoured with one another? Maybe, I simply read the whole situation incorrectly. Maybe what I sense and what I feel – what I think I know – is only what I want to believe is real.

I look at the clock again and it reads a quarter past six when only a moment ago it said five minutes to three. I must have drifted off unknowingly and sadly it's now too early to get up and too late to hope for a good night's sleep. To add to the misery, sleet and howling wind beat hard on the window as if mocking my insomnia, knowing that with little sleep I will have barely enough strength and resilience to fight against its bitter penetrating iciness when later on this morning I'll have to venture out. A chill runs through me that not even the addition of a thick woollen blanket, thrown over my usual bed covering, can guard against, and it's a miserable feeling.

Even though she's lying slightly angled away from me I can still tell that Gemma too is not sleeping. The barely discernible movement of her head and occasional tremor gives her away but I resist the urge to talk to her. I know she'd much rather have her peace and be left to mull things over herself. I have no choice but to continue to watch the clock between failed attempts at counting sheep and trying to clear my mind.

Thankfully the clock finally reads seven, which is a reasonable time to get up, so I muster the motivation, moving as stealthily as I can from my bed, out the door and downstairs to get some breakfast.

With tea and toast in hand I move sleepily to sit at the table, wrapping a large wool blanket around my shoulders in the hope of some warmth and comfort, and it's not long before I hear the creak of floorboards from above my head.

"Morning!' says a rather neutral-looking Gemma as she sweeps in through the kitchen door.

"Morning hon!" I almost whisper as I ponder for a moment, if it is at all possible for misery to enhance beauty in any way. Who knows! Still, I've never seen Gemma look so stunning in all her life. Her flowing pale grey pyjama suit and loose cascading blond hair gives her an almost ethereal look, like the persona of love's wandering soul, a beautiful spectre, destined to roam the world for all eternity, searching endlessly for what's lost.

"How're you feeling?" I ask cautiously.

"Grand. Not a bother." She replies, somewhat unconvincingly as she heads to the grill to put on some toast. "I was thinking I might help out up at the Community Centre today, if you could use an extra pair of hands? What time are you heading out at?"

"We certainly could use the help, thank you!" I state with absolute certainty. "That would be great. I told Breda that I'd be up there for nine to help set the room up, so whenever you're ready. I'll head upstairs now and get washed. It's a bit harsh outdoors today by the looks of it, so we'll need to dig out the extra woolly woollies." I say, in an effort to sound light and perhaps amusing. My gut feeling is that Gemma is going to get through this the same way she gets through most everything in life and that's by throwing herself into work and responsibilities, her own and everyone else's, which will eventually wear her out, no doubt. But for now, there's no harm in indulging her.

Taking the last sip of my tea, I place my cup in the sink, give it a quick rinse and head upstairs to wash and dress, and it's not long before myself and Gemma are bearing into the ferocious wind and sleet as we make our way up to the local Community Centre. The classes, which we'll be taking names for today, will be run over the course of next week, and even though it's only for the Monday, Wednesday and Friday, being the last week, we anticipate that we will be running twice the amount of classes as normal. The last week is always the busiest and this morning will be busy too. But it'll be the distraction Gemma is looking for. Still, even though I am genuinely happy to have her with me today, I'd much prefer to see her on this rare morning off keeping better company than with heartbreak, and doing something more exciting than taking names for classes.

When we finally arrive at the centre, the caretaker is just opening up and Breda, who is the chairperson of the committee, is with him. Breda also happens to be a very talented violinist herself, who has in the past worked with me over the summer months. She's very passionate about teaching youngsters traditional music skills and I reckon that if I ever decided not to be involved in the community classes, she'd probably come around to my house and drag me up the road kicking and screaming. She's a force to be reckoned with and I have to admit I sometimes find myself hopping to attention when she starts to dole out the orders. Today is no different from any other time I've been under her command and almost as soon as the Community Centre doors open, she has myself and Gemma instructed and hard at work. Gemma is putting out tables and chairs and erecting signs for the various classes like fiddle, guitar, tin whistle, etc. Strangely, I wasn't looking forward to today, mainly because of having to venture out in the frosty weather, but as I set my station up a wave of relief washes over me at the thought of having this opportunity to include Gemma in such a pleasant and rewarding distraction. Today is one day less that I will have to worry about what's going on in her head and how that is taking its toll on her, and when I take a quick glance over in her direction and see her talking to one of the other volunteers, I'm reassured that everything is okay for now.

As the morning wears on people file in and out in a nice steady flow and by the time lunch hour arrives our classes are full to bursting and Gemma is clearing up, repositioning tables and chairs and taking down signs with the focus and energy of a woman possessed.

On the walk back home, I struggle with deciding whether or not to talk about it or whether to act like nothing is going on. All the signs are that she is deliberately trying to distract herself, so small talk is probably the best option, which I manage till we get as far as the local shops.

"I know this is just another banal cliché, Gemma, but if it's meant to be it will be, hon. You know, it's hard for me to think of you being sad. I wish I could say something or do something. But words, with all their power, are just not enough sometimes," I finally say, unable to keep up the pretence.

"Oh Rhian, don't worry about me. I'll be fine. Yes, I'm disappointed! Yes, I feel sad. I expected more from him. But you know what they say about expectations?" she asks before answering herself. "Expectations are the mother of all disappointments. I have nobody to blame but myself, so I'm just going to concentrate on work, my life and of course Christmas, and move on from this. Besides, 'What doesn't kill you …' isn't that what they say?"

I smile consolingly at her and we walk the rest of the way home in silence, relishing the ease and calm of early Sunday afternoon, the sleet cruelly bearing into our half-shut eyes, turning the tips of our noses a bright red. I humour myself and imagine that mother nature is trying to numb our hearts, starting from the outside and working her way in and by the time we get to the front door of our house I'm almost sure that the job is half done. The cold has deprived my toes and the front of my legs of any feeling at all and I'm as glad as I've ever been in my life to close the door behind me and embrace the warmth of the indoors. The comforting smell of turf and roast beef greets us immediately and it's enough to dispel the gloom and despair for just the shortest while. In the kitchen, Dad is perched contentedly beside the roaring fire watching a wildlife show on TV. The volume is turned as low as it will go and the Sunday papers balance precariously on the edge of his knees. The girls, who are all sitting around the table expectantly, are rigorously quizzing Amy on various aspects of her personal and work life while Mam stirs gravy on the hob, glass of wine in hand, gazing into the pot.

For a moment I linger, eyes squeezed shut just briefly, and allow myself to believe that everything is as it should be. Turning to Gemma, she flashes me a reassuring smile, letting me know that she finds consolation in everything around her too and I know that even though, deep down, she is undoubtedly pained, right now she is comforted in the same way as I am. Aubrey wanders in from the sitting room, still in her pyjamas and still appearing to be half asleep. She promptly takes her place among the gaggle at the table and almost immediately seems to come to life as if in some way connected to the energy of the group.

After offering our assistance to Mam who declares herself to be sober and capable, with everything under control, we sit down and join the girls in their chat. Dad gives us a sideward glance when he hears the laughing elevate briefly to near roaring levels, but almost immediately turns back to his TV. I see a smile flash across his face. From the corner of my eye, I can also see Mam gazing over at us and she too has a contented smile on her face, though that could be the heat and the wine.

The girls are all intrigued with Amy and it's clear that Amy too is enjoying the attention and the camaraderie. She appears very comfortable with all aspects of our unpolished and inquisitive interaction with her and is not one bit fazed by the questions, probing and liberal discussion. Admittedly, she is quite a bit more polished than we are, maybe even a little more sophisticated and worldly, but I get the distinct feeling that she doesn't see that; I think she's genuinely at ease on every level. The girls are outlining the complicated yet natural arrangements that are meal times in this house.

Dinner on Sundays, which is really lunch because it's the next big meal after breakfast, is always later than on any other day. Monday to Friday, lunch is around one o'clock, whether you're in work or at home, and dinner is in the late afternoon at five o'clock sharp. On Saturdays it's kind of a free for all, with no real timetable for meals but that in itself is very much set in stone, strict adherence to casual, with no big meal as such. However, Sunday is the feast day of sorts and religiously the lunch/dinner meal is served between two and three o'clock and will ultimately require elasticated pants and forty winks afterwards to recover. We normally have a fry up on Sunday morning which helps us to last till the later hour but which also helps seal the deal for a future with clogged arteries. Inevitably if you have dinner in the afternoon, come evening your next meal will then be your tea which is really your dinner but nothing like a dinner, more like a lunch. It's all very confusing to anyone but an Irish wan.

Trying to explain the difference between your tea and a cup of tea to Amy is a wonderful source of amusement for the girls and a comical conversation to hear if ever there was one. At first, she couldn't understand how a mealtime could be referred to as "tea" and how that didn't confuse us all with regards to a cup of tea and, despite the fact that her mother is Irish, she insists that she has never come across the concept of lunch and dinner every day of the week except one day when you had dinner and then your tea in the evening. Apparently, that was not the way in her home, though in fairness she spent most of her younger life in France. Whatever the reason, the concept got lost in translation somehow and remains alien to her.

Of course, when you have a few drinks in you, any subject can turn into hilarity at the drop of a hat and that's exactly what the tea discussion becomes. At some point I notice Dad giving up on trying to hear the television and picking up his newspaper instead, although I'm sure he wasn't reading it but probably trying to make sense of the absolute rubbish spouting from our mouths like: "are fishnets classy or trashy?"; "is crimping your hair bad, full stop, or is it okay now and again?"; and, most importantly, "how do the punks get their mohawks to stand up so perfectly?"

I doubt that anyone would argue the fact that, while waiting on dinner in this house the big issues, the real issues, are laid bare and in the process, sense is made of this maddening universe. But with all the chat and fun I hadn't noticed Gemma slip off over to help Mam at the cooker, and when I look up my heart is warmed to see a brief hug between the pair as Mam then demonstrates how to make the perfect gravy, sharing what she calls her secret tips. The pair toil away, prepping and plating up our dinners and it's not long before heaped, steaming plates are placed in front of us and the blackberry wine is flowing freely.

Plates come and plates go in a hue of berry-induced sedation and even Gemma can't help but get caught up in the big discussions that continue, like how it's never okay to wear white shoes with black tights. Dad looks momentarily perplexed at this and simultaneously amused at the discussions before he decides that it's time for a board game, while the tea and coffee are brewing.

The evening wears on quite pleasantly and before we know it, we've all exhausted ourselves of chat, games and eating and one by one each of us slips away upstairs to bed.

Earlier on in the day, Mam had set up a bed on the floor of Jade's room for Amy to stay over which she had been duly directed to at some stage before myself and Gemma had arrived home earlier in the day. By nine o'clock sharp the house is a calming hum of low voices coming from behind closed bedroom doors and a restful contented mood settles throughout and all around.

Despite Gemma's protestations this morning, the barely audible sound of sharp intakes of breath and clear but subtle sounds of sobbing, can be heard coming from her bed just after the lights go out, and my heart breaks for her. She must have thought it safe enough – that I was asleep by now and finally allowed herself the release that tears would bring. Unfortunately my brain is holding me back from the threshold of slumber and painfully I lie listening, powerless to ease her pain. Yet the truth of the matter is that there is nothing anyone can do. Sadness must wait to grow its wings before it can take flight and finally depart. Right now we move as time takes us and keep watch by her side. The harsh howling wind and beating rain intensifies, drowning out the soft, low sound of her grief; windows rattle rhythmically and doors, all around the house creak and thump in their frames. I'm not even sure now if I can even hear her sobs and my eyelids are growing heavy, thoughts scrambling. Perhaps she's finally asleep.

Christmas is just around the corner and that's always a good distraction – something to look forward to for all of us.

HOPES AND DREAMS

And we did look forward to Christmas. We turned our minds from the unfathomable riddle that is love – the quandary that so often weighs heavy on the hearts of young people – and we threw ourselves blindly into work and responsibilities. But healing takes time and the pain of heartbreak lingers. The chaos that seemed to define the previous weeks was replaced by an almost tranquil order which gave volume to the screaming disillusionment, making it very hard to ignore. On some level it all felt a little like the calm before the storm.

For me of course, occupying the position of observer, things were easier. My path still lay before me, just as it had a week ago, or several weeks ago, or for that matter, last summer – my vision remained on course. Classes for the winter project had concluded and Christmas Day was tantalisingly within reach. I could almost smell the turkey at this point and beyond that, I had little in the way of expectations, apart from surviving the holidays and pledging, as my New Year's resolution, to be a better and more organised person. Honestly, this is the same pledge I make on a regular basis – the sum total of my aspirations.

But that wasn't the case for Gemma, who soldiered on as if the hopes and dreams of young girls, which are too often hastily formed and just as swiftly shattered, had never been within her grasp. She dealt with her disappointment the only way she knew how and that was by working herself to the bone, eagerly volunteering for every extra shift that became available, which at this time of year is quite a few. However, by doing that she inadvertently earned herself a reward, and that was getting rostered for Christmas Day off and an early shift on Christmas Eve, though I suspect she would probably have preferred to be working through, given half a chance.

The thought of not having everyone together on Christmas Day is not a thought I relish in the slightest and so I secretly applauded her stoic work ethic while worrying madly about her, as well as simultaneously frowning upon the efforts of one other sister. Literally, while Gemma is working herself to distraction, in total contrast there's Aubrey, who seems to put the same amount of time and effort into aiming for the exact opposite. She's currently breaking boundaries in her endeavour to avoid having to work at all cost. As it turned out, just around the time the hamper run got underway, Aubrey, to everybody's amazement, managed to secure herself a full-time job working in the supermarket just up the road from us. Very convenient you might think. But not for her, at least not for long. The novelty rapidly wore off and soon after starting the job funnily enough became a source of annoyance to her. It began to get in the way of her newly invigorated social life and if it hadn't been for the season of goodwill and a shortage of retail personnel I suspect that management would have sacked her long before now. Her constant moaning, tardiness and frequent sick days must be making it very difficult for the shop to keep her on but right now they just don't appear to have much choice in the matter. Still, in her defence, the dedication shown in the pursuit of a life of idleness and hedonism is so unwavering as to be somewhat commendable.

However, it is neither the worry of Gemma nor the frustration of Aubrey that plays on my mind at this moment. It is Kathy who is more of a concern. Her almost constant absence and uncharacteristically coy behaviour are very disturbing. At the moment she is a mystery to us all. We know at least that she is still seeing Bill, but beyond that, nothing. On the rare occasion that she is around these days her morose countenance and general distancing of herself from us has left everyone feeling a little unsettled and so we fall back on the wise words of our mother to give us comfort. For some things, nothing but the passing of time will bring forward the inevitable, and therefore we wait and we fret and we hope for less worrisome days to come.

The flickering light in the present gloom, however, comes in the guise of Jade and Amy. They are our vision of hope moving forward. Happily, the pair are now officially an old-married-couple-in-the-making and Amy has even taken to spending most of her time here at our house. She ticks along quite nicely with us, and in some ways, it just feels like we are now a family of eight instead of seven. Simon and his posse, of course, are lost to us – not a word has been heard from any of them since that phone call to Gemma, and life goes on as before. Given that Kathy's boyfriend Bill has worked for them and to my knowledge still does, then I'm sure she must have some understanding of things, some information that she's not sharing.

"It's like she's ashamed of us," says Aubrey, as we all sit poised, waiting for Dad's piéce de resistance – the Christmas Eve breakfast special. All of us that is, except for Kathy and Gemma. Gemma is on the early shift in work and Kathy has mysteriously disappeared again, up and gone before any of us had a notion of opening our eyes this morning. Another vanishing act.

"Well, you can't blame her for being a bit cagey after her

last disaster," I offer by way of a little support.

Mam, Aubrey, Jade, Amy and I all sit around the kitchen table, a beautifully aromatic fried breakfast sizzling and popping its way to our plates, complete with Dad's homemade sausages. He was up very early this morning despite the fact he had his Christmas work-do last night and is today a little worse for wear. But like an enduring trooper, he sticks rigidly to tradition and cooks the Christmas Eve breakfast. Not only that but he'll do it all over again tomorrow morning as well, though hopefully in a less wretched state than he's in right now. We all love Dad's contribution to the Christmas festivities, of course, and although he's not exactly a domestic god; on the odd and truly rare occasion that he does participate, he comes up trumps. Christmas is the appointed time for such delightful miracles. Another little contribution of his is to take responsibility for cooking the turkey and ham, as well as acting as Mam's assistant on the big day, while she exhaustively puts together the amazing banquet that will be our Christmas dinner.

"Go on! Eat up, girls! That'll put hairs on your chest," says Dad placing a serving dish in the middle of the table piled high with sausages, rashers, pudding and potato cakes. He adds another dish to the centre of the table that's equally piled high with bread and toast, as well as the non-traditional additional item of croissants, served up as a tribute to our newest family member, Amy, as well as a pan of fried eggs. We all tuck in hungrily and for just a little while, in the eerie silence of consumption, it's possible to forget worries and woes. Spirits are high and seasonal cheer is creeping steadily in, flowing hard against the tide. Everyone is looking forward to what tomorrow brings.

Stories of old, of previous Christmas antics, flow around the table and Amy is horrified to hear tales of how our parents would visit family on Christmas Day, driving from one house to the next, drinking at every stop and then get back behind the wheel of the car to drive us all home again. The look on her face is comical as Aubrey describes how they were barely able to stand – two sheets to the wind, lolling and lagging under the weight of inebriation – and yet still felt it was okay to drive a car. Of course, they don't do that now. Well, not as much. Times are changing and drink driving has fallen somewhat out of favour in recent years; in fact, it's rather frowned upon. But there was a time, and I remember it well, when the five of us girls would all squeeze into the back Dad's rusty old Cortina, giggling at the ridiculous spectacle of our drunken parents, none of us with seatbelts on and thinking it was all such perfectly normal behaviour. In particular I remember a year when we made our last Christmas morning call into see my Auntie Rita's on the way back to our house. Rita was near plating up her own festive feast and all the adults in the house were so drunk at this stage that for some unknown reason they thought it would be a good idea to eat every single roast potato. When my cousin finally arrived at her parents' house, no doubt for her much-anticipated feast, she was horrified, disgusted at the notion of not getting roasties with her Christmas dinner, so much so that she went mad. I don't think she has ever forgiven my parents for that incident.

Anyway, Dad decided on that particular day, after a lambasting from the victim herself, that from then on we'd stay put on Christmas Day. It wasn't worth the grief when you could just as easily get legless in your own front room. As a trade-off, he sits at the foot of the stairs every Christmas morning after breakfast and phones each one of the same households that he would previously have driven to. In keeping with tradition, he makes his calls with a hot whiskey in hand and the end result is pretty much the same except for the driving and without the possibility of an early demise. More importantly though, everyone gets roast potatoes with their Christmas dinner. Not that any of it ever took the shine off our feast because no matter how drunk and how out of it our parents get, they have never once ruined a Christmas dinner (of ours). It's the one meal of the year that is always guaranteed to be superb over-indulgence.

"So what time are we heading into town, Rhian?" asks Jade, excitedly.

We have a lot of traditions in our family, but drinks in town on Christmas Eve is just one of those with longevity and endurance – an absolute steadfast. Most bars, to my knowledge, close early on Christmas Eve and the last buses leave town round about nine o'clock, so we head in earlier and leave early and there is a wonderful sense of measure and celebration to it all. There was a time when we would go to Midnight Mass afterwards as well, but that was a long time ago. (Apparently, it started to turn into a bit of a social event rather than a genuine expression of piety so Mam banned us from going and, funnily enough, nobody put up a fight.) In Mam's opinion we made too much noise, and who'd have known, but Midnight Mass is not where you go to pick up boys. Consequently, we are left with no option but to drag our tipsy backsides home to consume more alcohol and rip pieces off the freshly cooked ham – very indiscreetly. Then after a couple more hot ports or hot whiskeys, it's off to bed to wait for Santy, who usually crash-bangs his way up the stairs not long after us.

"We'll head in for about six o'clock if that suits everybody," I say, scanning the faces to see if that's met with approval. "Gemma will be well finished before then and she can meet us in town. I'm not sure about Kathy though. She knows the ritual, so either she's going to be there or she's not," I say as the girls begin to clear their plates away and prepare to leave the kitchen.

After they've all left the room, I help Mam finish the cleaning up and then we peel and chop potatoes and veg, make the stock for the gravy and prep the stuffing for tomorrow's feast. Mam goes into the sitting room to arrange her presents under the tree and Jade and Amy head out together, having been up, washed and dressed from very early on.

I decide to wrap my presents and put them under the tree as well. As part of our shopping trip, we always buy seven different types of wrapping paper and dole them out among ourselves making sure that everyone has their specific wrapping paper to identify what they bought. I wrap my presents in red and gold paper with tiny glittery stars and spend ages adorning the gifts with ribbons and bows. This year I bought Gemma a top. She was admiring it in the boutique window up the road from us and so I went back and bought it at a later stage. For Aubrey I got a new hairdryer. The one she has smells of burning hair; there's that much of the stuff caught up in the workings, that we're all expecting it to burst into flames any day soon. For Kathy I got a nice new handbag and Jade, the purple Doc Martens she was hinting at for ages. I also bought Amy a small gift of slippers and PJs because she's going to be stopping with us till after Christmas. Understandably she's fed up with travelling every year and her Mam and Dad are just so pleased that she's in a relationship, they have no objections.

"Rhian! Would you go to the shop for me? I want to get another box of Christmas crackers. I don't think we'll have enough," Mam calls from the kitchen. And so, I head out into the hall to get my coat and hat on, glad of the opportunity for some fresh air.

Mam comes out into the hall with her purse in hand and starts rifling through her change.

"Mam, I'll get them. Put that away," I say to her.

"Are you sure, pet?"

"Yes, of course! Is there anything else you need?" I ask her and we both stand contemplating for a few moments.

"I can't think of anything else, Rhian. We're all stocked up, I'm sure of it," she says before gasping in a sudden expression of realisation. 'Oh Jesus! Pick us up something for Amy. I have nothing under the tree for her. Suffering Lord above, what kind of host am I?' she says laughing before resuming her purse rummaging.

"Mam! Seriously? I can pick you up something," I say as I head out the door.

Our house is only about a hundred yards away from the local shops, which is a small nest of essential businesses all in one large, two-storey structure. It consists of a reasonably sized supermarket, a newsagent, chemist and boutique, all of which are on the lower ground floor. Just above these three is a hair salon that does piercings and some beauty treatments and a very small shoe-menders where you can also get keys cut.

After wrapping myself up well against the elements I head off, deciding to go to the chemist first to pick up something in the way of toiletries for Amy. As I push open the heavy glass-panelled door and step inside, I immediately notice that a couple of the local ladies, who were chatting rather loudly as I entered, quickly hush themselves up before giving me a look that in my understanding conveys a mixture of derision and embarrassment. I resign myself to ignoring it and instead stroll methodically down the first aisle before selecting a nice basket filled with Christmas-themed beauty treats. When I approach the near end of the aisle where the group of ladies still stand, mute, glancing and glaring at me for who knows what reason, the atmosphere seems to becomes a little more tense and uncomfortable. I turn at the top of the aisle to quickly scan the items on the other side, just to make sure there's nothing I would rather have than what's in my hand, and I'm painfully aware of them taking ever-lingering and more scornful looks at me though at one point I almost have my back to them. The whispering becomes less discreet as each second passes.

"If ye have something to say I suggest you get it off your chest before the strain puts another wrinkle on that sour face of yours, Mary Burke," I say, directing it at the one woman out of the three who I've identified as the individual most aggrieved by my presence. I can almost taste the hostility radiating from them and my annoyance begins to bubble to the surface.

"Nothing te say, Rhian. What about yourself? Got anything you'd like te say te any of us?"

An overwhelming sense of being out of the loop hits me like a hurling stick to the jaw – as if I'm meant to know something that I don't or I've somehow offended and I'm just not aware of how I've done it.

"Nope! My conscience is clear," I say looking her square in the eyes.

Why I'm feeling the need to defend myself is a mystery even to me right now, but when you're backed into a corner it's a natural reaction. So I continue on, my annoyance pushing aside any hope that I was ever going to be polite.

"Just picking up a small pressie, before I head home. Ye know how it is? Get in, get out. Don't wanna be out round the streets too long in case some scanger starts brawling in public, showing themselves up and terrorising decent people like meself. Happens ye know! But of course, you do know, Mary!"

I see the fire ignite in her eyes, tinged with an edge of shame. Exactly the reaction I was hoping for and with that she turns to me, spitting venom.

"Ya might well say ye have a clear conscience missy but that sister of yours sure doesn't. And don't try to pretend yiz didn't have some notion of it either," she says with a smug grin on her bitter-looking face.

Now, if there's one thing that will set me off it's an affront to any member of my family. So I charge round to the other side of the aisle and stand with my nose a hair's breadth away from her face.

"Now, lady, if you've got something to say then spit it right out. But take heed, you better have the evidence to back it up or you'll be out that door tramping the street to make the money for your solicitor's bills," I say with great restraint.

Joanna, the girl that works behind the counter darts out from behind her till and edges her way in between myself and Mary with a nervous smirk on her face.

"Now, ladies. There's no need for trouble, not in here. If you'd like to step outside," she says, whipping up breakables left, right and centre.

Mary's two companions pull at her coat sleeves urging her to leave with them and, with her nose slightly less raised than before, she accompanies them out through the door, holding my stare till the bitter end.

"Them fecking McCarthys think they're above everyone," says Clare Dunphy, one of Mary's companions, a woman I've known since I was a child, a woman that I would have called a friend, before today. "Ye wouldn't catch any of us robbin' people blind."

And with that they're gone out the door and I can see them as they stomp over to the crossing and down the road out of sight.

"What the hell was that all about?" I say, turning to Joanna in desperation.

"Beats me, Rhian. But they were talking about your Brian before you walked in, that much I do know," she says with a sympathetic look on her face.

"Our Brian! He's hardly our Brian. He was somewhat dubiously married to our Kathy for the sum total of ten months and two weeks and in that time, I've seen more of you than I did of him and I'm not thinking of taking you home any time soon. Feck it, sure I've had toothbrushes for longer than that blackheart was around. You do know that they got married in Las Vegas and it wasn't legitimate?"

Joanna giggles and gives me a reassuring pat on the shoulder before placing all her breakables back in their designated spots.

I feel the tears well up in my eyes but blink rapidly, trying to stem the flow before picking up a larger hamper with what looks like much more interesting bath stuff in it, swap it for the smaller one I had been holding and then pay and leave. After a quick run into the supermarket for the crackers, I head home, vowing to myself to say nothing of what happened to anyone, especially not to Kathy, also minding that I'll have to try and discreetly find out what the hell is going on.

For the rest of the day I ponder over the whole sorry mess.

Kathy and Aubrey both may be high-spirited, and I know the neighbours like to gossip about that, but when it comes to honesty and integrity, I would swear my soul to the devil on theirs. In my mind, Mary Burke is just a bitter old hag. What would she be minding anyone's business for anyway, especially if it didn't affect her?

To take my mind off the incident in the chemist I wrap some gifts for Mam, including the one for Amy, then I taste-test a few of her practice canapés for tomorrow before getting ready for our night out. My plan is to get the five-fifteen bus and meet the girls in town in our usual haunt for six o'clock sharp. But the incident from earlier hangs on me for the whole time it takes to get ready and I hardly even notice the journey into town with how it occupies my mind.

Still, the time on the bus gives me some much-needed pause for reflection – a respite from the gnawing unease. Despite that though, I can't settle my mind completely and the sight of Gemma, Jade and Amy waiting at the Central Bank with no Kathy in tow, reignites my sense of discord. It's time for answers. Apart from all else, it's the only thing that is going to restore peace to my universe.

As it turns out, my universe finally catches a break because Kathy luckily is in the pub when we finally make our way over there. I spot her the moment we walk in. She's sitting off to the left of the bar in a cosy little booth with Bill to her right and Aubrey and Declan seated to her left. The foursome are engrossed in conversation, with all eyes transfixed on Kathy, mouths agape and as we near the group Aubrey looks up and beckons for us to move faster.

"What are yiz talking about?" I ask as the conversation comes to an immediate halt, all heads turning to look at us.

"Brian O'Farrell, the dirty blackguard," says Aubrey with a measure of theatrical horror.

"I thought as much!" I respond quickly, and with a seasoning of my own theatre add, "and would it go any ways to explaining why that article, Mary Burke and her posse, had a go at me in the chemists earlier today?"

"What did that aul' bat have to say for herself, Rhian?" asks Jade a little defensively, and I can't help but notice how cagey Kathy and Bill look in this moment.

"Nothing I wasn't able to handle but I suppose I'll have to give Ma and Da heads up so they don't get ambushed like I did. You know Ma wouldn't be able for that shite," I say in a deliberate attempt to make Kathy come clean.

"Rhian! Don't say a word to Ma and Da. They don't need to know!" she implores, finally.

"Well you better tell me everything now or I'll have no choice. Not having me Ma treated like that. I'd be done for murder, sure."

"It's nothing, Rhian … really. Well … just that Brian is trying to drag me into this whole sorry mess of his with Simon and Matt, and others … you wouldn't believe it if I told you – some of them are even local. Like, who shits on their own doorstep?" she asks incredulously, turning to look around the group inquiringly, her hands thrust out as if waiting for an answer to fall into her partially outstretched arms. "Just because we were married at the time that he stole some of that money, he's trying to say that I was in on it. Actually, what he said was that finances were my responsibility and he just handed it all to me so I must have spent it, or something. Anyway, I snook over to the flat a while back to see if I could find it or find anything. All I managed to get was some paperwork which I didn't think much of at the time, but would you credit it, the eejit had kept hand-written notes and accounts. Bill thinks he's hung himself – more or less. Talk about being the greatest gobshite that ever walked the planet. We also have some bank stuff too and we have it all kept somewhere very safe. One thing is for sure. He's not going to have me tarred, not so long as there's a breath left in me body. Having said that though, the fecker knows I have stuff on him. He knows I have him by the short'n'curlies and he's trying every trick in the book to get me on side. Anyway, Rhian! You're not to be worrying yourself! When this goes to court, Mary Burke and her lackeys can ask me arse. You know I wouldn't steal a penny and I won't rest till I've cleared me name too," she finally concludes, turning to look doe-eyed at Bill in the process.

"Ladies! If I might interject," says Bill in his haughty British accent, while looking directly at me. "I've had dealings with Mr O'Farrell and his crew on a number of occasions and even though we weren't initially aware, it did soon become apparent that something wasn't quite right. This goes back way before your sister ever met the scoundrel. Rest assured, I will do everything in my power to clear her good name – you can count on that," he says in conclusion before turning to look at Kathy with an adoring, intense gaze and in that instant, a thousand worries dissolve and cascade from my shoulders. I nod in understanding at Bill and immediately resign myself to putting it all aside for now and enjoying the rest of the evening. No sooner have I settled myself into that well-fitting thought than Gemma springs to her feet with an offer to get a round of drinks in. Clearly I'm not the only one this thing has being weighing on. The lightness in Gemma's demeanour radiates from her in the moment and it feels good to see her less burdened, if only just slightly.

I accompany her to the bar and we bring a tray of assorted drinks back to the table, to the awaiting throng of eager faces, and after distributing them and returning the tray and empties we sit sipping our drinks as I fill everyone in on what transpired in the chemist earlier. Everyone seems suitably amused by the tale and when I have cause to go over aspects of the encounter the story becomes somewhat embellished. Everyone adds their bit of comedy to the now vastly elaborated report. Jade surmising that a good shag would sort all Mary's woes for her while Amy decides that Mary is, right now, pitching herself up on top of a neighbouring building with sniper rifle in hand waiting to take me out on my next shopping trip. Aubrey on the other hand reckons that Mary would have definitely had to go home and change her underwear afterwards because, apparently, I'm scary when I'm angry, which thankfully Gemma disagrees with as does Bill, who declares that to be highly unlikely. Nevertheless, it doesn't stop Aubrey from suddenly scooching herself across the chair with comical flair then off towards the lady's toilet, mimicking someone who may just possibly have soiled their underwear. I take a momentary glance at Gemma and see genuine amusement etched across her tired face, the weariness still evident but for the moment overshadowed by the frivolity. Despite the fun, I can't help but be glad that tonight we're only out for a short while. Long hours as well as other things on top of that are taking their toll on my poor sister.

I drift back to thoughts of Bill's declaration of support for Kathy and it comforts my mind anew as does the sight of Jade and Amy, heads pressed closely together, laughing and smiling. A warm sense of satisfaction further envelops me at the sight of Declan's face lighting up to greet Aubrey as she returns from the lady's toilet.

She sighs loudly and pats her bag with a wide grin on her face.

"Always keep me a spare pair of undercrackers in here

in case Rhian ever kicks off. You never know when some poor eejit is gonna need them," she says to a howling audience, before sitting down and continuing on her humorous tirade. The evening fills up with fun and laughter and before long nine o'clock looms. Everyone starts to gather their coats and belongings, knowing well that the options for getting home on a Christmas Eve, if you miss the bus, are slim to none. Kathy says goodbye to Bill as he climbs into a taxi outside the front door and we all wave him off before heading towards the bus stop.

Once back in Tallaght, Declan also says his goodbyes to Aubrey and just as it's meant to be, we all march towards home.

When we opened the front door the mixture of aromas that hit the senses ignite food lust and we scramble to get ahead of each other through the kitchen door. Dad is just this very moment, taking a large succulent-looking ham from the oven and transferring it to a foil tray. Mam has a row of hot whiskey glasses lined up on the kitchen counter beside the kettle and everyone gathers round.

"So! Who's for Irish coffee, hot whiskey or hot port?" she says, and the orders roll in. Once again, the lightness shines and worries are dispelled.

Dad slices thin slivers of the delicious hot, freshly cooked ham for us to pick at and of course the mince pies soon make an appearance too. Everyone takes their drinks into the sitting room and squeezes into the two large couches adjacent to each other, all except for Jade and Amy who sit on an array of large cushions thrown in front of the fire. Dad sits in his armchair and debates whether or not to open just one pressie before bedtime, but Mam, being the voice of reason, puts a stop to it before it happens and we all sit watching a recording of White Christmas, singing along to the signature tune, Aubrey of course showing us all up with her phenomenal voice.

The combined effect of the heat from the fire and the

hot drinks conspire to take us down and before the credits have a chance to roll the low sound of snoring begins to swell out from the corner of the room where Dad sits, the continuing, melodious hum of the television failing to disturb him in the slightest. Soon after, barely audible raspy breathing noises start to emanate from various spots around the room, followed swiftly by stifled giggles as Aubrey's boisterous snoring forces everyone that was nodding off to come to life again. The sound is so comical that we can't help but be amused by it. The laughter and slagging soon becomes loud enough to wake Dad from his sleep too so Mam decides it's time for us all to go to bed. Again, it's a sight to see Gemma laughing along with the rest of us for a bit, though I know that deep down, her heart still weighs heavy.

CHRISTMAS DAY

Generally speaking, Christmas is considered to be a wonderful time of year for most people, and we McCarthys are definitely most people. We spend weeks preparing for it, endless amounts of time focusing on it and thinking about it. Why, exactly, is still a source of ferocious debate. It could be the coming together, the indulging with abandon, the craic, the movies, the food, the presents – maybe even the hangovers and the occasional bouts of heartburn. But most likely it's all of it together. Christmas is like a smorgasbord of an occasion and no matter how old we get, that sense of anticipation never dissipates. For some of us, it never ceases to be the pinnacle, that something to work towards and to look forward to all year long. The only downside is Kathy and Aubrey hauling everyone from their cosy nests (as they usually do) at the crack of dawn, like a pair of over-eager, expectant toddlers. And all just so they can open presents an hour or two earlier than they would otherwise be opening them. It's painful – literally.

So, imagine my surprise when Christmas morning 1994 finally arrives and for the first time in my entire life I open my eyes, quite naturally and untrammelled, to the sound of seamless silence. To my left, Gemma's slumbering form is buried beneath bulbous pillows of white cotton, deep in unearthly repose. Not even the barest hint of nearing consciousness, no faint intake or release of breath, just the vaguely visible rise and fall of the duvet. And all this, despite the prodding beams of light streaming in through the cracks in the curtains.

It's only when I sneak from the bedroom and tiptoe across the landing that I at last hear the faintest sound of soft breathing and snoring coming from the other bedrooms and know that there is still life in this house. Continuing on down the stairs, as quietly as possible, the low tap of Delft being placed on a hard surface can be heard coming from the kitchen, where unsurprisingly I find Dad busying himself in the kitchen with the Big Day breakfast preparations.

"Oh, I thought you were in bed," I say, as I set about helping him lay the table. "I take it your current mastery at stealth and minimal-noise-prep is to save your sore head and not to allow us a few more minutes in our leabas?" I say in amusement. "On a scale of one to ten, how sore is your head, Pops?"

His moderately bloodshot eyes gaze at me contemplatively, before he moves slowly to retrieve a milk jug from the press.

"Oh, I'd reckon a good nine, maybe nine and a half, a little improved on yesterday morning, that's for sure," he says drowsily. "But still better than your Mam's, I reckon. Too many Irish coffees, you see," he says before turning to look at me again. "Rhian, before anyone gets up can I ask you something? Actually, I feel it's a bit of an insult to my daughter just to be even thinking about it but Lord knows I need a bit of reassurance, is all. Our Kathy, will she be okay? Will this all work out okay?"

Despite his clear and concise question, by the look on his face he's anything but clear. I would guess at troubled, and to see my dad so uncharacteristically bothered is distressing. Evidently, he has heard the gossip and, knowing well the characters of his children, the conflict must be confounding for him, something I genuinely can relate to.

"Dad! You have nothing to worry about," I say, projecting real confidence. "She's not a stupid girl. A bit high-spirited and you know that, but not stupid and certainly no thief or liar. Besides, she has Bill on her side now and he'll let nothing happen to her. He's no fool either," I say, as reassuringly as I can, and I see a look of relief come to settle among the creases in his face. His bloodshot eyes seem to lighten before me and he looks a little less strained.

"Well, we'll say no more on it this Christmas then. Don't want to spoil the fun and I certainly don't want your mam getting wind of it and worrying herself sick. She doesn't have a notion and with a bit of luck it'll stay that way till the truth comes out," he says before moving to survey the table briefly.

We continue for a few moments more, positioning and repositioning items on the kitchen table and, by the time the first sounds of floorboards creaking underfoot begin to emanate from upstairs, the table is laid out in such style that it would rival that of a royal banquet. Dad cooked all the food before I came down and placed it in the oven to keep warm. The only thing left is to get the rabble from their beds and start the celebrations and I have a perfect idea for how best to do that.

With the devil as my guide, I sneak back upstairs just as Mam is coming out of the bathroom looking a bit worse for wear. I give her a scolding shake of the head before heading in to see if Gemma would like to partake in the enjoyment of payback with me. Gemma is sitting up in bed yawning and stretching and, when I've explained, she's eager to join me in reaping revenge. Some might even say she is uncharacteristically enthusiastic about my proposal, bounding out of bed with a little giggle while rubbing her hands together like a miserly character from some children's fairy tale. Quietly, we tiptoe from our bedroom into the bathroom stifling the giggles before running our hands under the cold water tap for a few moments. Then, after a quick sign of the cross, we head back towards Kathy and Aubrey's bedroom.

"You take Kathy and I'll take Aubrey," I whisper to Gemma, who nods in agreement and I push the door open as gently as possible. Without even disturbing the flow of air we both sneak up alongside a bed each, hands poised, and then nod our cue. As if the powers that be had designed the setting for just such an ambush, both girls, who are lying comatose, also lie perfectly vulnerable. Aubrey has her duvet clutched to her chest, her back entirely exposed to Gemma while Kathy has one leg inside the covers, the other one out, just a hands width of her bare waist begging for my cold hands. All we have to do is hit our marks, which we do and woe betide, you'd swear we were trying to murder them the way they respond. Aubrey takes a swipe at me and misses by a mile. I stumble backwards laughing triumphantly, readying myself for a possible second strike. However, Kathy manages to grab Gemma pulling her down, forcing poor Gemma to flail around to regain her composure. This only makes things worse for Kathy but she's so desperate to get Gemma away that she continues on anyway. Gemma finally manages to get up and run out the door as I follow swiftly behind.

Jade and Amy have come to their bedroom door to see what all the commotion is about and we delight in telling them through our howls of laughter.

"Years of injustice have been put to rights, that's what's going on," I gasp as Kathy and Aubrey spring through the door after us, Aubrey trying to swat at us with her dirty socks.

Before long everyone is laughing and swearing

vengeance in equal measure.

"And that's what you call 'payback'," I shout exuberantly as Gemma and myself make our way downstairs for breakfast.

"Oh that was cruel, Rhian," says Aubrey as she runs up behind me and tries to pass. "I'll be having one of your roasties at dinner, as compensation," she moans, rubbing frantically at her arms and body to coax the goosebumps away.

"I'll tell you what! You can knock that off the list of things you owe me for years of the same crap," I offer.

"I never put me cold hands on ye," she says in her quite valid defence.

"Aubrey! Your excited squeals were like cold hands on my warm subconscious. It's pretty much the same thing. Now! I do believe we have presents to open." The mention of presents has everyone else charging down the stairs like half-demented, escaping convicts, bursting through the sitting room doors where Mam and Dad are already waiting on us by the Christmas tree, their presents piled beside them. The chaos that ensues is indescribable. As much as we try every year to do this in the most orderly and civilised way we can, it never happens. Frenzy ensues. A tsunami of sparkly, coloured paper, ribbons, bows and tags, billow all around us. The chatter, the oohs, the ahhs and the delight in the giving and receiving is more fun than the gifts themselves.

"Let's have a toast," announces Gemma, when we finally make our way back into the kitchen, turning to raise her glass towards Mam and Dad. "To the best Mammy and Daddy in the world! To family and also to good friends. Genuinely, all you'll ever need to survive in this world!"

We all clink glasses, nodding our approval and hugging. Everyone looks genuinely choked for a minute, looking fondly to each other before supping en route to the table. I watch fondly as my sisters gather around choosing seats and discussing the best spots for everyone, while Mam and Dad remove plates of food from the oven and place them at the centre of the table. The energy and the banter are genuinely uplifting and I'm reminded once again, of why I love Christmas so much.

Trying hard not to gorge myself I listen intently as the girls eat, chat and rib each other ferociously and ponder on how Christmas is such a wonderful time of ease and leisure – unlike any other time of year. We linger at the table indulging and enjoying the simple pleasure of company and banter. Even as we clear our plates from the table, clean up and ready ourselves for Mass, we do it at an ambling pace, the kind of pace you feel life should always move at.

Mainly because we want to get Mam to and from Mass without incident and also partly because it's an old custom of ours from old, we all decided earlier on to accompany Mam to Mass today. When we told her, she looked genuinely tearful, emotional even, though as we prepare to leave, I note a hint of suspicion in her demeanour. But she wears it well, delighted to have her brood as company on this rare and wonderful occasion no doubt.

Thankfully, Mass is a crowded affair and even though I notice a few more stares than we would normally get, nothing out of the ordinary happens and we manage to get home safely and without any encounter or incident.

Back at home, we all get stuck into organising the house for the feast ahead and even though it's only mid-day Mam cracks open a couple of bottles of bubbly and the day progresses in a wonderfully harmonious haze of alcohol-induced sedation, helped along also by sporadic glasses of mulled wine.

Declan pops in for a short visit sometime around one o'clock and Mam delights in the opportunity to stuff mince pies and mulled wine down another poor wretch's throat. Soon after, Bill calls Kathy, who happily sits for an age on the stairs giggling a cooing like a love-struck teenager. God help the poor man when his phone bill finally comes in.

Jade and Amy cosy up on the couch in the sitting room watching White Christmas over again, surrounded by the contents of several selection boxes, and from time to time through the early afternoon some of our neighbours and one or two family members pop in and out with Christmas greetings, stopping long enough for a tipple.

Soon there's a lull in the comings and goings so I settle myself in the armchair by the fire, book in hand, as Mam and Dad busy themselves, relay-style in the kitchen. Gemma tidies the remnants of the mess from this morning's present unwrapping and when she's finished, I join her in the kitchen along with Mam and Dad as we help pull all the components of the feast together.

Like most people, we've done this so often now that we all know whose job is whose, without anyone having to give direction. It's not long before the table is reset and has an enormous bronze turkey adorning its centre. The unquestionably delicious-looking bird is surrounded by every Christmas dinner delight you could dream of asking for, flanked on all sides as if to pay homage to its majesty.

After pulling crackers and eating ourselves into a near coma we somehow manage to clear up and make it to the couch to not watch television and fall asleep almost instantly. I can honestly say that there's not another day like it in the whole year and I can't help but imagine that Vikings and Saxons as well as medieval royalty must definitely, in their time, have known how I feel in this moment. I suppose when your days are numbered it's good to make them count, though I'm hoping that, unlike my ancient ancestors, I have a lengthy and fulfilling life ahead of me.

As I drift in and out of my food and drink coma contemplating my survival, a thought makes a confusing entrance into my mind. I imagine Simon ringing to tell Gemma he made a horrible mistake and that she is his one true love. I also wonder why the thought occurred. When suddenly the phone does ring, I swear my heart stops for a beat or two. Luckily, it's just my mother's friend ringing to wish us all a Happy Christmas. I look over at Gemma and feel relief wash over me at the sight of her sleeping face, undisturbed by the startling tone of the telephone.

The sleepy lull is soon broken by the appearance of the Monopoly box and all thoughts of Gemma's broken dreams and the past are pushed briskly from my mind as the house fills with laughter and energy once again. Judy Garland follows the yellow brick road somewhere in the background and the sight of Gemma's smiling face lifts me up again.

Almost as soon as the game starts, the bickering ensues and before long Aubrey and Kathy are at each other throats over minor perceived slights. To avoid the ruination of the wonderful evening atmosphere, Mam decides we've all had enough and that it's time for turkey sandwiches. To further dispel any lingering animosity, I take the fiddle out for a while and the girls are soon slapping their thighs and jumping around like drunken eeejits. All traces of the brewing argument quickly forgotten, Aubrey and Kathy link arms and spin each other round and round almost falling over at times. When they finally tire of the leaping and jumping a chorus of voices rings out, begging and chanting for Aubrey to sing a song. To everyone's delight, she willingly obliges, launching immediately into a surreal rendition of "O Holy Night" that brings the room to a reverent hush and calm. With eyes closed and bodies gently swaying it's as if the sound swells among us to nourish and heal in a way that can't be measured in any real and tangible way. But the feeling is pure and sublime nevertheless.

After that Dad joins her in a light-hearted performance, singing "Fairy Tale of New York" before begging off and heading up to bed early. In fairness, I don't know how any of us are still standing given the amount of alcohol consumed today. Not long after, Mam follows suit and after chatting among ourselves for a bit longer, we too, one by one, wane and wilt, our full, dizzy heads and happy hearts driving us up the stairs and into our beds.

Lucky for Gemma she's on the late shift tomorrow, which means that not one member of the McCarthy household will be up before noon and the thought of it is just pure bliss. Unfortunately, we won't have Gemma for dinner tomorrow but Declan will be a welcome addition to the Saint Stephen's Day festivities and he has already been allocated her seat.

Though I can't claim to have spent too much time in his company and have had little or no conversation with him, he still seems like quite a nice lad and, more importantly, he guarantees us a peaceful day, as Aubrey is less likely to argue with anyone while he's around.

With thoughts swirling their usual course around my weary but happy mind I eventually feel myself drifting away to that all-too-familiar oblivion and unsurprisingly I don't resist. Truthfully, I rarely resist the call to slumber.

TIME ROLLS ON

After the Christmas period, life quickly slipped back into normal routine. The big party we were planning for Gemma's 23rd was cancelled at her request and nobody argued, for a change. It was clear that her heart wasn't in it and so, in a break from normal practice, we dressed up and went to the local Chinese restaurant instead. It was a surprisingly pleasant and sober affair and we were even joined by our newest family members, Declan, Bill and of course Amy.

Soon after that, Jade and Amy flew to France for the New Year and the house began its eerie descent into near-lack-of-chaos. Kathy and Aubrey both absconded on the eve of New Year's Eve, to spend a few days with their respective partners and to ring in New Year in a more romantic vein. Gemma, too, was otherwise occupied for the New Year, predictably taking the most undesired of all shifts, consisting of not only New Year's Eve but also New Year's Day as well. This left me alone with Mam and Dad, counting down to the start of 1995, not that I'd have had it any other way but I will admit I pined a little for a genuine reason to fly the nest myself, if only just to feel like I had options, which I clearly didn't. We drank way too much of course and yet still managed to croon a relatively coherent verse or two of the customary "Auld Lang Syne" while slobbering emotionally over each other in the most embarrassing way possible. I guess I was hoping that the "way too much alcohol" would erase any memories of the year everyone had a boyfriend, or broken heart from a past boyfriend, except for me, which it didn't. I am still painfully aware of the fact that I don't even have a broken relationship to my name, never mind one in good working order, and dare I mention the obvious fact that my parents felt sorry for me as I am now the grand old age of twenty-two years and still steadfastly positioned on the proverbial shelf. As a counter-balance of sorts, there was of course another dimension to all this; it was a sense of relief and some measure of gratitude that at least I had someone to ring in the New Year with.

Word got about that Brian O'Farrell was due up in court in August charged with fraud, among other things, and that he planned on pinning some of the blame on Kathy. We couldn't keep it from reaching Mam's ears in the end but as it turned out she had known all along and had set a few people straight along the way. According to some of the neighbours who still spoke to us, she had quite vociferously warned some people that she could also hold council with gossips and was in a position, when it came to some choice individuals, to bandy about accusations with equal lack of fact and evidence and she would do so if, for example, those individuals were ever to speak a word against her daughter. Not that our mother ever used such crass language as "individuals". I believe the term she did use was "gossiping wenches with their knickers in a twist".

Over the Spring months I saw the sparkle creep back into Gemma's eyes and she even went out on a date with a young doctor who had recently started working at the hospital, though she still claims they're only friends. More excitingly though, she had, some ways back, been to the bank to discuss getting herself a mortgage for the purpose of buying herself an apartment in town and had told none of us until she got the approval. The excitement was immeasurable because she was set to be the first one of us girls to own her own home. Kathy and Aubrey spent hours planning possible parties and soirées that Gemma flatly declared would never happen, but that didn't stop them dismissing her and planning them anyway and to be honest, I don't think they do have any intentions of turning her future abode into party central – it's just the excitement of it all.

Jade rang home soon after the New Year to tell us that she was extending her stay in France to learn the language and had even gotten some evening bar work to help towards her keep while she was there. By all accounts she was having a ball and, surprisingly enough, Mam seemed more relaxed about it than I thought she would be. Like most Irish Mammies, our revered guardian spends at least 80 per cent of her time worrying about us: about what we eat, what we do, where we're going, how safe we'll be. Up until she called, the fact that Jade was in a foreign country had been Mam's new focus of stress and anxiety, but as it was evident she was living her dream and undeniably over the moon with herself, Mam had no option but to accept her choices and miraculously did a complete turnabout, seeming to reconcile herself to the situation entirely. Life was genuinely ticking along rather pleasantly.

By the time summer was on the horizon, life was on

such an even keel that I was kind of hoping something would kick off just to liven things up a bit more. The gossips had tired of the whole Brian O'Farrell saga, mostly because other stories about him were coming to light and people were beginning to get a true measure of who he really was. Kathy had officially started working for Bill as his PA and even Aubrey had managed to get herself a nice new job working in a printing company in the same industrial estate where Dad worked, and she took it much more seriously than we had ever hoped she would. Both her and Dad were like two happy peas in a pod, bounding off to work together in the mornings, lunches in hand, full of the joys of spring. The sight of them was enough to warm the cockles of the coldest heart. To everyone's amazement she completely gave up going out and drinking so that she too could save, and despite our reservations, she hasn't faltered on this yet. I think that when Gemma got her mortgage approval everyone began to believe that the same might be possible for them too.

As for me, well I was looking forward to spending a few weeks in the west of Ireland over the summer holidays, playing the trad sessions in pubs and venues along our usual trail. Mostly, I was looking forward to the craic but also I was aiming to earn a little extra money, which is definitely possible just as long as you're careful about how you organise your accommodation and food. As usual, the group had set out a schedule earlier in the year, planning on starting this year's stint by doing a few venues in Kerry first off, then on to Galway and finally we are hoping to finish up in County Clare, though these things are never set in stone. Too often venues will be looking for last-minute fillers for random, unanticipated slots and then it turns into a juggling act trying to work the schedule successfully. Our first stop is going to be Listowel for the Fleadh on the 22nd of June and six weeks from that date it will be all over and the gang will be finishing up and heading back to Dublin –

that much we know for definite. It's a long stint and though I could definitely do the full six weeks myself, the entire summer would be gone and I'd be left trying to cram a hundred jobs into my last few days off. So to preserve some of my holiday time I made arrangements, as usual, with Niamh, a fiddle player from Connemara, to divide up the work between us. I'll be starting off, doing the first three weeks, before she will meet up with us in Galway and take over. At this point, I'll head back to Dublin to reclaim some of my time off. Summer passes so quickly that I don't want to find myself facing a return to work having had no personal time at all. It has all worked well in previous years and I have no doubt it will do so this year too and as the band have been following this same routine for a good number of years now, we're all pretty comfortable with how things go.

So when the summer holidays finally arrived, I spent the first two weeks helping out with the local summer project before setting about doing a bit of painting and DIY at home. We had all been promising to do it for so long, that someone just had to bite the bullet. Dad taped off all the skirting boards, sockets and the fireplace the night before and the following morning, with everything laid out for me, I was able to fly through it with amazing ease: first the sitting room and then the kitchen, both of which still look as fresh and as pleasing on the eye today.

After that was done, we all banded together to draw up a plan for a back-garden makeover. Mam had mused about turning it into her little haven so often that we agreed a date three days before I was due to go off to Kerry to finally take some time off and set our plan in motion for her. We even sat down beforehand and physically drew out a design, though nothing that would ever end up in the Louvre, that's for sure. The girls all booked the time off work.

Our modest back garden, though not enormous, is very reasonably sized by anyone's measure. Nevertheless, for our makeover, the main focus is still to maximise space.

Today, our job is to dig the soil and weed it out for planting, in the soon-to-be vegetable garden section. Dad will erect a cute little picket fence around it at a later stage when we've decided exactly how large it's going to be, and there has been ferocious debate on how the picket fence will be painted. The general consensus is white with large pink spots.

Being that it's a Monday morning and typically a working day for everyone except me, nobody is too keen to get up early. But that's not going to be a problem because Mam and I, who are already in our wellies and ready to go, have devised a cunning plan. We're going to set off the smoke alarm.

After waiting patiently for Gemma to finish in the bathroom we lay sausage sandwiches out on the table covered with tin foil, plus a large jug of orange juice and glasses. Then the three of us sneak back into Mam and Dad's room to retrieve our lighter and copy paper. Gemma and I position ourselves with a baking tray, holding it firmly under Mam's hands as she lights a piece of paper and raises it up to the smoke detector. The sound is almost instant and deafening even though she immediately extinguishes the paper, dropping it into the baking tray, before retrieving her teacloth and standing poised to fan the detector into silence as soon as the girls make an appearance. It's not long before the sleepy faces of disgruntled McCarthys and one Dú Bois begin to make their way out of the various bedroom doors and down the stairs where Gemma and I have laid out wellies and work clothes.

Kathy and Aubrey are not too pleased to say the least and Aubrey even tries to get out of participating by claiming that a lack of sleep could put her at risk of myocardial infarction, a term she heard Gemma use a few weeks ago. Not only that, but apparently she may even have a life-threatening allergy to Wellington boots – not rubber per se but specifically Wellington boots – or so she claims.

Tiring of her incessant ramblings we all head out into the garden to start work and soon enough she trudges along after us. Jade and Amy get stuck in immediately, working up a storm so they can do their fair share, finish up a little early and head off to the cinema later. Kathy however, only too pleased to be out of the office for the day, decides that today she is just going to constantly fool around.

"Girls! Watch this," she says when Aubrey appears at the back door.

Everybody turns to look at her as she squats in the left-hand corner of the garden, knees bent, facing towards us, a strained look on her face. With one hand behind her back, she slowly lowers an elongated lump of muck that she moulded into the shape of a poo. Grunting and groaning the mud sculpture slowly appears between her legs and grossly enough it does look real. Soon everyone is having a go, each trying to be more authentic than the other, while laughing ourselves into hysteria.

"Jesus Kathy, what the hell are you doing?" roars Mam from the back door in horror.

"Relax Mam! It's only muck," she says and we all burst into ferocious laughter again, at the realisation that Mam thought the worst.

After a bit more giggling and messing around, we all get stuck into the work and by lunchtime the vegetable patch is completely weeded out and the soil turned over, all rocks and stones removed. It looks very nice indeed and Mam is beaming about all the vegetables she's going to plant.

The second half of the day, however, isn't as productive, as everyone tires and begins to lose interest. Soon they're all devising excuses to finish up and head off, promising earnestly to make an early start the next morning.

Of course, the next morning I'm left mildly perplexed by a sense of déjà vu as soon we're repeating the whole smoke alarm rigmarole over again coupled with endless persuasion. The only real difference today is that Kathy finds new antics to entertain us with. She plants herself in a large hole that she and Aubrey dug and then gets her partner in crime to compact the muck in around her lower legs, as hard as possible to see if she can free herself afterwards. With muck shovelled in over the top of her boots and the realisation that the thing tickling her foot is most likely a creature of some kind, she nearly bursts a blood vessel trying to get out of the hole and out of the offending Wellington boot.

In her efforts, she manages to fling it over the neighbour's wall before falling back into the hole which is now more like a small crater than a hole. Everyone finds this hysterical until the neighbour pops his head over the wall complaining that Kathy's boot flattened two of his best sunflowers and terrorised his dog. After apologising profusely Kathy pops next door to put support stakes in the ground to stabilise the sunflowers, which weren't damaged in the slightest, just toppled, and soon the harmony is restored to the garden enterprise once again.

Before long, the sun has gone down on day two and one by one the girls beg off again to do other things. When I'm just about to give up myself, Dad arrives home with the posts and rails he's going to use to make the fence strapped to a trolley, and I stay to give him a hand digging the rest of the holes. He'd probably do it quicker without me in his way but he never complains about the company and to be honest, I think he could do with at least another set of hands. By eleven o'clock even the rear security light is not enough for us to do any more work by so we both head indoors to wash and get ready for bed.

By late afternoon on the third and final day, which thankfully is another glorious summer day, I have to beg off myself and get ready to head off to Kerry. Even though we're not playing the first gig till tomorrow evening we thought it would be a nice start the trip off by doing a spot of sightseeing early Thursday morning.

Sadly, I have to leave the girls to continue on with the garden project without me and after a thorough scrub and a last look out from my bedroom window to see how work is progressing, I head downstairs to say goodbye. The garden does look very well and the ideas that were initially laid out are beginning to take shape. I'm a little envious that everyone else will be there to see it through to the end.

At four o'clock on the dot, the powder-blue and white-topped, rusty old Volkswagen van pulls up outside the house and Eddie Dignam, the driver and owner of the vehicle, hops out to help me with my gear. Eddie, who is the bodhran player in the group, also kindly provides the van for moving equipment about. He used to be a full-time musician at one point in his life, playing in several trad bands who had residencies in many of the usual haunts in Dublin city-centre. But now, since getting married and having children, he professes to only playing very occasionally, including the few weeks over the summer holidays. Normally we would all travel together in Eddie's van to wherever we were playing but the rest of the group wanted to leave as early as possible and both myself and Eddie had things we needed to attend to first. Just like me, Eddie alternates with another musician and he'll only be with the group for three weeks as well, heading back to Dublin a few days later than me and then re-joining the gang for the last weekend of the trip, by which time I will be long gone.

After loading my few bits into the back of the van I turn to hug and kiss Mam and Dad, as well as all the girls, who dribble out from the back garden swearing blind that they'll do their best to come to at least one of the gigs in the coming weeks. Before long Eddie are I are in the van and on the road heading west.

We estimate that, all said and done, it should be about nine o'clock by the time we arrive at our B&B, given that we can't drive too fast with all the gear in the van and will most likely have to make one or two pitstops along the way. That should amount to at least five hours of a journey, something I wasn't looking forward to up to a short while ago. However, when we finally get on the main road, that anxious feeling begins to subside and at last I begin to feel like the adventure has finally begun.

Admittedly, this trip is not shaping up to be very profitable on the face of it because sadly we haven't been too successful with regards to our accommodation costs – not that this will stop any of us getting into the spirit of things of course. Still, in years gone by we have been very lucky in that, on many an occasion, we were able to source a few places to crash free of charge, thanks to friends of friends and kind offers, which not only saved us money but also added to the fun of it all. This time around, we have only managed to amass a grand total of two nights' accommodation gratis and that's courtesy of some friends of Kathy and Bill's. According to Kathy, the couple in question are old school chums of Bill's from London who have a lake view, eight-bedroom house in Killarney which they only use a couple of times a year. They have kindly agreed to put the whole band up for the weekend of the 30th June and the only thing they want in return is for us to play a couple of songs in their local bar on the Monday night for a party the gentleman of the house is organising himself. We agreed because we have a gig on the Thursday and Friday in Killarney and in Killorglin on the Saturday and Sunday, or maybe that's Tralee on the Saturday. Wherever it is, the house is very conveniently located to all of these towns and venues.

ROAD TRIP

The road trip to Kerry is surprisingly pleasant, with Eddie and I singing along to a Mary Black cassette with genuine abandon. Of course, when questioned, he vehemently denies ownership of the tape, dismissing any postulations very unconvincingly. According to his extremely ruffled self it definitely, most certainly belongs to his ex-girlfriend Janet though, surprisingly enough, he knows every word and note off to a T, and it's his hand-writing listing the songs in the index. No doubt Janet would have taken it with her when she left, if in fact it was hers. Consequently, his protestations ring very hollow in my ears, especially when he gets excited at the suggestion that we play it over once again, which we do of course. By the time we near the end of our journey I'm just as note-perfect and just as addicted as Eddie is.

When I next look down at my watch I see the big hand move jerkily into position indicating ten minutes to nine, just as we pull into the driveway of the B&B. The stone-fronted farmhouse, which sits a little back off the main road, is located just outside Listowel town centre in a picturesque setting of rolling farmland. The vague stirrings of a session are the first sounds to greet us as we exit the van and make our way across the gravelled front drive. The B&B owner, who is a small motherly looking woman with an apron and her hair in a bun, appears almost immediately at the front door, eager to show us to our rooms. It's obvious she wants to return to the hive of activity at the front of the house as she hastily runs us through what we need to know. After off-loading all my bags and equipment, I follow the sound of uillean pipes to a room which is indeed situated at the front of the house and which has a small but beautifully ornate, handcrafted bar nestled in the near right-hand corner, complete with an array of beer pumps and equally ornate high stools. The bar is manned, by someone I suspect to be the landlord, a rather stout, jolly chap who stands leaning with one elbow on a beer pump, beaming and nodding at everyone that looks in his direction. As I walk into the room, he nods a greeting to me as well, and then to Eddie who trots up behind me, springing through the door with his last step and throwing his arm around my shoulders. Without missing a beat, he then turns and gestures at the beer tap the barman is leaning on, letting him know to pour a glass of the black stuff, and by the time he's dragged me with him around the entirety of the room, hugging and greeting friends as we go, his Guinness has rested and been topped up.

Unlike Eddie and the gang, I have no intentions of getting into this too early. In fact, my sad but well-thought-out plan is to start off this three-week stint as I mean to continue, so for now I'm sticking to the orange juice, and an early night is most certainly on the cards. Lingering just long enough to catch up with the rest of the group and also long enough not to appear rude, I soon head off quietly to my room and hop into bed, totally disregarding the book I placed on the locker earlier. It's been an exhausting day all round, between the early rise, the laborious garden toil, not to mention the long journey. I haven't got an ounce of energy left and as soon as I pull the covers up around me, I can feel oblivion calling.

The next morning after breakfast, which consists of a mindboggling array of continental offerings as well as the usual cooked delights, we all head out to Dingle as planned. We pass through the bustling town of Tralee on the way and after a short scramble around the harbour, choose a quaint location by the waterfront for lunch where we watch the fishing boats as they navigate into position along the dock to bring ashore their catch. After that we stroll through the town, joining the other tourists as they soak up the atmosphere and delights of the wild and rugged Atlantic coastline.

In the evening we play to a rapturous crowd back in Listowel, and then again for the next three nights after that, with little time in between for anything other than some brief band conflab, a few hasty rehearsals, eating of course and essential sleep only. As usual, the time is racing by and before I even have time to reflect on how the trip is progressing, the first week is nearing its end. It crosses my mind that perhaps the universe is playing a very cunning trick by deliberately speeding time up when everybody's distracted and not in a position to notice.

The following week we head to Killarney with the instructions Bill gave us to find our accommodation, our trusty map helping us to successfully navigate along the winding country roads that take us to our destination. The house in question, which is perched on the side of a hill, overlooks the glorious and breath-taking lakes of Killarney, the majestic mountain range of the MacGillycuddy Reeks standing sentinel over the glistening bodies of water. The structure can only be described as being of palatial proportions with a large three-vehicle car dock located underneath the main part of the building. Its size and elegance are awe-inspiring and when we park up and get out of our respective vans, the others push me forward to ring the bell, unsure and uncertain about the invite. Within seconds of ringing, the owners come to the door to greet us.

"Ah, you must be Rhian. We've heard so much about you, good things I might add. What a pleasure it is to finally meet you and to have all you wonderfully talented people here to stay with us," says this rather jovial-looking gentleman who opens his arms towards the group, in a welcoming kind of gesture. Mr Maguire, as I know him to be, is a tall, imposing man whom I guess to be around forty years of age or so. He has a full, thick head of speckled grey and dark brown hair and his accent is an odd mixture of what I surmise to be a bit of Irish, a little English and possibly even some German, all blended together. His wife, who he introduces to us as India, is a very attractive, slender woman with almost shaved dark hair. She's a good bit younger than he is and has the softest, most gentle countenance. They both welcome us with energy and enthusiasm.

"You're both very kind to put us up like this," I say when Mr Maguire has finished with his introductions.

"Call me Stephen please, and please come in and make yourselves at home."

"Thank you very much," I say again before turning to introduce everyone else. "This is Eddie, he is our bodhran player, occasional tin whistler and van driver extraordinaire," I say, gesturing to my right. "And this is Gwen, she plays the guitar and mandolin and most other stringed instruments. Clyde here is the master of the uillean pipes and Rory and Jake, well, none of us know with any certainty what they do. But they're fun to have around and occasionally they have been known to try and sing a little or blow into stuff, and now and again bang and shake things as well. But most importantly, they charm the crowd," I say to delighted laughter.

Jake pokes me in the arm good-humouredly before declaring that he does his level best to distract people from my awful fiddle playing and everybody laughs again before heading inside.

Passing on through the large, heavy, double front doors, we find ourselves in a surprisingly sizeable, bright reception room. Beautiful, tall, gothic style arched, paned windows refract the sunlight with an almost artistic style, casting dabs of colour in every direction, up the walls and across the floor ahead of us. Gazing around, we follow our hosts as they lead us out into the hall and left towards the bedroom area. With India narrating and guiding, I amble, trailing slightly behind, momentarily mesmerized by the scenery, glimpsed in passing. A quick look through, into the lounge towards a balcony on the far side of the room, and I'm captured by the panoramic view of the entirety of Killarney lakes. To say it's a breath-taking spectacle is something of an understatement and I make a mental note to stand there at the first opportunity and breathe it in so it will be mine to keep, imprinted on every sense possible, for all eternity.

The bedrooms which our hosts have graciously assigned to us are as truly impressive as everything else we have encountered since arriving, and we're like naughty boarding school kids sneaking from room to room, each checking out what the other one has. Eddie and Clyde share a beautiful twin room with views of the wonderfully tended gardens to the side of the house, a full-sized bathroom as their en suite. Rory and Jake also have a twin room. Theirs however, has a quaint, antique-looking set of French doors that lead out to the front garden. Outside, there's a small patioed area with cast iron table and chairs where visitors might admire the trailing roses that weave their way through a nearby wooden archway. The archway leads to a sectioned-off part of the garden that has been designed for an early morning stroll to enliven the senses, or an evening potter to accommodate contemplation and reflection. I imagine a sleepy carcass rising from their bed, throwing open the French doors and ambling barefoot through the grass that spans the distance from the patio to the archway and into the beautiful rose garden. For a split second I contemplate asking them to switch rooms so that I can have a barefoot stroll, but then decide that the room Gwen and I will share is definitely the best one of all. In our room there is an enormous double bed; bigger than any double bed I've ever seen in my entire life. Without doubt, it is a more compact room than the boys' rooms but it has the added feature of a mezzanine level which for all intents and purposes looks like somewhere you go to meditate. The entire floor area, bar a small passageway from the stairs to the balcony door is covered in oversized cushions and pillows and decorated in a beautiful bohemian style, with large colourful paper lanterns and a variety of hanging tapestries. The door itself, a large arched stained-glass panel door, leads out onto a small balcony which also has a cast iron table and chairs, just big enough for two people to sit, sipping coffee, breathing in the surrounding beauty.

It's all so truly therapeutic and Stephen and India are such superb hosts that when we come in each night after our gigs, we're careful to be respectful and quiet, in return for their wonderful hospitality. Originally we were only supposed to stay for a couple of nights, until after we played at the party being organised by Stephen, but our hosts insist on us stopping for a few more nights, until we have to leave for Galway.

The party, which is organised to celebrate the couple's tenth wedding anniversary and the pub where they're having it, which happens to be their local, is almost within walking distance of the house. By walking distance I mean you could walk it if needed, but it would be a fair aul' walk nonetheless, so when Monday finally arrives, nobody argues with Eddie when he insists on driving us all down instead. Happily, we all squeeze into the back of the van together, India and Stephen included, and have a short sing-song on the way. Eddie points out that walking is against his religion and though admittedly the journey is a little further than first anticipated, we all agree that it would be rude not to respect his spiritual sensibilities, not to mention that there is a serious lack of street lighting in this neck of the woods also.

When we get to the pub, I can't help but think that they chose this venue purely on the basis of proximity and how convenient it is, and not because of its desirability or appeal. The pub itself is situated on the side of a relatively busy main road with little or no parking attached to it, which makes no sense because it's quite a bit outside of the town and clientele will most probably come from far and wide, and far and wide requires transport. The décor is as tired and worn as the exterior and there is an overpowering dreariness and grottiness to every inch of the place. It lacks warmth and character and I'm doubtful of whether even our best performance will add any magic.

However, despite my initial trepidation the pub

miraculously undergoes a slow but significant transformation as people start to arrive. By the time it has filled up and the music is in full swing, the life and energy generated somehow manages to mask the weathered surroundings. You could be anywhere for all you notice of the décor. I'll even go so far as to say the night progresses towards being one of the best nights we've had so far. Usually in such circumstances, we are just the band, playing to the audience, but with Stephen's charm and the fact that he is obviously a well-respected member of the local community, we've somehow been elevated to VIP status. Throughout the evening the bar staff constantly supply us with fresh drinks even when we haven't finished the previous ones, and generally tend to our every whim and wish. During the short break that we afford ourselves halfway through the performance, the bar manager even lays food out for us and instructs his staff to get us anything we need. I almost don't want the night to end, it's so nice, but as usual the time gallops by.

When we settle back in to play the last few songs of the night the cheers from the crowd would almost lift the roof from the building, they're that loud, and I have a sense that I will remember this moment for the rest of my days. It is truly a magical night. Normally at gigs, particularly when I'm playing complicated parts, I tend to do so with my eyes cast down in concentration, looking up only occasionally to scan the room briefly before closing my eyes again as if to read sheet music stored inside my head. Consequently, I rarely notice much of what goes on around me. Tonight, not unusually, when it comes to the last song, which just so happens to be Murphy's polka and which mainly features Gwen on the mandolin, I look up to gaze around the room momentarily. I don't play in this tune so it's one of those rare opportunities when I do get to sit with my fiddle on my lap, clap along and absorb what's going on around me. These moments are welcome interludes for me, a chance to be on the other side as such.

As I scan along the faces, first at the front of the crowd and then further back I think I see a familiar profile in the crowd, and it catches my eye, not initially because of the familiarity but because of how intently they stare at me. The realisation is not immediate but quick nevertheless. It's the face of Simon's friend Matt, who for once looks slightly less miserable than I remember. Not happy, but not miserable either. He smiles and nods as soon as it becomes apparent that I have recognised him and I smile and nod back in the most neutral yet courteous way possible. He looks more handsome, more polished than I remember and I have a strange sense that I've just noticed him for the first time. This, though, conjures a patchwork of strange and conflicting emotions in me and I feel unsettled by what I feel is an invasion by unwelcome, alien feelings.

Almost at the same time as I nod to Matt the last song comes to its end and the audience erupt into gleeful applause. Without hesitation the band begin to stir from their positions, gathering equipment in the process. The crowd however, shift tack and start chanting for more, and after a bit of negotiating it's agreed that I'll play Swallow Tail jig for them – solo. It gives the rest of the group time to pack up and load the van. The silence in the room has plummeted to its lowest point of the night as everyone is waiting for the song to begin.

Picking back up my fiddle I launch straight into the jig and in turn, the pub erupts into whoops and howls. Stephen pulls India up into the middle of the floor spinning her round and round and jumping about like a drunken teenager. They're all having so much fun that I have to repeat the song over till I think they're content enough at having gotten what they wanted. When I do finally finish up the clapping and cheering is of deafening proportions and Stephen has to grab the mike to get everyone to quiet down so he can say his thanks, not only to us but to the bar staff and his friends and family as well, and most importantly his beautiful and beaming wife who places both her hands on her chest above her heart in a gesture of reciprocity.

"Stephen, there's no need to thank us," I tell him when he puts the mike back in the stand holder. "We should be thanking you. It's very kind of you to let us stay," I continue to shout, with genuine heartfelt gratitude while desperately trying to be heard above the noise.

While I stand talking to Stephen, I can see Matt out of the corner of my eye making his way towards us and when he reaches us, he puts his hand out to tap Stephen on the shoulder. Stephen swings around and greets him heartily.

"Ah, Matt. How are you?" he says with pure delight. "Have you met this beautiful young lady?" he immediately asks him.

"Yes! I have indeed met Ms McCarthy," he says a little awkwardly.

"Rhian! Her name is Rhian man, lighten up and get some drink into you," says Stephen slapping Matt roughly on the back. "We'll be going back to the house, soon to continue on with the celebrations and I hope you'll join us?" he adds before walking off. Matt's face is a mask of horror, as if he'd just been asked to do something unthinkable and I wonder for a moment if it's the thought of the gathering back at the house or the fact that he's now been left alone with me that causes it.

"He certainly knows how to have a good time, your friend Stephen," I say as I flip the catches on my violin case and then move to place a chair that Gwen had been using over against the wall, out of the way. Matt promptly picks up the case, along with the two duffle bags beside it, and turns to head out the door, which Eddie himself just recently exited with equipment to place in the van. It strikes me as a pre-emptive move to avoid response and therefore possible, further conversation and not for the first time I think that Matt is a strange enigma of sorts.

"I'll take these out for you. They look heavy," he says and before I can protest, he's on his way towards the door leaving me with no option but to follow him.

On the way across the room, people keep stopping me to say how well they think we did and how enjoyable it was and so Matt has to stand for a moment waiting on me. He stares quite probingly. Eventually we get out to the van where Eddie and Clyde help to put the stuff in the back.

"Well, we'll see you back at the house then ... if you're going that is," I say to Matt a little awkwardly as Eddie starts up the engine. I can't wait for a response as our driver is not a man to hang around, so I jump straight in and predictably Eddie wastes no time moving off – even before I've closed the door fully. I see Matt turn back towards the pub entrance and disappear inside.

Back at the house Stephen and India put some music on and offer everyone drinks. But our ever-prepared crew have brought their own beverages and our host is greatly humoured by the sight of Jake hauling a crate of beer into the middle of the floor.

"There's more in the van so help yourselves," he says with a mischievous grin stretched across his flushed-looking face. Just then India wanders back in with a couple of plates full of canapés, which I think in my house are called snacks but admittedly are not as fancy looking as the ones she has. She lays out the delicate morsels around the room and contrary to my earlier fears about this getting messy and boisterous the night proceeds in a very civilised and enjoyable vein.

I hadn't noticed when Matt came into the room because it was sometime later on and I had assumed that at this stage he wasn't going to bother. But he did arrive at some point and when I finally notice him, he's standing chatting with Stephen over by the far-right end of the glass-panelled doors. There's something about the way he frequently glances over towards our group that prompts me to take my glass of bubbly out on to the balcony to get out of view for a short while and to breathe in the scenery which is now only visible by the light of the enormous full moon. It's a beautiful sight nonetheless, enhanced by the memories etched on my brain from earlier. I think I could possibly stand here forever, content to just feel, and to be. However, I've barely drawn a breath when Matt comes out on the balcony and joins me. Instantly I'm inclined to hurry back inside before it's too late, but in my lack of decisiveness I miss the opportunity to do this innocuously.

"Beautiful part of the country!" he states, quite decidedly. "Stephen and India most certainly have a bird's eye view of it too."

I smile and nod at him then turn to gaze out into the darkness once more.

"You are a very talented woman, you know," he says a little awkwardly.

"Thank you, Matt!" I say with true sincerity. "I will admit; I feel blessed by times and certainly, I wouldn't choose any other profession. Well ... it's not like I have the patience and selflessness of, say for example, my sister Gemma, to work in a caring profession," I state quite pointedly, searching his face fleetingly for some hint of understanding before I continue, "or, for that matter, the type of mathematical brain that my sister Kathy is gifted with. Yes! I think my career choice may well have been decided by my general, overall lack of any other skills." I say, pausing for another moment. "What about you Matt? If you could do anything in this whole entire world, be anything in this whole entire world, what would it be?" I ask with a careful measure of confidence and a touch of flair, as my words seem to momentarily confound him.

"I've never given it much thought to be honest, Ms McCarthy. My business is all I know. I was introduced to it by my father at a very young age and I've never side-stepped ever. Well, except for when I joined forces with

Simon of course."

The mention of Simon's name pricks my nerves and I restrain myself from asking about him, opting to pretend as if he was of no consequence at all.

"Please! Call me Rhian. Ms McCarthy makes me sound like an old spinster …"

"And she's still only a very young spinster," interjects Jake who sneaks up behind me and twirls me around, trying to engage in what looks like the dance of the drunken leprechauns.

"C'mon Rhian, dance with me," he says before turning to Matt and looking him dead in the eye. 'Did you know? I have asked this woman to marry me seven times and still she won't succumb to my obvious charms."

"No he hasn't! You have not ye drunken fool," I say with good humour and an uneasy smile. I don't know why it bothers me that Matt would believe what Jake is saying, but it does for some strange reason.

"Have I not?" asks Jake, with a puzzling look on his face. "Well I've had a mind to on many occasions, Rhian, but sure I know ya won't have me. See, I resisted cos I'm too feckin' wise for me own good. Destined to die a lonely old man, me only hope being that ye'll take pity on me before I draw me last breath," he says before clutching at his chest as if his heart was broken. In quite dramatic style he backs away, off down along the balcony blowing kisses and winking before peering over the far end of the railing, turning and heading back in to the rest of the group, almost as quickly as he came.

"He's just joking! He's always joking. He's quite mad. Good musician but certifiable for sure," I laugh nervously and Matt smiles a sympathetic smile.

"I'd say this … this lifestyle is great fun?" states Matt, gesturing to the air around him.

"Oh, it has its moments, yes! But I'll be looking forward to getting home nevertheless. I miss my family: my sisters,

Mam, Dad, everyone. The girls promised that they'd try to find their way out to me, for at least one of the gigs. And given that next week is my last week. I'm kind of half expecting them, possibly this weekend. They have been known to drive up and down in the same day and on other occasions stay for a night or two, so who knows? One thing is for sure, by Thursday of next week, Niamh, another fiddle player, will be arriving to take over for the Friday night gig in Galway and when she arrives, I'm done; it's back to Dublin for me."

"Oh, you're heading to Galway. That's my neck of the woods, as they say" he announces in a somewhat surprised tone. "I have a small, modest home there, not too far from Salthill. It's a summer house really, but these days I seem to spend so much time there that I'm beginning to feel it is more than just a summer home. You're all more than welcome to stay if you like! Of course, you've probably already organised your accommodation at this stage," he says and for a moment I forget just how much he bothers me. The realisation makes me ponder on whether he might not be as bad as I first thought. It is a very kind offer after all.

"That's very generous of you, Matt, and a day or two ago the gang would have jumped at the offer, but would you believe it we got invited to stop off with a friend of Gwen's, in Salthill. It's within walking distance of the venue. When we started this trip off we had barely a notion of where we were going to stay for most of this time."

With that, I begin to edge my way back towards the indoors, while simultaneously talking and yawning, readying myself for a respectable exit.

"I should go back inside and mingle a bit. Plus, we're hogging all this beauty for ourselves. It's unfair," I say gesturing to the distant mountains and barely visible lakes which still manage to catch the moonlight in glistening dabs.

Matt follows me inside and we join our hosts who are sitting with the others in the sunken lounge area, discussing homosexuality. It suddenly occurs to me that none of them would be aware that I have a sister who's gay and because it's a topic I've been drawn into discussing on many occasions I find slipping into it is pretty easy.

"What do you think, Rhian?" asks India quite sweetly. "Jake is sulking because nobody will agree with him that it's not right."

Everyone looks to me for my response and so I pose before carefully picking my words from the many and varied collections that I've had to sort through over the years.

"Well, of course it's natural. It's of nature, isn't it! In all species too. There have been gay people, bisexual people, asexual, heterosexual people, since as far back as we can gauge. And anyone who suggests it's wrong will have no scientific or biological evidence to back that claim up with. Because none exists. In fact, correct me if I'm wrong but is it not the case that the prevailing opinion within all learned fields is that each of us is capable of loving either man or woman but a complex, myriad of things in our life will settle us on one or the other. You can feel it's wrong because it's not right for you. But as long as sex is between two consenting adults then it's none of anyone else's business. We should only have issue with anything in this world that impinges on the rights and freedoms of others and not when it's consensual love between two adults. Nature is a complex thing. It works within a diverse spectrum of creation. You can have general rules, general guides and just generalisations for anything and everything but invariably not everyone or everything will be defined by those generalisations. That's how complex and diverse this world is. There is a reason for everything. Just because you don't understand it doesn't mean you should demonise it …"

"It's not right Rhian! Two men ... together, ewww. Sex is for procreation. Double ewww!" says Jake with a bit more passion than you would expect in a rational discussion.

"Procreation is for procreation, Jake. Sex is for pleasure or expression, or for procreation if that's your aim. You don't make babies every time you have sex, do you? You mostly do it to be as close to the person you love as you can be. Besides, how many times have you drooled over the idea of two women?" I say as light-heartedly as I can, given that the subject puts me on the defensive. Someone I know and love is gay and truthfully Jake has probably never even brushed off a gay person in his life and yet feels well equipped enough to judge each and every one of them. It's ridiculous to me.

"That's different Ree," he says in bewilderment.

"It's only different because it doesn't threaten your rigid understanding of masculinity. I bet you even get creeped out by heterosexual guys who wear pink shirts. You always slag guys like that off. What is it? You can't be a man unless you're swilling beer and bumping chests?"

Jake and I debate back and forth for a bit longer and eventually everyone else joins back in again.

Suddenly a memory from some time back, storms back to my mind. It was the evening myself and the girls spent at that party in Ballsbridge and I remember something Matt had said hinted at aversion to gay people and I'm curious now to know for sure, it that is his view.

"Matt! You're very quiet on the subject!" I say quite pointedly as everyone turns to hear what he has to say. "What do you think?"

For a long moment he doesn't speak and I fear that putting him on the spot like that may not have been my best move ever. But I can't take it back now and frankly I wouldn't want to either.

"I must concur, insofar as I do believe it to be entirely natural," he states, confidently. "And I might also lay claim to having a more in-depth understanding due to the fact that there is someone in my life, a young person with whom I am very close and care deeply about, who is gay. Admittedly, at one point I was concerned that perhaps rebellion was at the fore of her choices with regards to this. Of course, I say 'choices' only because that is the language I grew up with. I don't mean choices in this respect. Anyway, I digress!" he says apologetically before continuing, "Ultimately, it wasn't the case that she was acting out, being contrived in any way, or indeed, being influenced. She was just trying to live her life, her way. In hindsight I may not have always been supportive or even said the right things but it can be hard … you know! When you grow up being constantly told something is wrong, but your education, your experience of life tells you differently." At this point Matt turns to face Jake directly, looking directly at him, before concluding. "It can be hard though, to shake values instilled in you at a time when you were incapable of truly measuring them, particularly in such a way as to instil fear. So, I completely understand how difficult it might be for you Jake, to see another perspective when perhaps fear is what guides you."

Matt continues to gaze at Jake who doesn't falter in his steely stance even though, knowing Jake as I do, the suggestion that he is in some way "afraid" would no doubt be very unpalatable to him.

"Do you know any gay people? Personally? Are you close to anyone gay; related to anyone gay?" asks Matt with poise and curiosity.

Jake rolls his eyes and throws his back before responding.

"No! But I don't need to eat crisp sandwiches to know crisps don't go between two slices of bread," he barks petulantly and the room erupts into roaring disapproval.

Of course; crisp sandwiches are a near delicacy and no question about it, so to say that I'm happy to see Jake lose face with such a frivolous and scandalous comment, is a wild understatement. To add to that, the absurdness of the crisp sandwich analogy almost seems to be too much for Matt to fathom and in this moment, he looks frozen in shock, like he just heard the most ridiculous thing ever – which of course he did. Looking briefly in my direction he smiles quite sweetly at me and I have a feeling that perhaps, and only just perhaps, there might be more to this guy than I had first thought.

The debate about crisp sandwiches soon reverts to point and eventually reaches its inevitable stand-off. I take the opportunity to wish everyone a good night before heading off to bed. Looking over at Matt before I leave, I have a sense that for some reason he appears to have recoiled back to a more sullen and pensive self. But I don't dwell on this as I amble away, off down the long corridor towards the room I share with Gwen, glad to be finally getting to kick off my shoes and slide beneath the cotton-soft duvet atop our enormous double bed, which truly is a piece of heaven.

GONE

Clichés, old wife's tales, well-worn, endlessly circulated adages; I love them all because they're more than just words. They're expressions that came into existence as a result of countless people's experiences, and most likely their difficulties in finding appropriate words to explain and describe what those experiences were like. I love them also because they're like life's little language lucky bags. Some have small treasures, nuggets of wisdom in them and some are just cheap worthless offerings. But it doesn't matter, they have their appeal and their uses. Some more than others of course, like "time flies when you're having fun"! That's one that gets called into use very often. Of course, we all know that time moves at the same pace, regardless, whereas this truth could not be further removed from the lived experience and sense of actual time passing.

It's a saying that quite aptly goes with my experience of this trip, and I wonder, fascinated at my very real and mindboggling sense of accelerated time. As I move towards the end of my three-week stint, there's this overwhelming sense of having only set out on this adventure, just to reach the end, almost immediately, in particular, this last week in Galway.

On arrival, our first gig was on the Wednesday

afternoon in a quaint thatched roadside pub not too far outside Galway City, on the road to Ballinasloe. The gig again was a favour to a friend of Gwen's who was organising a celebration for her grandfather's 90th birthday. Of course we were more than happy to oblige, given that the same girl had kindly agreed to allow us the run of her house back in Salthill for the remainder of our stay in Galway, while she obligingly stopped off at her boyfriend's place for the duration.

After the gig we happily packed back up and headed back to Salthill to off-load our equipment and immediately set off on a drive to Barna, stopping at a lovely bar and seafood restaurant where we had the most wonderful meal and one of the most relaxed and fun nights off together as a band that we've ever had. For the next couple of evenings we strolled the short distance from the house, which was located not far from the promenade, to the venue on the High Street, to play to a packed and appreciative audience.

After finishing our soundcheck each evening, it became customary for us to settle in to some quiet corner of the pub and have a quick bite to eat, just before we were due to start the performance. On one or two occasions, Rory and Jake went out to get rolls or take away, which they brought back to the bar for us when the offerings at the bar just wouldn't do. This evening however, it's been unanimously agreed that we will leave the bar and go in search of some good old-fashioned fish and chips in soggy brown paper bags – just the way fish and chips should be served. Jake thought it would be nice to take our leisure on the way back for no particular reason other than to soak up the atmosphere, life, hustle and bustle of this beautiful city. Rory, who ate his food in about half the time it took the rest of us to eat ours, steps up to the door of the pub when we finally arrive back, pushing it wide open for everyone to enter, a big cheesy grin lighting his face up. As soon as we enter the bar a rapturous roar of greetings pours from the group just inside. Kathy and Bill, with Matt in tow, as well as Aubrey, Declan and also Jake's sister, had all arrived earlier in the day, apparently conspiring with Jake to get me out of the pub so they could surprise me. We hug and squeal relentlessly with the joy of it and chatter incessantly as the pub begins to fill up. Unfortunately, Gemma couldn't come because she was working extra shifts. For as long as I can remember the hospital has been under-staffed and overloaded and as usual she seems to think that it's her duty to work all the hours possible to take up the slack. Kathy and Aubrey are not shy in voicing their disapproval with regards to this.

"Pity she isn't here", says Aubrey with a look of mock sorrow. "She'd have made sure we behaved ourselves. But she's not here – unfortunately! And because she's not here … well, I won't be able to control meself. It's just the way it is lads! Things are going to have to get messy, very messy – yiz have been warned. I'm on me holliers so, Declan!" she barks as if Declan were somewhere else other than sitting right beside her. "Go to the bar! Bring pints. Bring many pints!" she orders theatrically and the rest of the group laugh in response. Even Matt appears to crack a smile at this.

"Excuse me," I say, quite conspiratorially. "I think that's my cue to leave. I'm just gonna hop on over there with the rest of the sane people and do my thing, if that's okay!" I point to where the band have started to set up their gear in the other corner of the room and then get up and leave with a wink.

When the music finally kicks off, the atmosphere in the bar lifts immediately with an electric sense of revelry, and at times I think the band are enjoying this more than I've ever seen them enjoy a gig.

After about an hour and forty minutes or thereabouts, we decide to take a short break and so I take the opportunity to have a quick word with Gwen and Eddie before signalling to Aubrey to come join us. After agreeing a suitable song for Aubrey to sing I head over to the table where she had been sitting and nestle into her spot between Declan and Matt.

The brief silence is soon interrupted by the haunting sound of Aubrey, accompanied by Gwen tentatively on guitar and Eddie, more assuredly on oboe, as they manage at short notice to lend music and rhythm to her flawless execution of Jimmy MacCarthy's "Katie". The song itself, made famous of course by the wonderful Mary Black, is one of Eddie's favourite songs and I'm not a bit surprised he knows it so well.

Encouraged by the genuine outpouring of rapturous applause and praise at the end of the song, Aubrey continues on, enticed and encouraged to sing a few more equally haunting tunes, as requested by the audience. The interlude gives the rest of us a welcome break and I for one sit and enjoy the performance while, surprisingly, engaging in quite open and revealing conversation with Matt.

"I had no idea your sister was such a beautiful singer," he says with some amazement. "She has real talent!"

"There's a lot about my sisters you don't know. Good things, I mean of course," I correct myself awkwardly. "Do you live far from the City?" I ask him inquiringly, though I have a vague recollection of him telling me the answer to this already.

"No, not too far. Well … at a distance that affords me solitude and retreat but not so far that I can't come with ease, to immerse myself once more in life and people, when my own company gets too much for me."

For a moment I feel a little sorry for him. He appears to me as someone who craves company but abhors it at the same time. Society is both a scourge and a need for him, a bit like it can be for most of us. But for him it seems a little more difficult and the more I get to know him the more I begin to suspect that maybe, he's not quite as confident and self-assured as I first believed him to be.

We chat idly about our favourite things in Galway, versus Dublin versus London. Of course, my input with regards to London is limited as I was only ever there on two very brief occasions: once on a Christmas shopping weekend, and once as an overnight stop-off as part of a trip to Brighton. Therefore, my knowledge only extends to Regent Street, mainly Hamley's (as I can't remember any other shops), a Chinese restaurant on a street I can't remember the name of and the London Underground. The Underground, quite frankly terrorised me, because it was underground, which for some strange reason Matt seems to finds very amusing.

"I'm sure you were a little scared the first time you ever went on the Tube yourself!" I scold light-heartedly.

"Yes, but I think I was about four years old at the time. You, on the other hand, were a mature, grown, adult!" he says smiling sweetly, if not somewhat sarcastically.

"I was an adult! That part is true. But I certainly wasn't mature. I've yet to reach that milestone in my life." I say, with some degree of sincerity, and before he can respond, Jake's voice comes booming over the mike, summoning the "skiving fiddler" and instantly I'm startled to my feet, as I realise that I'd completely forgotten what I was here for.

The second half of the performance flies by and before long the barman is calling last orders, vociferously instructing people to drink up. For once in their lives, both my sisters appear to put up no fight when their respective partners usher them up and out. The long journey and fun-filled day is the only possible reason, not to mention the fact that they have a long road ahead on their return journey home tomorrow.

Everybody hugs and says their farewells and in the midst of it all I overhear Matt complimenting Aubrey on the way out the door.

In the quiet of the bar as I roll a cable up to pack away, I begin to reflect on what a truly wonderful venture this has been – more so than other trips. But despite how enjoyable it's been, with its many high points, I'm still looking forward to going home. Earlier on in the week, I had phoned home to see how Mam and Dad and all the gang were doing and sadly she told me that old Mr Byrne's health was on a downward spiral; things were not good and everyone was genuinely concerned. According to Mam, many of the neighbours including herself have banded together and worked out a rota for checking in and looking after him so he can stay at home, out of the hospice. His only wish is that he's not sent to any of those "death houses" as he likes to call them. He wants to spend his last few weeks/days on this planet in the comfort of familiar surroundings. His sister, who isn't very much younger than he is, moved in immediately to help with his care, but the general consensus is that it is too much for her on her own. Everyone is happy to rally round. The thought of never seeing the old rogue alive again weighs heavily on me and I want to get home to help out if I can. Inwardly I bemoan the rotation of the planet and the passing of time, stealing precious moments and loved ones from us all, and despite my real, genuine enjoyment of these last three weeks, I now can't wait for tomorrow, my final day, to come and pass.

At the beginning of this journey, all the members of the band including myself, despite my reasonable adherence to the self-imposed orange juice pledge, would sometimes partake in the odd lock-in or two after gigs. The B&B owners in Listowel loved to encourage the eruption of spontaneous song and dance in the evening and Stephen and India too; they were both quite partial to an after-gig gathering. Every barman and barwoman that we've come across so far have been more than generous in extending the celebrations beyond pub hours, whenever possible. But as the time wore on our after-hours activities dwindled to maybe a token drink or two, until soon it became just a "thank you" and "see ya tomorrow". Tonight, the band are already in the van and nodding a weary goodnight to the equally weary bartender, and I'm only too delighted to head straight back to Salthill with them, so I can hop into bed and drift off to the distant but audible lapping of the Atlantic waves.

When we arrive back at the house, as anticipated, the gang barely say goodnight to each other before they all head off to their respective rooms/beds, sleeping in much later than they normally would the next day. At about lunchtime, having only just gotten out of bed, I hurriedly wash and dress before heading out for a walk. Leaving the rather dilapidated yet quaint old cottage-style house on Upper Salthill Road, I walk towards the shops, a short distance away, to buy a few trinkets and gifts to take home with me. After that, I grab some lunch, have a leisurely stroll along the promenade and then head back to get ready for the last night. The beauty and wonder of the Atlantic coastline as well as the memory of last night's fun and excitement fills me with a simmering melancholy, as I ponder on Gemma's absence and the enjoyment that she missed out on. She would have loved this and it would have done her the world of good too.

Pushing this from my mind I focus on organising myself for the gig later on as well as packing the one bag that I'll be taking on my journey home. Tomorrow the band will play their penultimate gig here in Galway before heading on up country, to County Clare. After that, they plan to return to Kerry, to Kenmare briefly, before finishing up back in another part of County Clare. Dublin is another three weeks away for them, whereas for me it's on the horizon. I'll miss them all of course, but I want to be home now. It's time! I've had my fun, but thoughts and concerns are pulling my heart back to the pale.

Tonight, the bar is once again jammed to the rafters. In fact, it seems even more jammed than the night before. Life and energy radiate from every corner and space around me and though the crowd are shoulder to shoulder and back-to-back they move around with great fluidity and ease. Activity, colour and joyous euphoria lap at the banal and sedentary as the soul of the west of Ireland intertwines with the souls of all the many visitors; people from far and wide who dapple the already vibrant body of humanity flocking to this region during the busy summer months.

Tonight, there's a strange intangible something in the air and I can't quite put my finger on it. I'm jinxed at every turn, as if the universe is trying to warn of some impending disturbance to the milieu. Both Gwen and I break strings in quick succession, during a song, and honestly, I can't ever remember that ever happening before – not two in the same night and never at almost the same time. Luckily, we manage to pull it off though and to be honest the crowd are in such good form that they are further entertained by their good-humoured heckling of us.

Thankfully the night draws to an end with no more incidents and, though elated, I can't help but also note an eagerness in myself as I set about packing up and readying myself to leave.

Just as I'm about to close the clasps of my violin case I turn, and to my genuine surprise I see Stephen approach, the strangest, broadest, almost comical looking grin on his face, as if we were already in confidence on some hilarious conspiracy.

"Rhian, I thought I'd come and see your last performance before you desert us and head on back to the big schmoke, and I'm very glad I did. It was a brilliant night, as usual," he says with a somewhat slightly less goofy and sweeter smile on his face.

"Stephen! I didn't see you in the crowd, you must have sneaked in late and hidden yourself away. All the same, I'm very glad to see you and even more delighted to hear that you enjoyed yourself. Is India with you?" I ask as I scan the room looking for her.

"Unfortunately not! She had things to do back at home but sends her regards nevertheless and if you're ever back in our neck of the woods at any time she insists that you come visit us; you'll always be welcome you know. Actually, I came with Matt, I'm crashing overnight at his place. But I'm a little puzzled as to where he has gotten himself to right now," he says distractedly looking about the room before giving me a very odd, almost appraising look. "Yes! Just myself and Matt tonight," he continues, rubbing at his chin like an actor in character, overplaying a role in some budget stage performance. "What a fine gentleman he is. Best of sorts. But sure who am I trying to convince? You know him well enough yourself and seem to get on very nicely with him," he says with that same odd look on his face, a look that hints at conspiracy and yet for the life of me I'm not sure what it is I'm meant to be in on.

I just give him the barest, nondescript smile that I hope is both friendly and sufficient and then I feign more involvement in my task than it requires.

"A woman could do worse ye know. Such a loyal friend too. Since both his and Simon's parents passed away, well … Matt has been like a big brother to Simon. Did you know that, Rhian?" he asks. But without waiting on a response continues on, "He's always looking out for him. In fact, he's setting up and organising the Irish branch of the business on his own now so that Simon can stay in London and concentrate on with things over there. Apparently, Simon met a girl when he was here, got messed around by her a bit … very unfortunate. Poor guy! He is that genuine type though, the type, that unfortunately, being quite naïve, can be easily duped. Matt tells me the girl's family were rather dubious too but that thankfully, he was on hand to guide and support him and now he's stepped into the work breach here; so essentially Simon has been saved from a very bad situation by all accounts."

All the while I'm packing up stuff and tidying the area where the band had been playing, Stephen had been talking and helping with moving chairs, handing me things for my bag. And at some point, my brain switched to autopilot, collating only necessary words and phrases to stay tuned to the point of what he was saying, while not listening entirely. Suddenly however, at the mention of Simon meeting some girl, there was a shift in my focus and the realisation hit me full force. Matt was the reason Simon had left Dublin and broken Gemma's heart. He'd done it deliberately too, no doubt that night in Temple Bar: sealed the deal when Gemma had, for genuine reasons, not turned up. And as for Aubrey, well … someone must have put something in her drink. I believe her when she insists that she only had the one drink. But of course Matt had already decided that Gemma was either insincere or unworthy or I don't know what, and that our family were … well, I don't know that either. But poor Gemma hadn't even been given a chance to apologise or explain before being cruelly punished.

Suddenly a calm settles on me. Like all the rolling, rambling thoughts somehow finally manage to fall into place. Matt Devine is the reason my sister's heart aches like it has never ached before! And just as I was beginning to warm to the fecking blackheart …

Now, anyone who knows me will attest to the fact that I have words. I have an abundance of words. I have no shortage of words – ever. Words for any situation, any scenario. But right now, right at this moment in time, for some exasperating reason, I can't seem to locate the proper words or indeed discern the emotion appropriate to this moment in time. I have no response. As an interim move I hug Stephen, smile at him and thank him once more for putting us up. I'm lost right now and don't know what to do but I know I need to get away from Stephen before I betray myself.

"Stephen! If you ever come to Dublin, please look us

up," I manage to utter.

I can hear the words coming from my mouth but I'm disconnected from them. I have so much I want to say and want to ask but it seems too futile, too hard. All I can muster is one line.

Stephen gives me a warm, fatherly like smile, hugs me and then heads off, in search of his treacherous friend no doubt. I take my bag and case and hurriedly leave to go put them in the van, desperate for a blast of fresh air to clear my head. Annoyingly, the van is parked at the far end of the town as it didn't seem worth the effort to move it earlier on in the evening I now have to dash a few hundred yards when I can barely function, to rid myself of my burden. It seems like a monumental hike with, both my arms and heart so laden down.

As I approached the van, I see Matt pacing up and down at the edge of the path alongside. He appears unsettled and I'm now too close to divert in any subtle move as he's already spotted me. Before I have enough time to mentally prepare myself for what I need to say to him and much to my utter amazement, he almost charges at me speaking, even before I'm comfortably within earshot.

"Rhian! I need to talk to you!" He blurts out. "Sorry! You probably have things to be getting on with but I won't take up too much of your time. Truthfully, I'm not great with this kind of stuff so I'll just get straight to the point," he says, pausing momentarily before progressing more calmly. "I've grown very fond of you over this last while. Your family confound me a bit, I have to admit. They're a little rough around the edges if I'm to be totally honest but, well, nobody's perfect. Anyway, I digress. What I want to know is would you like to have dinner with me some time, please?" he says at last.

I'm stunned! For some reason, that right now seems totally absurd to me, I was expecting an apology for his misrepresentation of my sister, or indeed his lack of understanding with regards to her character and an assurance perhaps that he was going to put his wrong to rights. But he didn't of course, so with all the strength that I can reasonably muster I shove all my emotion and confusion to the recesses of my soul and calmly and collectedly respond.

"You're very kind, Matt. But I don't think that would be a very good idea, to be honest. Thank you very much though!" I say, quite concisely, while desperately suppressing the desire to say more – much more. An overwhelming urge to run and hide in some corner takes firm hold of me and pent-up emotions threaten to undo me but all I do is smile politely.

"Oh, okay," he states quite incredulously and with a rather surprisingly animated facial expression. "May I ask why? Just to satisfy my curiosity," he says with just a hint of disbelief and a vague but unmistakable look of shock on his face. Honestly, I don't know if the look is what tips me over the edge or whether I was just fooling myself that I could act in a restrained manner, but I suddenly let rip.

"You may indeed ask why, Mr Devine!" I say with fiery animation, before launching into a near tirade, "First off, no human being in good conscience ever asks another out while insulting their family in the same breath. It's ungentlemanly for one and not conducive to the desired response – truth be known. Secondly, I have not a shred of a doubt in my mind that you are the reason for my beloved sister's broken heart, and I dislike you fervently for that. Do you know why she wasn't here with the rest of the gang for the fun and the life afforded to everyone else?" I ask. But without waiting on a response, I barrel on, "Because, Matt! She's working – again. She works every hour she possibly can because she can't sleep at night knowing that someone is suffering and needs her help. She's afraid to come home from work lest she goes in the next day and something has happened and she wasn't there to make things better. Her heart is full of compassion and love and she wants to make a difference. So, if someone were to think her capable of 'messing' a decent, honest man around then they would be very, very sadly mistaken indeed. She is the best of people, as are all my sisters and yes, I will accept a little criticism of their energy and decorum, at least the younger ones. I would be dishonest if I were to deny being embarrassed by them on occasions myself. But I will not, ever, accept criticism of their honesty, integrity and good natures." I pause for one moment to organise the thoughts that are now rolling in chaotic heaps into my head, just dying to be vocalised, cautioning me, urging me to deliver a monumental blow of wit. But, all I managed to come up with is, "You, Matt ... are a snob."

Before Matt has time to respond, Stephen and Eddie stride up to where we stand and I can see by Stephen's face that he thinks something completely different has transpired, an innocent, beaming smile on his face. Eddie, eager to get to some soirée, urges me to hurry so he can drop the equipment back to the digs and I willingly oblige. Waving and calling out a heartfelt goodbye to Stephen who looks on somewhat perplexed, I eagerly hop into the van. Matt turns and walks away briskly and for one second Stephen seems uncertain; but then turns and follows him, catching up quite easily, engaging him immediately in some discussion. Eddie finally starts the engine and pulls away from the kerb and Matt is now thankfully out of view.

Sitting in the back of the van with the equipment, I seethe with unspoken words. I've no interest in returning with Eddie to join up with the others for a nightcap so I beg off, insisting that I'm exhausted and need sleep for my journey home tomorrow. After he drops the gear off Eddie goes back out without me and I head eagerly to my room, climbing immediately into bed, the tiredness and the emotion sapping me of any lingering thread of energy.

The events of the last few hours get regurgitated and

over-processed, churning around in my brain, dragging me to the edge of exhaustion and back again, over and over. I can hear the words from Matt's lips. I can see myself moving around him, placing my things in the van, stacking them neatly. I go over the words I said and the words I wish I'd said and soon I wear myself out.

Next thing I know, the sun is creeping into my room and I find myself lying, fully clothed on top of the bed covers. But sadly I can't linger to eke any pleasure from the warmth of the sun's rays, or the cotton softness of the bed. I have to hurry to catch my train, an exercise I plan on carrying out as swiftly as possible and without saying goodbye to anyone. All the plans had already been laid out the evening before so there's nothing left for me to do other than collect my stuff from Eddie on Sunday when he will finally make the return journey himself.

The early train is mercifully quiet and with only my small backpack to take, I feel very light in luggage and heavy in heart on the long journey home.

When I finally arrive back in Dublin, I decide not to mention a word to anyone about what Stephen told me and certainly nothing about what had passed between myself and Matt. To take my mind off things I throw myself immediately and entirely into Mr Byrne's care, which means that nearly everyone that has been helping out to date gets some much-needed time to themselves. It's hard watching him so frail and lifeless in the bed and I almost wish he'd jump up out of the bed and start midering me to come here, to do this, to do that. Sadly, it's at times like this that you begin to question whether you could perhaps have put more time and effort in, when time was not so scarce.

The nurse assigned to his care drops in every day while I'm there and her face tells us all we need to know. The only pleasure to be got is in seeing him smile at the sight of me when I pop in early in the morning after she leaves from her morning shift. He is genuinely happy to have so many people around him and it suddenly dawns on me how different people are when they're not plagued by loneliness. In stark contrast, he is so easy to be around when he doesn't have to vie for your attention. It saddens me to think of his loneliness, but warms my heart to be able to converse with him in such satisfyingly in-depth ways at last.

About a week after getting back from Galway, while I'm sitting having my breakfast one morning and planning what time I'll head down to Mr Byrne's, Mam walks into the kitchen and hands me a letter, before heading directly back out into the hall and up the stairs again. The address on the back of the envelope tells me it comes from Galway and instantly I know it must be from Matt. For a moment I toy with the idea of throwing it in the bin, but curiosity gets the better of me and I open it up instead, much to my annoyance. The letter reads;

Dear Rhian,

I hope this letter finds you well and that all your family are in good health. When we last met, that night in Galway, things didn't go quite as I had imagined they would, and I think you will agree that what did transpire was, at the very least, unpleasant – for both of us. Sadly, I never got to respond to your admonishment of me and so I dearly hope you will oblige me by allowing some defence of the criticisms you levied at me. Firstly, I truly never meant to insult any of your family and please believe me when I say this, but I genuinely am horrendous with words. Admittedly, where at first your sisters did indeed shock and confound me, I soon recognised the qualities in them that you so succinctly outlined on the fateful night. In fact, I now know that I am, on occasion, too quick to judge and will endeavour to correct this trait from here on. Family is not something I am overly familiar with, as I have none of my own now, and my only recollections are ... well let's just say they're somewhat less embracing than what I see within your own. As for the situation with

Simon, well, he and Kelly are the closest thing to family that I do have and I realise that I may have gotten a little overzealous in my desire to protect this. Simon has been hurt in the past and your sister Gemma didn't seem all that keen. I see now that I was wrong but you must believe me when I say that I was driven only by my fear of seeing Simon hurt again. I don't think he could have suffered another blow. For that, I sincerely apologise. As for being a snob ... well, I never considered myself to be, but I can understand how it may appear so. Again, with regards to your family, I can wholeheartedly say that I would trade all I have in a heartbeat for a portion of what you have. Your family, the love, the camaraderie, the talent, the unwavering conviction of all your sisters; it is indeed something you should hold dear, and defend, as you do.

Please can you forgive my foolishness, and hopefully when we next meet, at the very least, maybe we might do so on better terms.

Regards,

Matthew Devine

After reading the letter over several times more, I finally manage to shake off the numbness that almost immediately gripped me on first reading the words. My mind races to recover memories, conversations, interactions – trying desperately to make sense of the progression of events. As things come to mind, I begin to truly marvel at how simple everyday actions, even commonplace words and statements can get so skewed, misinterpreted, or even misunderstood. I wonder at why we so often feel that instantly we know and understand the very essence of someone on just the tiniest grain of information about them, or perhaps some brief interaction. People are so much more than just one thing in isolation, out of the multitude of component parts that go into making their personalities.

Right now, more than I've anything I've ever wanted in my life, I want so badly to able to think, to analyse, to regurgitate the actions, words, events that I find so hard to understand. But unfortunately, I can't sit and contemplate; I can't linger anymore. In my heart of hearts, I know there's nothing I can do to change any of what has gone before and even if I could, right now, there are more pressing matters to attend to. Right now, I need to push this from my mind and focus.

As if to reinforce that ultimate realisation, a soft knock on the front door prompts me to slide the letter back into its envelope and move from the seat where I have lingered longer than I should have. But before I manage to go anywhere, I hear Mam trample down the stairs at speed to open the door almost immediately. Seconds later a loud sob, penetrates the peace and quiet of the house and I run down the hallway to stand by her side. Arm in arm we look out at Catherine, her dejected form telling me everything I need to know, negating any need for her to repeat the words.

Mr Byrne passed away peacefully on the 21st of July 1995, about an hour or two after I'd left him last night. He went with just a gentle gasp as Catherine sat reading to him, his hand softly resting in her open palm. He was eighty-six years of age and our community lost one of the most colourful characters to have ever trodden the local paths and byways. In the latter months of his life, when he could still get about, Mr Byrne, who was known to have been a very talented and avid wood-turner, had been busy turning little gifts for many of his close neighbours and friends, tasking Catherine with the distribution of these on his passing. The time and effort that went in to these little treasures can only lead to a belief that to some degree he must have had an inkling that the end of the road lay just ahead. Before leaving, Catherine hands Mam a small white cardboard box about 4 inches wide, 4 inches deep, and about 6 inches in height. Inside the box is a beautifully turned yew mushroom, polished to an extremely high sheen. Inscribed on the mushroom, hand-painted with a fine-tipped bush are the words: From the earth comes life and to the earth we return.

Looking at the mushroom I recall our last conversation and though I can never be sure, I wonder nevertheless if perhaps the gift was on his mind at the time. We had talked about our mutual dislike of mushrooms, as a foodstuff, and Mr Byrne was intent on coaxing me into giving them another shot at some point in my future life. However, I also remember him turning his nose up at the mushroom soup that was offered to him later that very same evening by his sister and not because he wasn't hungry but because he wasn't going to eat fungus, no matter how bad things got. I also recall him explaining in detail how essentially fungi were a necessary component of the cycle of life and I recall being fascinated at how insightful he was on the subject. As part of that same conversation, I had told him all about Matt and what had happened on my trip to the west. He was enormously entertained by such gossip – by just the simple tales of the lives of silly girls like me. I guess when you're facing the end of your own life it's the life around you that you hold onto. He had tried to draw a comparison with my revulsion to mushrooms and my relationship with Matt. In all my days I had never thought much more about Mr Byrne other than he was the old guy down the road who sometimes seemed a little needy and always a little unkempt. But in the last few days and indeed the last few weeks, for me anyway, he had proved that there was so much more to him I first thought.

The very vivid recollection of that conversation with him sets me into a state of uncontrolled sobbing and I head upstairs to my room to duly soak my pillow.

According to Catherine, Mr Byrne is to be buried next Tuesday, and that morning, I have no doubt, will be as sombre a day as ever there has been in the McCarthy household.

'MOMENTS'

The morning of the funeral I awake early and head downstairs to help Mam with the breakfast. Understandably, things are not as they would normally be, and as part of that apparent shift, there is the conspicuous absence of a cooked, meaty offering. It appears to be the case, so I'm led to believe, that we eat way too much pork in this house, and so the all-powerful Mammy has declared a ban on fried foods for now. Given current circumstances it might well be a wise move if everyone involved was to let this one slide for the time being. I can't help but pine a little, though, and ponder on the consensus that this new regime is a tad excessive given that we only ever have fry-ups on "occasions" and definitely not on a regular basis.

Still, the Mammy is the boss, and so it would seem to be that we're all going to walk the healthier path in life, at least for now. Therefore, on this less than joyous morning, breakfast is to be as sombre as the mood itself, consisting of cereal, brown bread and freshly squeezed orange juice. As a concession we're allowed pancakes also, but only on the condition that we put yoghurt and fruit on them and not lemon and sugar, and definitely not golden syrup; most certainly not icing sugar. As anticipated, the girls are less than impressed with this turn of events but remain silent on the matter for now.

While pouring myself a coffee and trying to persuade them all that it's just a passing fad that won't last too long, Gemma puts her head around the door to ask me if she can speak to me for a moment upstairs. I rush eagerly up after her, happy to get away from the mumbling complaint of the girls. Gemma got in late last night having worked the late shift and of course by that stage I was already asleep and didn't get the opportunity to chat with her. After following her into the room she moves behind me to gingerly close the door in a somewhat covert move.

"Rhian! I was dying to talk to you last night but I didn't want to wake you," she says excitedly. "Simon rang me yesterday, in work. He's back in Dublin. He apologised for running off and begged me to give him another chance. We're meeting up for coffee during the week and going out to dinner on Friday night," she concludes, looking at me expectantly. I stare at her, stunned. A multitude of thoughts run riot around in my head and I'm momentarily incapable of forming any immediate response.

"Rhian!" she reiterates. "Isn't that wonderful? Oh my God, I am so excited I can't tell you …" she says, unable to further elaborate. Finally, I manage to find my tongue and form words and sentences but for a moment before getting them out I open and close my mouth as if to limber up and loosen my jaw.

"Gem! I'm delighted. He's a nice guy and I'm sure he never meant to hurt you. Men are a strange breed, truly. I genuinely don't think they're great with the whole emotional world," I posit, not fully knowing if that's true or not but genuinely struggling to form any coherent thoughts. "But don't let him off the hook too easily either!" I continue. "Order lobster at the very least. Or don't! I take that back. They torture those poor creatures. Order one of everything on the menu instead, and don't eat half of it. That blackheart needs teaching," I say in jest, before drawing a deep breath. "Or maybe just kick his arse. That would make me feel better … and it's all about making me feel better Gem. Yep, that's what's important here," I continue, half in jest and half in overwhelming relief and looming, barely contained hysteria.

After I stop rambling on, we chat a little while longer about her feelings on the matter and understanding of the whole situation but I disclose nothing of my encounter in Galway. However, we have to cut things short and head back downstairs to have our breakfast so we can start getting ready to head out for the funeral. When we walk back into the kitchen, I can hear Kathy informing everyone about details of the upcoming trial.

"So, yea, they're dropping the complaint with regards to any transactions done during the time I was with Brian so that Brian can't drag me into it. It's going to cost them thousands. Though I wasn't meant to tell anyone that."

She looks up at me and Gemma when we walk through the door and tries to sidestep a little. "Sorry, I got a bit excited. My mouth runs away with me you know. Anyway, Brian will still be going to court because there are other charges against him. But girls, please don't tell Bill I said anything. He was very clear that I do not mention it to anyone. But you are my sisters. I know you can keep it to yourselves."

Mam places a plate full of pancakes into the middle of

the table before making a declaration about her intentions towards aul' Mary Burke up the road, who will be getting the sharp side of her tongue the next time they cross paths. Because for sure, nobody can back up any of the accusations about her angel Kathy at this stage. Silence descends over the breakfast table and so I take a look around at every one of my sisters and at Mam and they all seem so deep in thought, none of them with a notion of what has been occupying my thoughts of late, and indeed, I with little notion of what occupies any of theirs.

Suddenly Dad bursts through the back door, stomping his boots on the floor mat and putting the heart crossways in us all as he shakes off the grass and any dried mud.

"Jesus, man! Are you trying to secure us a spot next to old Mr Byrne's?" says Mam between gasps of shock.

"Bloody hell! It's like the funeral is happening in here and not down the road at the church. Will yiz liven up and come out here and have a look," says Dad with a cheesy but encouraging grin on his face.

We all leap to our feet and scramble towards the back door like excited pubescents heading to their first disco and the sight that greets us leaves a giddy feeling of elation and delight. While we were busy stuffing our faces full of healthy breakfast options, poor Dad had been equally as busy putting the finishing touches to our little garden design. He must have been up since the crack of dawn too, because he not only managed to paint the door of the shed with a wonderfully vibrant glossy shade of red, reminiscent of some quaint French gîte d'étape, but he also gave us our white picket fence with large pink spots, along with various other intriguing finishing touches. As we all stand mutely admiring the display I can easily envision Mam contentedly tending to her vegetable patch with its neat little rows of herbs and colourful vegetables, and it's enough to bring light to this dark and mournful day. Maybe, she might even fancy sitting for a while, sipping tea by the apple tree, perched on one of the chairs belonging to the new garden furniture set, or pottering around the surprisingly large greenhouse which already has a few tomato and pepper plants needing her attention. It all looks so good that we can't help but buzz about like oversized bumblebees, ideas of barbecue nights and garden parties beginning to formulate and flow with a rush of enthusiasm, before Mam sternly reminds us that we have a funeral to go to. This prompts a quick retreat back inside as we hurriedly set about getting ready to give Mr Byrne the best send-off we McCarthys can give, and it's not too long before we're all dressed in our very appropriate black frocks and sombre fascinators, heading for the front door.

The church where the ceremony will take place isn't too far away from our house thankfully, making it quite easy and pleasant to walk there. As a group we must surely cut a striking pose as we trudge, in procession, two abreast, up the road. People turn to watch us as we file past, Mam and Dad heading the small convoy hand in hand, with Gemma and I at the rear. In between, again in pairs, is: Kathy and Bill who also walk hand in hand, Aubrey and Declan and Jade and Amy. As we march up the road we're soon joined by Declan's surprisingly well-behaved friends and a couple of neighbours that seem to somehow fall into formation as if we were the official procession group demonstrating a new style of funeral march.

When we finally arrive at the church the crowd that has gathered is a testimony to how much our community is going to miss this amazing character. And because most people, for some odd reason prefer to loiter outside the church rather than sit inside, there's plenty of seating to be had, despite how large our group has become. Sitting listening to everybody recount their most cherished moments with Mr Byrne I realise once more that I should get to know my elderly neighbours, much better, while I still can.

After the Mass ceremony is over we head in various cars to the graveyard which, oddly enough, is sparsely attended, before we return home to abandon the cars and walk the short distance to the village pub, where soup sandwiches and snacks have been laid on by friends, helping Miss Byrne organise a send-off for her beloved brother. Although not too many people ventured to the graveyard, everyone, it would seem, decided to cram into the not-too-sizeable bar and as a result it's impossible to find a single seat anywhere. We're forced to stand near the bar which suits us all very well because no sooner have we done so than the barwoman comes out with platters of sandwiches, cocktail sausages, chicken wings and chips, placing them easily within reach along the bar top and surrounding tables. We order a round of soft drinks and decide to linger just long enough to eat some food and pass our condolences to Betty, Mr Byrne's sister.

After about an hour or so of mingling and offering consoling words to the few remaining family members, Betty approaches asking if I might accompany her godchild in playing a tune. The owner of the bar kindly provides a violin belonging to one of his children to make that possible and so I agree. Unfortunately, the only remotely appropriate song that we both know is "The Lonesome Boatman" which I know is definitely going to rip the heart out of half the pub in an instant. But as Donnie, the young lad in question, is unable to convince me that "Stairway to Heaven" constitutes an appropriate tune then it will be only piece that will be played, I fear. After unsuccessfully trying to persuade me one more time to play his choice of song, Donnie finally agrees to "The Lonesome Boatman" before grabbing his tin whistle. The barman immediately turns off the background music and the pub falls to a mournful hush as Donnie raises the instrument to his lips. The sound pouring from this whistle is truly haunting and the young lad plays it extremely well. The melody lifts and lifts till it reaches a heart-swelling crescendo as tin whistle and fiddle together meld together in musical lament. Half the pub are brought to tears and I feel my own heart bear the strain.

Lovely as it is, I'm glad when the tune ends and slightly amused when Donnie continues on, launching straight into a pepped-up version of "Stairway to Heaven" on his own which, to my surprise, gets everybody singing along. I watch and listen for some time before returning the fiddle to the barman. When I turn around I see Gemma and Simon standing holding my cardigan out towards me. My heart misses a beat and I suddenly feel hot and uncomfortable from my head to my toes at the sight of Matt also, staring at me with a look I can't understand, painfully etched on his face. For a moment or two I'm detached from reality. Donnie had finished up his tune and the barman resumes playing the background music. The song now playing is Spandau Ballet's "True", which seems surreal to my ears right now, like it's carrying me on a wave of notes over to the group, my feet not touching the ground.

"Hi! How are you Simon … Matt?" I stuttered, my mouth suddenly going dry.

Gemma gives me an odd questioning look as Simon launches at me for a surprisingly enthusiastic and slightly strangulating hug.

"I'm very sorry for your loss, Rhian. I hope you don't mind us imposing like this. I wanted to see that Gemma was okay and offer my condolences. She told me a bit about Mr Byrne so I know he was very dear to your family. We've also blagged ourselves an invite back to the house with you all and because Matt's sense of direction is deplorable, forcing us to get a taxi over, we can now walk back with you all as well," he says. "I hate to say it, but he let me down badly on this occasion," jokes Simon, before slapping Matt heartily on the back. "Truth is, I rely on him far too much anyway," whispers Simon, conspiratorially and loud enough for Matt to hear quite clearly. Matt just rolls his eyes and follows us out of the pub.

"No! Of course we don't mind. We're delighted you're both here," I say with a startled tone that I have no doubt is what is prompting Gemma to continue looking at me curiously, which I pretend not to notice. "Yes! It's the end of an era for us. We grew up with him always being there. It's very hard to think of him not being around anymore."

I struggle to keep the tears back and for a brief moment they threatened to overflow and destroy my facade of strength and resolve. Thankfully Gemma and Simon, encouraged by Bill and Kathy, are already turning to head out the door and up the road after the rest of the posse. Mam, Dad, Amy and Jade are already way ahead as Bill and Kathy run to catch up.

Gemma and Simon hurry on ahead too as Matt and I follow close behind.

"I'm very sorry, Rhian," says Matt after a moment or two of silence.

"Thank you, Matt!" I say with a raspy croak in my voice. "It's not like we weren't expecting it though," I continue.

"No! I mean I'm sorry about everything. And your loss, of course."

"Oh it's okay, Matt. I haven't been the person I like to think I am, in all this either. You did a very honourable thing. Most people wouldn't have bothered. I mean look at them. They're the cutest couple in the world."

"They are indeed and I must admit I've never seen him so enamoured in all my life. Rhian, I truly am sorry. I misjudged you all and that's the thing that I most regret," he says quite poignantly.

"I did as much myself, Matt. The first time I laid eyes on you I christened you 'Grumpy'. I reckoned you were the most miserable looking so-and-so I'd ever laid eyes on. So, what do you say to forgetting all about what went on before and starting afresh?"

I turn to look at him, extending my hand for a

reconciliatory shake but instead he hesitates. For one awful moment I think he is going to pass on the handshake and I feel my heart sink. Maybe confessing to calling him names wasn't my best move and as the seconds tick by I feel overwhelmingly like I might just scream out, shout his name and shake him.

But instead, he reaches out and pulls me to him, burying his head in my neck, breathing deeply into my hair. The pent-up emotions immediately and smoothly dissipate and I take a deep breath myself, hugging him tight, an almost indescribable sense of something unknown, a life force, coursing through me. The world disappears around us and nothing else in this moment matters more than this, our contact. I never imagined that one single moment could hold so much peace and promise and soothe the soul so perfectly and entirely and in my mind's eye I see a vision of Matthew Devine, his smiling face gazing longingly, lovingly down at my upturned face. I open my eyes and it's real.

Taking me finally by the hand we walk on up the road towards home.

ELLIE TAYLOR-BROCK

ABOUT THE AUTHOR

Just someone, who keeps at it, even when it seemed almost impossible.

Printed in Great Britain
by Amazon